Octave Thanet

Otto the knight

And other trans-Mississippi stories

Octave Thanet

Otto the knight
And other trans-Mississippi stories

ISBN/EAN: 9783743308916

Manufactured in Europe, USA, Canada, Australia, Japa

Cover: Foto ©Andreas Hilbeck / pixelio.de

Manufactured and distributed by brebook publishing software
(www.brebook.com)

Octave Thanet

Otto the knight

OTTO THE KNIGHT

AND OTHER TRANS-MISSISSIPPI STORIES

BY

OCTAVE THANET

AUTHOR OF " KNITTERS IN THE SUN," AND " EXPIATION "

BOSTON AND NEW YORK
HOUGHTON, MIFFLIN AND COMPANY
The Riverside Press, Cambridge
1891

The Riverside Press, Cambridge, Mass., U. S. A.
Electrotyped and Printed by H. O. Houghton & Co.

CONTENTS.

"Sist' Chaney's Black Silk" and "The Conjured Kitchen" are reprinted from "Harper's Bazar" by permission of the publishers.

OTTO THE KNIGHT.

AUNT BETSEY GRAHAM, who kept the plantation tavern, stood in her wide gallery-way, waiting for the mill whistle to send her boarders to supper.

There was not a kinder woman in Lawrence County, or, in a homely fashion, a better cook.

Look at her, now, in the shadow of the old-fashioned porch, built when bears were shot in the cypress brake: her portly form is clad in a red and black striped cotton gown and white apron; her gray hair is as thick as a girl's, her little brown eyes twinkle jovially, the hardy late roses bloom on her tanned cheeks, and nobody on the plantation has such beautiful, white, store teeth.

She sees the road, a broad, then a narrow, then a fading streak of yellow, cutting the cotton-fields and defining the borders of the brake. Some of the houses that she sees are trig and painted; some have crooked, dark roofs, and chimneys bulging sidewise against black-gray walls. It is the old South and the new. Looking obliquely to the right, she sees the smithy under its great "water oaks," and, almost at right angles, the carpenter shop and the gaunt black shape of the old mill. Further down the river bank is the new mill, which has men crawling over its roof and rings with the click of hammers.

But soon Aunt Betsey's eyes returned to Otto Knipple, splitting wood just in front of the porch. She thought, sorrowfully, that he would never make out with that hickory; but what could you expect of a boy raised in St. Louis and come down to the Black River with those "ornery," trifling St. Louis carpenters?

Otto was a scrap of a lad, carrying a premature age in his sallow, careworn, eager little features, that were the sallower and more eager for his mat of sunburned white hair and his big, melancholy blue eyes.

"An' so" — Aunt Betsey was pursuing a conversation already begun — "so you paw's dead, but you Uncle Bruno, he holps ye all?"

"I guess we'd be in the poorhouse, if he did n't," said Otto. "He got me this chance. Mr. Bassett's a Knight, like my uncle."

"A witch?"

"A Knight of Labor, you know."

"Never heerd on 'em," said Aunt Betsey, placidly.

Otto straightened himself, his eyes flashing and his narrow chest swelling.

"You ain't!" he cried; "why, they're jest the grandest order ever was! They're going to make all the bad rich people quit oppressing the poor, and make all diff'rent laws"—

"Oh, sorter like the Ku-Klux?"

"Oh, no, mum, not a bit like the Ku-Klux. They are all good men, and they shall make all the poor people own their own property, and Uncle Bruno kin come home at four o'clock"—

"Sekrit soci'ty, hey?"

"They've got to be, mum; 'cause else them bloated capitalists would find out all their plans."

"That 'ar sounds powerful like Ku-Klux," said Aunt Betsey, critically. "They all was mighty biggity, but I never seen nuthin' come er thar braggs 'cept folkses ketchin' cole, romancin' roun' nights, by the dark of the moon. I know all 'baout them sekrit soci'ties. I read a book 'baout 'em oncet. Thar was a man taken a oath on a skull, wilst two men hilt dadgers over him iz was dreepin' with jore. War n't that orful?"

"Yes, mum; please go on!" cried Otto, reveling in the lurid picture.

"By the fitful gleam er a dyin' lamp," Aunt Betsey continued. "Must of ben one er them

grease lamps, they 're allers devilin' someway.
I disremember jes whut 't was he swore, but I
know his ha'r, iz was black like the ravin's wing,
turned plum w'ite in a single night. His folks
did n't know him. But he hollers out (in a *holler* voice, the book said) ' I done kep' my vow ! '
an' he jes natchelly died er sorrer right thar."

" Why for ? " exclaimed Otto, rather startled.

" Kase he had ter do sich a sight er killin' ;
some on 'em the folks he set most store by. But
he cud n't holp it, kase he 'd of ben false ter
the fatil vow an' ben a fool traiter. That 's
what the book said. My, my, my ! I wisht I 'd
of kep' that book. 'T had a sorter purplish
back an' right big print, an' — my word, Otter
Kaynipple, how ye done bust them pants ! "
screamed Aunt Betsey, as her eye got its first
full view of Otto's figure ; " it 's lucky I got a
pa'r ready fur ye. You wait ! "

She turned her broad back on the boy to
reach into the gallery for something, which,
presently shaken out, revealed itself as a pair
of blue flannel trousers, decked with crimson
streamers.

" Thar, store pants an' gallowses ! Make
haste an' putt 'em on ! "

The boy, red with pleasure, could hardly
stammer, " Oh, ain't they beautiful ! Who gave
'em to me ? "

" Waal, he said not to tell."

All the glow faded out of the lad's radiant
face. " I know. It was Mr. Dake," he said
sullenly. " I 'm much obliged to him, but I
cayn't take 'em."

His voice shook over the last words, while,
apparently not daring to trust himself to look
on the dazzling temptation, he flung his axe
down and fled across the grass.

" A - bustin' his pants at ev'ry lick ! " was
Aunt Betsey's comment, eying the wild little
ragged shape ; " an' he ain't got nare nuther
pa'r on earth, nur nuthin' ter mend 'em with
'cept pins ! "

She shook her head dolefully, and carried the
rejected gift into the house.

In a large unplastered room a table was
spread before an enormous fireplace, bare and
black now, since the Arkansas spring sun is
warm.

Marty Ann, Aunt Betsey's daughter, was plac-
ing the squirrel stew on the table, and Baby Boo,
the one little orphan grandchild of the house,
was already in the high chair that Dake the
carpenter had made for her, reaching perilously
after the custard pie. Those sturdy little legs
and arms of Boo's (or more properly, Elizabeth
North Carolina's) were only quiet when she was
asleep ; but no lover of children could see her

restless, curly brown head and shining eyes and
sweet little round face so dimpled and rosy,
without wanting to kiss the pretty lump. Possibly, were the lover a man, he might feel a like
inclination concerning her aunt, who also had
curly brown hair with red gleams in it, and
sparkling dark eyes ; and whose thinner, oval
face kept a childish and innocent charm in
the soft, fine skin, pure coloring, and smooth
curves. As her light figure moved about, she
showed an artless kind of grace, such as these
forest people often have. She wore a fresh
white apron over her blue cotton frock, and had
a bit of white lace and a knot of blue ribbon
at her throat.

"Well, maw, what is it?" said Marty Ann,
noticing a slight pucker at the corners of Aunt
Betsey's eyelids. "Do you reckon that light
bread is a little sad?"

"Law me, naw, Marty Ann, I was jis studyin'
'baout Dake an' that Dutch boy. He p'intedly
won't take them pants."

"Then I 'd let him go bare," said Marty Ann,
carelessly.

"He are 'baout that a'ready," Aunt Betsey
chuckled, recalling Otto's figure running.
"Waal, I cayn't cipher it out, nohow. Thar 's
Dake doin' oodles er things fur Otter, lettin'
him sleep in his room t' the store, an' a sight

more, but Otter won't have no truck with Dake. Wonder w'y."

"If I was Mr. Dake I'd find out, or I'd quit fooling with Otto — one!"

"*You* mought, Marty Ann; but Dake, he are a patient, long-suffrin' critter, an' terrible kind tew children. Look a' how he muches Boo!"

Marty Ann's pretty chin went up in a significant tilt, as she answered, "Other folks much Boo, too. Say, maw, did ye ever hear anything 'bout Mr. Dake's wife and child?"

"Nuthin', cept iz how they is dead."

"Well, *I* heard how he deserted his wife, and ayfterwards he tried for to steal the child."

"Shucks!" retorted the old woman with disdain; "*you* heard from Bassett, I bet a bale er cotton. I wisht ye wud n't take up with that 'ar feller, honey. He kin w'ar store clozes an' julery an' mock plain folkses talkin'; but he ain't got no real merits like Dake. Nur he don't set haff the store by ye. But ye jes toll 'em on. Ye got sorter mean turn with men persons, Marty Ann."

She shook a moralizing and reproving head at her daughter; but, in so doing, she happened to look out of the window, and what she saw made her forget the lecture. "Marty Ann, come yere," she exclaimed; "thar's a turrible to-do at the new mill!"

Marty Ann, looking over her shoulder, could see the St. Louis carpenters standing around two horsemen, the owners of the plantation, Mr. Francis and young Caroll. Topping the crowd was Bassett's handsome black head. He gesticulated furiously, and Marty Ann, too far away to distinguish words, could hear the angry rumble of his voice.

A short, slim man looked on, a little apart; and impassively stroked his mustache.

"Dear, dear, dear!" ejaculated Aunt Betsey, "ain't that Bassett a r'arin' an' chargin'! An' look a' Dake, cam 's a stone statchuary — my Lord!"

The old woman leaned out of the open window in her eagerness, when she saw Bassett fling the crowd to either side and aim a swinging blow at Dake. Dake dodged. Simultaneously, a thin line of light flashed in his hand. "He 's drored 'is gun on him!" cried tender-hearted Aunt Betsey. "My Lord, I hope they won't fight. Dodge ahind the winder with the baby, Marty Ann! I are so int'rested, someways I don't guess I 'll git hit. Naw, ye need n't, Mist' Caroll's putt 'is hoss atween 'em. Good for *you*, boy! Now, they 're all goin' way. Do look a' that Otter tryin' ter take big steps like the men! Waal, fightin' or no fightin', they 'll want t' eat; so less fotch in the coffee."

The four St. Louis men trooped noisily into the house, omitting their customary toilet at the pump. But Dake took his towel down from the nail and went out there.

"Well, Mrs. Graham," said Bassett, who passed for a wag and a man of ready wit, "git out your handkerchief, the Sam Eller's rounding the Bend and we 're going off on her."

"Reckon I better git out the *bill*," answered Aunt Betsey, dryly. "Say, whut you all ben doin'?"

"We 've given the old man the grand bounce," Bassett said, taking his place at the table; "we 're not going to be bossed any longer by a d— scab. If Francis wants us back, he 'll have to bounce Dake, that 's all."

"What did Dake do tew ye?"

A quiet-looking man explained, "He ain't done nothing to us, ma'am; but he sold out a strike once, and he was a Knight of Labor and spoiled a boycott."

"Well, all I say is, just give me another chance at the d— traitor," said Bassett. "Bet ye he dassent show his ugly mug 'round here."

The unexpected answer to this was Dake's entrance.

The head carpenter's mild blue eyes and thin brown face bore no marks of agitation. He sat down calmly, in his seat next to Boo, and began to cut up the child's food.

Bassett glowered at him across the table. To be defied by a man of such puny sinews was a blister on the giant's vanity. "I despise a scab, don't you, boys?" said he, loudly.

But here Aunt Betsey lifted a fine round voice. "You hush, Mist' Bassett! I ain't goin' ter have no sich fool talk afore Marty Ann an' the baby. Nur I won't have no men persons hollerin' an' fightin' in my haouse like a passle er wild haogs. Ef I hear ary nuther ill word, Marty Ann an' me 'll git up an' light out — an' we 'll cyar' the victuals with us!"

"Give us a rest, Jim," said one of the men. "I want to eat my supper." And another added in a surly tone, "Don't you know there is a heap of fellows with guns and knives in this cussed swamp? You 'll be having them all down on us!"

"Who 's afraid?" sneered Bassett; but he said no more, and the meal went on in a sulky truce. When the men rose, he lingered in the gallery to settle the bill. Dake followed the St. Louis men out on the porch. He held Boo in his arms.

"Boys," said he, clearing his throat, "I dare say it ain't no use for me to tell you there 's been a lot of lies told to you" —

"No, it ain't," said the surly man.

"All the same, have I ever treated a man among you mean in any way?"

The men had halted on the steps so that they faced the head carpenter; the quiet-looking man answered: "That ain't the point; we ain't got no use for a man that sides with the bosses against his friends. I don't believe in licking you, like Jim; but I don't want no truck with you, and that's the fact."

Dake made no reply; he stood on the porch, holding Boo in his arms. The murmur of voices from the gallery reached him, soft bursts of laughter shaded by deeper tones.

Dake held Boo's small palm close to his cheek; now and then he would take it away to kiss it.

Suddenly he put the baby down and strode into the gallery, where Bassett was holding Marty Ann while he kissed her hair in default of her face, which had dodged under the shelter of her shoulder.

"I won't! I won't!" shrieked Marty Ann, laughing and crying at once; "you're real mean! I told you I — had n't — made up — my mind. Lemme go!"

"Let her go," said Dake.

"You dassent hit me," said Bassett, tightening his clasp.

The two men glared at each other for the briefest instant, a space of time to be contained within the flash of an eye or the click of a pistol trigger just behind Bassett's ear, before Dake's tone of concentrated fury seemed a part of that fine cold rim pressing on Bassett's brain : —

"I don't mean to hit you. Let her go, you brute, or I 'll *kill* you ! "

Then Bassett did loosen his hold enough for Marty Ann to wriggle herself free, crying : "Oh, please don't hurt him, he was only fooling ! "

"Get along, now," said Dake.

The carpenters, outside, ignorant of their comrade's plight, were bawling for him to hurry.

Bassett flung his clenched fist sidewise as he ran.

"I ain't through with you yet, Bill Dake," he shouted. "I 'll git you where I want you, some day, and your d— popgun won't help you, then ! "

"Great Scott, Jim," yelled a voice, "the boat 's whistling ! Say, write your girl the rest."

Dake, who had advanced again to the porch, was in time to hear Bassett cry, "I will ! " and to see him clear the steps with a jump that had nearly landed him on the grass head foremost, for he tumbled over Otto Knipple. Under the lad's arm was a bundle done up in a newspaper, too small to cover the contents.

"Hullo!" said Bassett, "you ain't going?"

"Ain't I?" cried the boy, eagerly; "ain't I going to strike?"

Bassett muttered something too low for Dake's ears. Then, "Yes, I 'm coming, d— you!" he shouted, and ran after the others.

Dake watched him, sombrely, until a sniff and a gurgle diverted his gaze to Otto, who was wiping his eyes with the knuckles of his forefingers and choking with sobs.

"Poor little fellow!" said Dake.

He walked towards the shabby little figure; but after looking at it intently he seemed to change his mind, and going back whispered a sentence in Boo's ears instead. Boo danced gayly off to the boy. And he, kissing her and drying his wet cheeks on her soft hair, felt a vague comfort that perhaps Dake missed as he walked down into the brake, alone.

After a while he sat down on a log, and in spite of his heavy heart, the beauty of the scene won his eye. In the later spring a cypress brake is a sumptuous revel of color. The fern-like cypress foliage and the short limbs above the high trunk make the tree seem more like a gigantic plant than a tree. The water in the brake is a mass of lily pads, and spattered with yellow cow lilies. The cypress roots are beautiful with moss. Even the hideous "knees" that spike the ground are transformed ; painted by this magical brush of spring a dull pink, with the texture and gloss of satin, they show like fairy tents among the lilies. Crimson blooms on the maple boughs, rich tones of red on post-oak leaves, brilliant green leaves on the huge gum-trees, a scarlet gleam from the " buck-eye " flowers, a flush of pink on a " red bud " tree, terraces of white dogwood blossoms against gray-green bark, — the eye is lured by them through all the gamut of color, whether they dapple the clumps of cypress greenery, or hatch the pale joints of the " elbow brush," or fleck the forest shadow with brightness.

Where Dake sat, the brake climbed up into the higher ground, ceasing thereby to be the brake. The river makes a blunt and wide incision, variously named " The bay " and " The big bayou ; " and the unwooded bank on the swamp side forms a kind of rude levee, which the ancient tradition of the bottom avers existed before the Spaniards or the French. Doubtless it is a relic of that mysterious, prehistoric race whose mounds are scattered through the Black River valley.

The levee was green, the short-lived Arkansas grass covering it with velvet; only, it was not altogether green, because the spring had bespattered it with blue and yellow-white from violets, cinquefoil, and oxalis. The water of the bay glittered softly like an opal; for the sun was setting, and shifting hues, red and purple and gold, were burning in the river as in the sky.

Dake, who had learned to love this landscape, turned from it with a kind of groan. "Lord, I hate things to be so pretty when I 'm so miserable," said he to himself. "I was a fool to dream she 'd get to liking me. Soon 's the mill 's done I 'll get out. I 'll go " — he tried to laugh — "I 'll go and get drunk!"

A sound that was not the echo of his laughter — although that was harsh enough — made him start. "Pshaw, it 's nothing but a hog," he said aloud.

"Naw, 't ain't a haog," answered a voice out of the brake, between grunts of exhaustion, "hit 's me!"

With a mighty push Aunt Betsey rent a tangle of muscadine vine in twain and emerged, puffing and disheveled but smiling, and bearing aloft a plate of custard pie. "Waal, suttinly this yere slash is pesky bad walkin'!" she panted. "I seen ye lightin' out an' ye had n't teched you pie, so I jes gethered a piece an' run ayfter ye. Thar," said the kind creature, who perhaps had noticed more than Dake's lack of appetite, "rest you plate on the log an' eat. T'-night them St. Louis men eat like their stummicks was a cotton baskit, faster ye throw hit in, the better. Bless the Lord fur victuals, I says, an' don' gredge the time t' eat 'em!"

She watched Dake eat, talking on cheerfully, yet with a wistful gleam in her eye. "I kin tell ye, I are plum glad ter get shet er they all, 'specially that Bassett. He war too biggetty; stepped 's high 's a blin' hoss. An' how he wud lie! Lie iz easy iz ye kin bat you eye. What do ye reckon he tole 'baout *you?* I says t' Marty Ann, I aimed tew tell ye, kase ye 'd orter knaw."

Dake put his plate on the ground; luckily he had finished the pie, since he had no appetite for more now.

"I most wish I *had* shot him," he muttered.

"Aw naw, ye don't," said Aunt Betsey, soothingly. "I ben 'lowin fur a right smart I 'd jes' ax ye pintblank 'baout you wife and chile. Then I cud talk up to Marty Ann, ye understand."

Dake sometimes addressed Aunt Betsey as mother, in his English fashion. "I 'd be glad to, mother," said he. The story that he told his sympathizing listener was not uncommon: a young English artisan coming to America to "better himself," and there marrying a pretty, ambitious, vulgar American, who has brought sufficient tawdry education from her high school to despise her plain husband, but is quite helpless to understand his moral aspirations. Dake had never complained of her during their discordant married life; he said nothing now of her fretfulness, her hysterical impatience with poverty and perpetual nagging him for not earning more money. He showed Aunt Betsey the picture of their little one, a boy. " Elsie was a good mother," said he. After he had carefully replaced the photograph he went on; " Well, mother, we 'd been married five years, and if married life was n't jest all I 'd looked for'ard to, still we got on with the rest, and I daresay as much my fault as hers, if not ; and we both thought the world of the boy. Then, this is 'ow the trouble come. I 'd always belonged to the union " —

" Sekrit soci'ty ? " said Aunt Betsey, sternly, lifting up a fat forefinger in the manner of an exclamation point.

" Why, certainly ; they all are. Well, I have a good friend, Bob Tomlin by name. Nobody was more interested in trades unions than we were, nor gave more money. That was one thing fretted poor Elsie. But we got disgruntled, after a while. A lot of hot-headed blowhards got the upper hand, and sent us on fool strikes till we were mad. It 's kinder hard on a good workman who can always command good wages to stay idle a third of his time 'cause a few hot-heads are dissatisfied. By and by come the big strike over the boss taking on some non-union men. Bob and I did our best to prevent that strike ; but when 't was no use we went out peaceful. Tomlin had a lot of sickness in his family and his savings run low, so he went to the secretary for help. What do ye suppose they told him? Why, jest that he 'd a cabinet organ and a Brussels carpet, and the help must go to them as needed it. 'But,' says Bob, 'Cowles gits 'elp reg'lar!' You must know, mother, that this Cowles was a drunken rip and keen for the strike. Well, they' said, Cowles needed it, he 'd nothing laid by. At that, Bob, who 's a bit 'asty though the best 'earted feller, he loses his temper and cussed 'em. 'And I 'm to mortgage my house to pay Hal Cowles's strikes, am I?' says he. 'I 'm d—d if I do!' says he. And he went back to work that very day, but before the week was out they fetched him 'ome on a shutter."

"I knowed hit," cried Aunt Betsey; "'t war the sekrit soci'ty. War he cut onywhar with dadgers an' sich?"

"Oh, no, only pommeled. He was 'round in a week ; but that got my mad up, too, and — well, the strike failed, and they laid it on us."

"Did n't they try fur to kill ye?"

"They talked pretty rough, but I got a revolver, and when a gang of them set on me, I shot one fellow in the leg. They did n't complain of me to the police; but after that they served me out other ways. You don't know it, of course, but those big strikes mostly end the same way. The old men come back, beaten or not. And the bosses, after swearing by all that 's holy to keep on the non-union men that have come in and helped them through, they begin to quietly weed the scabs out and get their old men back. You see, usually, the good workmen belong to the union and they won't work with the scabs, and the bosses find it cheapest to give in, on the sly like. And the unions promise big, and so the poor devil of a scab goes by the board. That 's the way they treated me. I went to two or three cities, but I could n't get work, having no union ticket; but I got a good job out in the country and went home for my wife to take her out. We 'd been having words, she wanting me to make it up with the union; but still I did n't suspect nothing. Mother, she was gone. Her folks — her father and brothers — were union men, and they persuaded her to leave me. She went off and she got a bill of divorce — for desertion and non-support, though I 'd sent her three fourths of my money. And, next thing I knew, she was married to a walking delegate, a fellow that gets a big salary for bossing rows."

" Waal, the triflin', deceitful critter!" said Aunt Betsey.

"I expect Bassett told ye I stole my child. I tried to; but there was a hue and cry, and they got him 'way from me. One policeman whacked me over the head, and my poor boy cried. I never saw him again, mother. They kept so close I could n't find them. But every Christmas and birthday I 'd send a present for the lad, what I thought he 'd like, to his grandfather, and I asked him very civilly if he 'd only tell me if the boy was well. But I never got a word till he sent me a marked paper. My boy's death was in it."

"Oh, ye pore, pore boy!" said the old woman, whose six tall sons were in their graves; "an' the only chile ye got?"

Dake nodded, shivering a little. "Yes, ma'am, that 's so. I guess I 'd 'ave gone to the bad then but for Tomlin and his wife. I 'd lost everything, and it 's awful, mother, the loneliness when a man's own mates turn on him. I confess I took to the devil's comforter, drink. But they got me out of it, God bless 'em. May be I had ought to thank the Knights of Labor too, for we both joined them 'bout that time."

"Another sekrit soci'ty?" cried Aunt Betsey. "Ye onfortinate boy!"

"Well, we pretty soon discovered that we 'd got more fights on our hands than in the union; we 'd everybody else's wrongs to right as well as

our own. I 'm blessed if we did n't strike once
to help some cigar-makers, and the walking delegate that come on to attend to the matter was
him — my wife's 'usband. He went white 's the
wall when he saw me, and marched off. The
next time I saw him he was bossing a boycott
on a poor widow woman who would n't turn a
scab carpenter out of her boarding-house. By
that time I did n't want no more Knights of Labor in mine; and I took sides with the widow.
So now the Knights are down on me."

" Ain't ye never seen *her* agin ? " said Aunt
Betsey.

" Jest once. I run up against her on the street
that same time. She looked most awful pale,
and wore mourning — for him. When I saw
her that way, somehow I seemed to see her like
she 'd look nights when Willie was restless and
we 'd take turns walking him. She 'd 'ave the
baby's little 'ead on her shoulder, and her long
black braids hanging down her nightgown; and
she walking and singing. My God, mother, a
man can't get over feeling *something* for the woman that 's carried his baby in her arms ! ' Elsie,' I says, ' don't look so frightened; you ain't
got nothing to fear from me.' Then the poor
thing cried and coughed, — for she was dying
in consumption, she only lived three months after that, — and she said she did n't know where

I was or she 'd 'ave told me 'bout Willie's sickness, and her father was mad, and so on.   Poor
Elsie! I never felt so bitter 'bout her again.   I
felt cruel hard before. She told me all 'bout
our boy and sent me a bundle of his little things.
Poor Elsie! Well, mother, there 's the story. I
come down here to get rid of the Knights; but
you see I have n't."   He laughed drearily, as he
added, "They beat me, every way."

"Ye mean 'baout Marty Ann," said Aunt
Betsey, who had no false delicacy; "but ye
need n't feel so mightily down. Marty Ann 's
kinder out o' fix, now, but she 's got a heap er
sense ; an' she 'll see ; I 'll be you mother-in-law,
yit. So guv me a buss on that!"

Dake kissed his homely comforter with a will;
and she leaning on his arm, as if he had been the
son she hoped for, they went back to the house.

Mr. Francis took the strike very coolly. He
found some Arkansas carpenters, who worked
well enough under Dake's supervision. Young
Caroll made light of the whole affair. "That
Bassett was a chump," said he; "he talked too
much with his mouth; I 'm glad he 's gone —
well, children?"

Otto said that he was only showing Boo the
red wagons in the store.

But evidently Boo had her own intentions;

she twitched the boy's sleeve. "Boo 'oves tandy," she observed with much sweetness of manner; "*tandy* won't make Boo sick!"

"Will you let her have *one* gumdrop, sir?" said Otto. "I shall pay you out of my wages." He flushed up to the eyes when Caroll tossed him a handful of candy, and he pushed the parti-colored heap back, excepting one piece, saying, "I'd like for to take more, sir, but I should send all my money home that I kin."

"Oh, take them," said the young man; "that's all right!"

Young Caroll had his clothes sent him from his tailor in the North, he rode a fine horse, he polished his finger nails, he never seemed in a hurry; Otto hated him.

Poor Otto, he deemed it his duty to hate everybody that had very much money or very much land. Just as his talk had a little twist of German idiom, so that good anarchist, Uncle Bruno (in very truth, one of the best of men), had twisted his moral sense awry. He was confident that not only did the rich inflict hideous misery on the poor, — they also gloated over their victims' humiliation. Tears of shame and anger burned his eyeballs as he picked up Boo (both fists full of sweets, but very loath to go) and hurried out of the store. "He laughed that I should not have enough to buy but one gumdrop!" he said between his teeth. And innocent young Caroll was saying: "That's a nice little fellow; do you reckon Aunt Betsey would make over my corduroys for him?"

Otto passed by the new mill. He could hear Mr. Dake whistling over his work. The head carpenter had rigged up a workshop in the mill, and worked there until late every night, making a chest of drawers for Marty Ann. The chest was to be a birthday present. Otto was not above peeping through a crack, thereby seeing very plainly that Dake was smiling.

"He thinks he has conquered," was Otto's instant reflection, "and he shall have Bassett's shaatz, too. Ya wohl, *will* he? Denn muss ich den Teufel anführen!"

He shook his fist at the store; "I despise the scab, but the tyrant I hate!" said Otto, who admired the sounding phrases of his uncle's newspapers. "Yes, I was sorry, I hated to do it even to bring the boys back; but now you have made me cry, look out!" He laughed fiercely, recalling a speech of Mr. Francis: "If the mill had n't been so far along I should have been bothered; for we *must* have the gin by October."

"I will do it," said Otto. "They thought I was a boy, I could n't help the strike. They will see!"

Little did Dake, still smiling over the chest of drawers, imagine how important to him was this soliloquy of Otto's; he only thought of Marty Ann and her possible pleasure. He laughed at himself, but he knelt down and kissed handles that might be touched by her fingers.

" Dearest lass, sweetest lass," he murmured. " Oh, I'd take such care of you, I'd work so hard! And we'd have the dear old mother and Boo with us, and, may be " — His eyes were full of tears. " Oh, good Lord, *can* I be going to be happy, after all!" said he.

Yet surely Marty Ann's behavior had changed to him. She was so kind and gentle, not making excuses to get away from him as she used to do. And how pretty she would look up at him if there was a little joke, to catch his eye; and what a sweet, sweet laugh she had!

So a lover's hopes and fancies played a fairy game through his head, until Mr. Francis's voice broke the spell. To-day was an unintentional holiday, owing to an accident to a saw; and the planter meant to improve it by driving the head carpenter about the plantation to discuss future building.

The two men spent the day thus; and did not return until evening. The supper-room looked bare to Dake without Marty Ann. Aunt Betsey explained that she had gone to see the new baby of a friend, "Cap'n Bulah Griffin, on the yon side the Creek."

"She laid out t' cyar' Boo, but she rode the claybank, an' he 's sicher ill hoss, she dassent. Boo begun tew beller when she seen 'er goin', but Mis' Francis come by an' she tolled the bad little trick off tew the new mill. An', by gum, she ben thar the enjurin' ev'nin', playin' doll 'ouse with the boards, she an' Otter 'n' Lizzie Vict'ry an' Seerayphine Dake. She putt Seerayphine tew sleep an' leff her thar fur the night."

Seerayphine Dake, be it explained, was not a little live girl like Lizzie Victory, but a beautiful wax doll that could open and shut its eyes, and cry in the most natural and affecting manner if you squeezed her stomach. Dake had bought her in St. Louis and put her on the Christmas tree for Boo.

"She did n't leave her," Otto spoke up with an unaccountable flush, "I brought her home."

But Boo had not heard, being absorbed in a new table pastime; namely, tilting her spoon so that the milk should trickle gently over the point and form wee rivulets in the creases of her oilcloth eating apron.

"Lammie," said her grandmother, placidly, "quit that, or I 'll have t' throw ye t' the big b'ar! Marty Ann 'lowed she 'd shore be back by sundown, knowin' iz I 'd be skeered up, the hoss is so mean."

But the sun set, throwing no rays on the "claybank," or Marty Ann.

Aunt Betsey paced the gallery, declaring that she did n't know "what got her, she jes' taken the all overs." Gradually, as the west dimmed and the long shadows devoured the forest vistas, leaving only the vast dark bulk of the swamp, Dake's nerves felt the contagion.

"Like 's not he 've throwed 'er," said Aunt Betsey, "an' thar she lays in the road, hollerin' on us. I are goin' down a piece to look."

"And I guess I 'll go by the other road," Dake said; "she might take that."

He borrowed a horse from young Caroll, and rode all the way to the Griffins'.

Marty Ann had left their house before dark. They were much concerned, and Jeff Griffin wanted to join the search, but Dake assured him that there was no need; if Marty Ann was not found before morning, he would send him word.

A sinister fear, very different from honest Jeff's anxiety, goaded him both into this refusal and his own feverish hunt.

That day one of the "renters" had told Mr. Francis a long story of seeing Bassett in a little town among the hills. "He sorter dodged outer my way, but I knowed by his favor[1] 't war *him*."

Now, why had Bassett come back? Dake

---

[1] Looks, appearance.

would not confess to himself that he feared that
Marty Ann had gone secretly to meet him; but
he rode madly through the brake, yelling her
name, and, being a poor horseman, might have
broken his neck over a cypress knee had not the
horse carried a cooler head than his rider.

Nobody answered his shouts until he came in
sight of the lights of the hamlet, when he heard
the peal of a horn, such as the stockmen use on
their rounds, and Aunt Betsey blew daily to
summon her boarders.

Approaching, he perceived first a lantern
swinging vigorously, then a ragged boy.

"Otto!" he called.

"She's come back," shouted Otto; "she lost
her way!"

The relief which was Dake's first sensation
was succeeded by a revulsion of suspicion so cold
and biting that it turned him sick to the very
heart.

"Go on back," said he; "tell Aunt Betsey
I'm going to the mill and won't be up."

He would not be fooled by another false
woman. A sentence that an old German, a former member of a religious community in Iowa,
used to quote, kept running in his head:
"Woman is a magic fire."

Well, he was burned. He returned his horse
to the stable and tramped savagely over to the
mill.

Lost in the swamp? she that was born there! Yet the dominant instinct of fairness in Dake's English blood would have its word. "She never told me she cared for me," he groaned. "I only imagined it. I ain't got no right to blame her."

He tried to work, but the contrast between his frame of mind in the morning and now was too bitter — he threw his tools aside.

It may seem strange that Dake should decide against himself on such meagre evidence; but his hopes had no vitality, they were cowed by suffering. He sat a long while thinking, or rather trying to think, for only visions of past woe and betrayal would crowd into his brain. At last he rose and betook himself to the store where he lodged; Otto and he occupying a chamber in the second story together.

The store is a plantation's social centre. Dake found the office full of men. The stove, gleaming in its summer coat of whitewash (which saves blacking), made a convenient shelf for divers heels. Otto's heels did not aspire to the stove; his legs dangled from the window-sill while he listened with a rapt air to Winter the blacksmith's eulogy of Bassett's strength.

"The ox, he sulled," [1] — thus the current of Winter's eloquence flowed on, — "an' Jim jes' guv 'im one on the head; knocked 'im plum

<hr>

[1] Jibed, sulked.

dead.[1] Tell ye I wud n't bunch rags[2] with
him; I 'd cyar a gun handy, if I was Dake."

"That Bassett brags a right smart," said a
quiet, fair man, who looked like what he was, a
prosperous farmer, "but he lets off too much
steam to ever bust the b'iler. He was fixin' to
kill off Mist' Dake an' most of the Bend, mightly
briefly. R'ared an' charged on the boat, I 'm
tole, all the way to Newport. But we 're all
movin', still."

" He 'll do us a meanness yit, Mist' Shinault,"
said Winter, gloomily.

Dake passed through the crowd, greeting them
briefly, and went up to his room. Very soon he
was followed by Otto. For a little time they
could hear the laughter and creaking of chair legs
and shuffling of heavy boots, then the gossips
departed in a body, and a deep hush succeeded.

The river lapped the bank like a thirsty dog.
Some wild creature of the swamp sent forth a
quavering, melancholy cry. Dake lay still in
his bed that he might not waken Otto. Otto
was feigning sleep lest he should be suspected
by Dake.

But the boy's flesh crept, his heart was thump-
ing against his ribs : now, now at any minute —
ach, Gott! what was that ?

---

[1] Senseless.
[2] Fight. Negro expression, but used in jest by the whites.

Hurried footsteps shook the wooden platform, and a clamor of blows and shrieks filled the air.

Dake sat up in bed. "Seems to want to get in," he observed coolly. "Say! you down there, don't beat the door down! We'll need it to-morrow."

A woman's voice screamed back: "Mist' Dake, Dake, come an' holp us! Boo done run away!"

It was Aunt Betsey's voice; and nobody was there except Aunt Betsey, pounding on the door with a stick; clad in a remarkable toilet of Marty Ann's gown slipped on by accident, therefore knotted round the wearer's ample waist by the sleeves, and a patchwork quilt for a shawl.

She panted out her story: how Marty Ann, awakening suddenly, had missed Boo.[1] They had searched the yard in vain. Now Marty Ann had run to the river.

Otto interrupted the recital. "Her doll — the mill!" he cried hoarsely.

"She 'lowed she lef' it thar, fur a fact," Aunt Betsey said with a gurgle of relief. "I bet she 's thar this minnit! Otter — will ye look at the critter split the mud! Dake — he are gone, too. Waal, quicker they all run, less need er runnin' fur Betsey Graham. I ain't precisely

---

[1] Doors of dwellings are rarely locked in this part of the country; so that any one could go out, easily.

built fur the run neither." With which reflection, she followed at her own pace.

Otto flew across the green like a hare. He darted into the great black hollow structure, into the shadows crouching under the rafters like beasts asleep. There by the chest, Boo was sitting, crooning to herself while she played with a trail of fire.

A yell tore Otto's dry throat.

"Run with the baby!" shouted Dake, "run for your life!"

He was jumping on the sparks; he gathered the mass attached to the fuse in his arms; he leaped through the door. Aunt Betsey, trotting ponderously along, saw Otto run from the mill holding Boo while Dake flew to the river bank, hurling his burden into the air; and simultaneously came the crash of a dozen claps of thunder rolled into one; a shower of dirt, branches, water and boards whizzed about her ears, and Dake tumbled headlong against a tree.

The next second Boo shrieked with delight, "Did Boo hear the bang! *Big* bang!"

"Good Lord er earth an' heaven!" screamed Aunt Betsey, "whut's that?"

But she was not a woman to be deprived of her wits by any catastrophe. Instantly she grasped the child and felt her over, commenting: "Ain't broke nowhar. Nur you, Otter, hay? Whar's Dake?"

"He — he's there!" Otto's chattering jaws managed to gasp, as he pointed a shaking hand at the cypress stump.

The black heap tumbled athwart the roots neither stirred nor moaned when the old woman touched it.

"Oh, my boy! my boy!" she cried; but directly in a changed tone she said: "Naw, his heart beats strong. Jes' hit his head agin the tree an' knocked 'im dead. Hope the devil's trick, whutever 't is, hain't no more go off in 't. Otter, you 'n Boo don' come too nigh! Holler on Marty Ann, she 'll be plum crazy hearin' the noise — Thar she comes — *wild!* Marty Ann, Boo ain't hurted!"

Marty Ann turned once towards Boo, standing solidly on her own plump legs by this time, then she ran straight to Dake. Aunt Betsey's lantern struck out a ragged medallion from the intense darkness, wherein lay Dake's profile resting on the old woman's arm, and a ghastly, terrified face with staring eyes and panting lips, above. Blood was on Dake's hair and cheek and on the hand that Marty struck against her breast.

Otto's head reeled; he caught at Boo, tumbling down on the ground to hide his face in her little white nightgown.

"That 's right, Otter," cried Aunt Betsey,

"wrop er up! The pore little trick 'll be chillin' if — yere," — flinging the quilt at him, — " putt that on 'er. Now, holler right loud, all er ye. Ary words come handy. *Murder! Fire! Holp! Holp! This a way! Whoop-ee-ee!* Git up the tree an' shake the lantern, boy! Marty Ann, w'y don' ye holler? Guv me that 'ar shawl; my gownd 'll kiver you all over, an' yourn won't *me! Holler! holler!* "

Really, however, the settlement needed no rousing.

The explosion had startled them out of their slumbers for miles around. Lanterns began to twinkle like fireflies, in every direction. They poured out of their cabins, half dressed; while their shouts and calls woke the echoes in the swamp. First John, the watchman, emerged from the old mill, rubbing his eyes. Then Mr. and Mrs. Francis came and the Carolls. Within five minutes a score of men, women, and children were on the spot, and Dorrance Caroll was spurring his fastest horse down the lane after the doctor.

Mr. Francis and Winter took one of the heavy shutters off a store window and laid Dake on it, still senseless.

"Tote him to we all's, in cose," said Aunt Betsey; "he saveid my gran'chile this yere night, an' nobuddy else shill nuss 'im.""

Every moment men on horseback came galloping up to the lanterns, having heard the noise.
The crowd streamed after the shutter, buzzing
like a hive of bees; with questions, ejaculations,
surmises, threats.

"Whut war 't onyhow?"

"Do you reckon 't war a yearthquake?"

"Naw, naw, brudder Sharon, dey did n't ben
no 'quake! I done seen piece er dat 'ar trick
done it, my black seff. Mist' Francis does 'low
hit 's dem *dynermite ca'tridges* dey does blow
out de stumps wid. Reckon dey all aimed blow
de whole settlement sp'ang up!"

A white man at Otto's elbow was explaining
the operation very correctly. "Ye unperstand
we got a heap er them cartridges, an' these yerc
vilyuns stole 'em an' hid 'em in the mill. Most
like, they set 'em off with a long fuse wud be
a hour burnin'. Then, they jes' lights the fuse,
lopes thar hosses, an' Mist' Francis may whistle
fur 'em!"

"Dad gum thar ornery hides, I 'm fur swing-
in' them up soon 's we git 'em!"

"Fust we got ter *cotch* 'em. I 'm trustin' t'
thar gittin' mired up in the slashes!"

"Dad burn 'em, blow 'em up 'ith they all's
dinnermite" —

"'T war n't they all's, 't war we all's."

"Naw, sir, hangin 's the best. Ye takes a
wagon" —

"Say, bud, you was thar, tell us."

Wedged in the throng, Otto must answer unlimited questions.

At the house, the talk veered appropriately to the merits of the injured man. A farmer told of a gate mended, for nothing; and a woman of a rocking chair made for her old mother. "Wud n't take a cent. Said we 'd give 'im many a dinner when he was workin' out our way. I had n't nary rocker but the one, an' I hated terrible not to rock."

" He was always so good to the little tricks, that 's what I think on," said a young mother.

" Thar war n't a better cyarpenter in Arkansaw," almost sobbed Winter; " jes' hurted him to do a pore job; an' honest? — my Lord, the man that wud do Dake mean wud rob a dead man."

" We 'll *make* 'em dead men ! " howled the crowd. But they were hushed instantly by the doctor's approach. A bag hung over the medical arm, from which projected divers steel handles glittering ominously under the lanterns. A shudder ran through the crowd, and Otto's next neighbor remarked in an awestruck tone : " Reckon he got many 's dozen knives in thar ! "

" Must hurt turrible ! " said another man.

" Say they all kin cyarve a buddy all t' bits, inside," pursued the first speaker with a kind of ghoulish enjoyment of his theme, " an' then putt 'em all back int' fix, like they was a clock. Fur my pyart, though, I 'd be sorter jubious they 'd fergit suthin', or turn some little trick er me wrong side up."

Otto sickened at this vision of the horrors that might be inflicted on Dake. Uncle Bruno had held a low opinion of doctors ever since they insisted on vaccinating the family, and mamma Knipple sided with the board of health. Otto began to feel a painful sympathy with Dake. " Oh, I did n't go for to kill him, or to hurt him neither," he was always saying to himself. " I would n't take the things 'cause he 's a traitor, but he was good to me. I don't want him to die ! " Mr. Francis's praises of his conduct were like a thorn pressing a raw wound ; but he did not dare to repulse them. He longed to fly, but his anxiety for some word from Dake kept him passive. He waited, in his torture, until he saw Mrs. Francis's pretty, kind smile through the crowd of faces and the lights, and heard her declare that Dake's hurt was not serious ; then he slunk away.

He crept under the shadow of the cypress-trees, along the edge of the brake, to the new mill. He looked at it, not a beam shaken, not a stone of the chimney jarred.

He looked a little while, then he walked back to the store.

The door stood open, just as they had left it, in their flight. Otto walked up the dark stairs, feeling his way; but when he came to touch the door, he recoiled. An uncontrollable, utterly irrational terror seemed to swoop down out of the night and clutch his soul. His knees knocked together and the chatter of his own teeth scared him, yet he could not for the life of him keep his jaws still.

"Oh, Lord," gasped poor Otto, "how 'll I ever live through this night? If only a rat 'ud come!"

But with a desperate effort he flung the door back and, running swiftly, he crossed the floor, jumped into bed, and cowered under the blankets. But the blankets are not woven that shall keep out fear. Otto was not repentant, he was frightened.

His imagination had armed his nerves beforehand against one train of shocks; instead, there came a horror for which he had not prepared; and they were defenseless. The homesick boy loved Boo; over and over again he saw her laughing at that devil's plaything. He saw Dake's pallid face and the woman's wild eyes. He heard the oaths and threats and curses. Somehow, Otto had expected that the poor people about would rather exult in the planter's misfortune; was he not, by rights, their oppressor? But now they raged against the man who had tried to kill Dake. They would kill Otto, if they knew. There was a step on the stair! No, it was nothing! The rustle of leaves was like voices. It was not the click of hammers, only the rattle of a sycamore bough in the wind. So the hideous hours wore on until, exhausted by his torment, the poor little lonely sinner slept.

Meanwhile, Dake was hardly less wretched. He uttered a deep groan in the middle of the night, startling Aunt Betsey, who was in the act of pouring some medicine into a spoon, and naturally shook the spoon. But she gave him the medicine just the same, conscientiously adding an extra half-spoonful. Then she looked down upon him with great tenderness and emotion.

"Mother," said Dake, "why do you cry?" for the tears were twinkling on Aunt Betsey's lashes and, holding the bottle of medicine in one hand, she was gently stroking his hair with the other — and the spoon.

"Law me, honey," she answered briskly (after a sniff), "I ain't cryin', my eyes is jest weakly, like."

"Am I 'urt bad?" said Dake.

"Naw, boy, Lord be praised, you ain't. Doctor says a board struck ye, an' knocked ye agin the tree, an' ye got a *confusion* (that 's what he calls hit), in you head; an' you leader unner you right knee got tore by suthin'; but no bones is broke, and you 'll be peart agin in no time."

Dake sighed and turned his face to the wall.

"Talk er *me* cryin'!" the old woman went on. "ain't I got good reason fur ter cry an' praise the Lord fur whut you done for we all this night? Me cry! Ye had orter see Marty Ann, she cried a haff hour studdy, when she war n't kissin' an' muchin' of Boo."

A quiver passed over Dake's face. Not a word did he say, being, truly, past speaking.

Drearily his memory had been plodding through the past evening. Bassett? Of course it was Bassett. But how much had Marty Ann helped him? He acquitted her, promptly, of any guilty knowledge, but he suspected that unconsciously she had given Bassett all his information. Through her he had learned of Dake's habit of working in the mill at night. It was at him, William Dake, that the blow was aimed. His single glance that night had shown him the hiding place cunningly contrived in the hollow behind the chest of drawers and covered with boards. By what miracle had the baby, pulling it out, escaped firing the horrible thing?

The fuse, most likely, was burning all the while he was in the mill — had he remained his usual time — "By ——, I wish I had!" thought the wretched man. Then it was that he had groaned. The desolate loneliness, the sense of being hated, the shadow of entailing misfortune upon whomsoever befriended him, which had poisoned life for him before, had in it now the venom of a woman's deceit.

" Woman is a magic fire," muttered Dake, with his face to the wall that he wished was his grave.

" Fire ? " cried Aunt Betsey. " Be ye chillin', honey? Marty Ann, fotch in the big blanket! "

Marty Ann appeared, the prettier for the violet shadows under her large eyes and the pale cheeks and tremulous mouth. She stammered a few words of gratitude, which Dake received gently and coldly. She could not understand him.

Neither could Aunt Betsey nor Mr. Francis.

He was the best of patients, quiet, morbidly cautious about giving trouble, joking, in a dry way, over his pain, and pathetically grateful for every kindness. " But someway, for all his funnin', the critter 's mightily down," declared Aunt Betsey.

" I wisht you 'd go in sometimes, Marty Ann," she said once to her daughter; " you kin chirk him up better 'n ary un else."

"No, I cayn't," answered Marty Ann quickly; " cayn't you see yourself he don't want me 'round? "

"Hev ye ben ill to the pore critter? I 'll bet ye hev."

"No, I ain't, maw," said Marty Ann. "I don't know what 's the matter. Nor I don't care neither."

Why, then, did Marty Ann go and cry over Boo until the child howled in sympathy?

Dake could not help noticing her changed looks. "She 's fretting because her scoundrel sweetheart done such a mean trick," he thought dismally. Nevertheless, his heart yearned over her. Bassett was a boaster, a coarse fellow, but may be he would be good to her, and he was Marty Ann's choice. "I 'll not stand in the way," said Dake.

The next day he spoke to Mr. Francis. "They 've downed me," he said. "What 's the use? I 'll go away. There 's a good carpenter in Portia and he 's a Knight of Labor, so they won't make a row. You can get Bassett back, then " — .

" I don't want him," said Mr. Francis.

" He 's not half a bad fellow," said Dake, " and a first-rate workman. I know how the decent workmen feel about scabs; I used to feel that way, myself. They 're fellows that make a good bargain for themselves at the expense of their mates; the decent Knights or union men won't lift a hand against them, themselves, but they don't feel bad, I assure you, when the rough fellows do them a mischief. If I stay here, they'll do something to you. I'm going, that's all."

Mr. Francis's indignation, appeals, protestations, were equally vain. The planter fumed, young Caroll swore, Aunt Betsey cried; Dake looked miserable, but his determination was not shaken one whit. Meanwhile the swamp had been scoured, a couple of detectives were prowling about in disguise, and nobody was a pin's point the wiser.

Bassett rode defiantly to the store with a couple of witnesses, who swore (and he offered to bring a dozen more who would swear the same) that he spent the whole evening from seven until eleven of the night in question, at a certain saloon in Portia. "And I ain't that kind of a fellow," said Bassett to the scowling faces, happily few, that day, which met his. "I fight fair, I do; and I'm ready to hold up my hands to anybody that doubts it! D— 'em! D— you all!" he yelled. In fact, Bassett had primed up his courage for the trip a little too heavily.

The planter, Shinault, and a few of the cooler heads got him off the place with all speed.

Otto, who was in the store buying quinine for Dake, witnessed the scene in indescribable agitation. The lad was a creature to be pitied. He spent most of his spare time in Dake's room.

At first he had shrunk from seeing Dake, but very soon the only relief that he could get was there. Against his will he grew fond of Dake. It is hard when a man's eyes brighten at the sight of you, when he likes the touch of your hand, when you lift his weak head, when you see him suffering but always with a smile for you — it is hard, even if you are a young anarchist, to properly hate that man. Before a week was over Otto surrendered; he knew that he could not hate Dake ever again.

"That 'ar boy 's plum changed up," Aunt Betsey declared; "to my mind, now he sees how that 'ar sekrit soci'ty done Dake, he are 'shamed, an' he got a anxious notion of makin' up tew Dake fur bein' so mean. Got them blue pants on him, t'-day, done so. Then, I made him h'ist his legs up on a chair so Dake wud shore see 'em. Dake smiled right pleasant when he seen them legs. But that boy, he looks so puny an' down, hit 's jes' *turrible!* Won't eat a mite. Makes me feel right bad."

There was reason enough for Otto's looks. Harassed by the criminal's galley slave, fear, which made him look askance at every new-comer's face to see if it darkened at the sight of him, and strain his ears to catch the words of any voice roughened by anger, the unhappy little dynamiter cried out: "Am I *always* going to be scared like this?"

It never occurred to him to give up his job; his people needed his wages too much.

The threats which are always uttered, on such occasions, in primitive communities kept his dread at fever heat. Apparently, the least he had to expect was to be butchered with bowie knives, or strangled on a high limb of the great overcup oak facing the mill.

Neither was fear his only torturer. He was a frank lad, with a sturdy self-respect of his own, witness his declining Dake's gifts though his rags hardly covered his skin, yet now he must be praised on every side for snatching the baby up and running; he must be clapped on the back by a score of hands, black and white, and receive a miscellaneous array of tributes ranging from Marty Ann's Waterbury watch (you can buy a very good one at the store for two dollars and sixty cents) to the package from a burly admirer that contained a bowie knife and a popcorn ball — it was intolerable!

But Otto remembered the threats, and his heart failed him; he dared not attract suspicion by refusing.

"How they'd hate me if they knowed!" he thought. Neither had he any longer the poor comfort of being able to hate and despise the givers, because it is so difficult to hate and despise people who are kind to you.

Very worst of all, Otto was beginning to have ghastly doubts about the righteousness of the cause. He was so utterly solitary, poor little wretch! Winter, the blacksmith, voiced the universal opinion: " 'T war a skulkin', pusillanimous deed."

He addressed a crowd of farmers waiting their turn before his forge.

"Them fellers, them Knights er Labor, done it, to my mind," he continued. " Bassett, when he war yere, he tole me of a heap of meanness they all done to folks iz displeased 'em. ' 'T ain't safe to mad *us*,' says he."

" He tole me," said a red-haired youth, "that when the Knights got thar will, nobody had need to work more 'n eight ·hours a day. That's 'nuff, he says."

" An' how 'd we all make a crap on eight hours a day, do ye reckon?" said Lum Shinault. "Shucks! ef ye want money an' truck, ye got to work fur it! Them Knights is the durndes' fools! W'y, that ar' Bassett he 'lows land had orter be free like water. By gum, I got a good farm I paid for, my wife an' me workin' hard. Does he reckon we all goin' to sheer with any triflin' feller comes 'long ? "

" Whut I cayn't enjure," said an old farmer, " is the way he done we all. He did n't have no gredge agin we all, yit yere he tries fur to cheat us outen our gin, when he knows the ole un ain't big nuff!"

"'T war a mean trick on Mist' Francis," said Shinault; "tell ye, he done a sight er good, yere. I kin remember when thar war n't nary sightly houses, an' the store did n't sell nuthin' much 'cept white whiskey, an' the whole settlement wud git r'arin', chargin' drunk Saturday night. Yes, sir, they wud so. Look a' the place, now. Look a' them fine painted houses an' the heap of winders! Look a' the school'us that's a church house, too! An' ain't the store the best all sorts store onywhar'? an' don't sell a drop of licker. Ain't we all's farms more vallable kase of j'inin' this yere estate with the gin an' the store an' the steamboat landin'? I tell ye, Francis an' Caroll done a sight of good."

"Dey's kin' gen'lemen fo' a fac'," agreed a tall negro. "Dey did guv me credit to de sto' fo' meal an' po'k endurin' de winter w'en I ben down wid de antedelarious fever, nur dey did n't know wedder I evah git up fo' to mek a crap fo' dem."

"Waal, to my mind," said a big farmer, he of the bowie knife and popcorn ball, "ef a man got a gredge 'gin a yuther man, let him go to 'im an' have it out fair an' square. In co'se take 'is gun. This yere blowin' up mills — w'y, it's ondecent!"

A hollow-eyed man in butternut jeans was stirred to reminiscence, and told a long tale of how a man set fire to his brother's cotton gin in revenge for a bad debt.

"War ye shore 't war him done it?" said Shinault.

"Shore?" cried the man indignantly; "did n't Dock most lick his hide offen him? Shore! Be you uns shore Jim Bassett an' they all done this yere meanness?"

"Waal, now, ef ye ax me," said Shinault, "I ain't."

"Who did, then?"

"That's what I dunno."

Otto, on the outskirts of the crowd, swallowed a lump in his throat.

"Waal, shore or no," said the big farmer, whacking his boot leg truculently with his ox whip, "thar's a right smart of good men an' true a goin' to pay Mist' James Bassett a visit —an' find out!"

"Leave 'im t' the law, boys. Ye better!" said Lum Shinault; he was Esquire Shinault now, a justice of the peace, and with a profound respect for legal methods.

"Oh *we* all ain't goin'," said the farmer, and there must have been some occult pleasantry in the remark, since the crowd broke into a rough laugh.

Otto was afraid of their mirth; he hurried away — to think.

Now, as it happened, the farmer was merely bragging; and had he not been, Bassett was safe in St. Louis. But this Otto did not know. He said to himself that either he must confess, or Bassett would be sacrificed. The idea of confession was not new; it had come to him once or twice before; and this morning he had felt a desperate longing to thus prevent Dake's going. For Dake was going that day. Otto overheard part of the conversation between him and Mr. Francis.

"Dake, I am sorrier than I can say," said the planter; "it's all nonsense, your notions about my being exposed to danger if you stay. A lot of trifling blowhards, I ain't afraid of them. Why, confound it, I reckoned you'd stay and marry a pretty Arkansas girl and settle down."

Then Dake's voice came with a tremor in it: "I swear I wouldn't ask any girl to take a man for a 'usband that might be brought in dead to her, any day, or all crippled up and useless, worse than dead. I'd think too much of the girl I cared for, to ask *that!*"

And, directly, the voices having grown duller because Boo was drawing Seerayphine Dake and a new wagon through the gallery, Aunt Betsey appeared, blowing her nose and wiping her eyes and slashing the air with her big red handkerchief, in a state of mingled wrath and woe.

"The critter's deestracted," she wailed, "fixin' t' go t' Porshy t' see the cyarpenteer thar, ef he 'll come — in co'se he 'll come, dad burn him! — then, he are goin' fur good. An' he ain't nowhar nigh well. Ain't sot up yit. Goin' off by his lone, pore boy. Declare, I wisht them sekrit soci'ties was all sunk en the river! They done hit, they done hit. Boo, you hush!"

She hurried away, crying.

Otto had wondered if he could not tell, but his heart failed him.

It is so seldom that we act from simple motives, in this world; we do in fiction, we do in the newspapers, and we are continually presuming that other people do; but we ourselves — how often can we even decide which one of our medley of motives casts the final vote?

Was it his remorse for the wrong that he had done Dake, or his disgust with his false position, or his still ardent loyalty to "the order," impelling him to protect Bassett at any cost? Otto did not try to decide. He only knew there was nothing left but to tell.

Was Uncle Bruno, who was so good, right? Or was Mr. Francis right? he was good, too. And Dake was good. But did good people oppress the poor ? How could it all be ? It did not matter, anyhow, he had only done mischief; he, not Dake, was the traitor; he had disgraced the order. Yes, there was nothing left.

"They all think so kind of me," he thought with an ache in his throat, "and they trust me so. He will feel awful bad," — he meant Dake, — "but it ain't no use, I 'll tell Mr. Francis and beg him he shall not tell Mr. Dake, and they kin hang me to the blacksmith's tree, for his bed is the other way, or they kin wait till he is gone so he shall not know — but oh, meine Mutter und die Kleine !"

His tears choked him, bitter, — like death.

Still he held to his course. There was nothing else left. He walked on to the store; but slowly, because his legs did not seem to belong to him and trembled and sprawled without his being able to control his steps. He could not eat this last week; and his sleep, when he slept at last, was a succession of nightmares. After all, he was only a child trying to sin like a man, and his strength, never robust, had snapped under the weight of fright, loneliness, and remorse. His head had been troubling him lately; it had a curious, empty feeling, as if it were a mere shell. At the same time he continually heard false sounds. Voices of anguish and terror, blunted by distance, sobs and moans and the hoarse murmur as of a frantic mob approaching; he heard them all more plainly than he heard the wind rising in the cypress brake. Did he stop and listen intently, such noises would cease, and he would realize that his imagination had feigned them, but they added to the constant strain on his nerves. Even now that the worst was come, that he ought to be absorbed in the moment (for he felt his feet stumbling against the steps), even now he caught himself wondering was it really Marty Ann weeping back in a dim corner of the empty store, or the same old noises of a dream.

No one was in the store.

He crawled down the long room, feeling his way, for he could not see.

Behind the gilt wire screen which protects the office proper from the small room in the rear of the store, Mr. Francis sat poring and frowning over the biggest ledger of all.

Otto did not see a head leaned against the wall of the safe, a head with haggard features and a white cheek, or a thin hand that clutched the safe-door knob to hide its trembling. Neither did he perceive Aunt Betsey towering above the screen in a yellow sunbonnet, flapping with her motions as she rocked her high stool by bracing her two hands against the desk. All Otto's dim eyes showed him was Mr. Francis's stern face.

He staggered into the office and steadied himself against the leg of the desk.

"Mister," said he, "I done it all. If they hang me, you send my mother the wages. Don't let them hurt Jim, I done it all."

"What in the devil" — said Mr. Francis; he was not a profane man, but he had been sorely tried, to-day, losing Dake. He shut the ledger with a bang. "What do you mean?" said he.

"The explosion — that blowed up the mill," faltered Otto; this anger was the beginning. "I done it all; nobody else knowed nothin' 'bout it."

Aunt Betsey jumped from her stool with a thud.

"I don't believe you," cried Dake, hoarsely.

"I done it," repeated Otto; "I done it to make you take the boys back. I stole the cartridges and hid them in the mill once, and ayfter Mr. Dake came in I ran quick and lighted the fuse. I done it, all, myself. Jim and the boys never knowed. They ain't to blame. I did n't mean to hurt Mr. Dake. The boys ain't to blame."

He spoke in a dull, weak voice, repeating his ideas a little, and his knees were shaking. His skin had gone a kind of gray-white like tree bark in winter. His eyes were glassy.

"How did you know about making a fuse?" said Dake.

Otto lifted his head with a strange, forlorn expression of pride. "Oh, I 've known that a long time. I 've seen lots of bombs and things."

"His uncle!" cried Mr. Francis under his breath to Dake; "of course he knows. Dear, dear, dear, I 'm afraid he ain't lying."

"Bassett put him up to it," said Dake, doggedly.

"Otter," said the old woman solemnly, "did you do that thar wicked trick?"

"Yes, mum," said Otto.

"Boy, fall down, right yere, an' bless the Lord! Ye war on the brink of a precept,[1] an' the Lord mussifully slewed ye off! Don't be too hard on the critter, Mist' Francis, 't war'n't his deed. Them thar owdacious, triflin' knights jes' tolled him on, pore, innercent chile."

"Nobody — nobody — but me," said Otto again, more faintly.

"Thar! jes' like the man in the book. He 's taken the fatil vow!" Aunt Betsey cried. "Oh, I wisht ye 'd of read that thar book, you cud jedge proper then — Otter! Otter!"

It was time to catch the swaying little figure in her strong arms, since Otto, making an ineffectual effort to say something about hanging and Bassett, had fainted.

---

[1] Mrs. Graham had precipice in her mind.

Mr. Francis, like most planters in lonely re-
gions, was a bit of a doctor; he hastily grasped
Otto's wrist and felt his forehead, just as Marty
Ann rushed in, hearing her mother's scream.
Her eyes were swollen; even blind Dake could
see that she had been crying. "He is in for a
fit of sickness," said Mr. Francis.

"Then take him straight ter we all's," said
Aunt Betsey. "Law me, Mist' Francis, ye won't
let 'em take the pore chile t' the jail. 'T war n't
his deed."

Suddenly, she rose to the full significance of
the moment. There was heard the crack of a
whip and rattle of wheels, outside.

"Ef *Otter* done hit, an' not the sekrit soci'ty,
fur w'y must Dake go?"

Dake looked at Marty Ann; he struck his
lips together, trying to speak, and gasped.

Aunt Betsey remained mistress of the situation: "Marty Ann," said she, firmly, "tell him
t' stay. Ye know ye ben cryin' fit ter kill kase
he ben a-goin'. Mist' Francis, holp me h'ist
this yere chile; an' we'll tote him 'cross the
road. You all kin foller when you ready. Guv
me Dake's bag, he won't want it."

Mr. Francis bit his lip and obeyed. Marty
Ann and Dake were alone. Marty Ann recov-
ered herself first, and commanded Dake to sit
down, he was n't fit to stand.

"No," said Dake, "not till I know if I 'm to go or to stay."

"*I* ain't telling you to go," said Marty Ann; and blushed furiously and tossed up the corner of her apron with a pettish movement.

Dake was trembling exceedingly. "I *can't* believe what I want to," he cried. "Say, Miss Martha, did you see — did you see — Jim Bassett, that night you was lost?"

Marty Ann laughed out sweet and clear: "It was that, was it, you were studying 'bout and fretting over? Yes, I did, Mr. Dake — when I went to the Griffins', on the way. And I come back through the swamp so I would n't meet up with him again. And, if you want to know, he said he come to Portia to see *me*. So there!"

"Martha," said Dake, taking both her hands, "you know what I think 'bout you. You know I love you. Say, did n't you" —

"No, I did n't," said Marty Ann, lifting her sweet eyes bravely to her lover's; "I did n't care for him, but I was n't sure but I did, 'cause he was so lively and handsome; but when — when I seen you lying on the ground — I *hate* him!" cried Marty Ann.

"But you don't hate *me*," stammered Dake, in a daze of bliss; "may be, then, you — you could" —

"I reckon," said Marty Ann, very low.

About five minutes later, Dake, looking out of Paradise, saw Otto's ragged hat.

"Poor Otto," said he, "we must forgive him, dear lass."

They did forgive him. How can one bear malice to a boy that one has nursed through a brain fever?

Mr. Francis was merciful; he kept Otto's secret. Perhaps his mercy was Otto's punishment. The lad winces to this day when the talk at the store drifts into the subject of the still mysterious explosion. To this day, the tongues of the plantation orators belabor the Knights around the store stove.

Mr. Francis, who is not a friend of the order, only laughs, and remarks philosophically to young Caroll, "Oh, well, those Knights have done so many mean things I reckon one more does n't matter."

Dake's helper, strange to say, is Uncle Bruno. The widow Knipple is making a crop, just beyond the Grahams'. Frau Bruno has an account at the store and money to her credit; but Uncle Bruno is not likely to have any such prosperous showing on the ledger; all his spare dollars go to needy comrades, or to pay for those wild-looking German sheets that come to him through the mail.

Nevertheless, he keeps on the best terms with

Dake (whom the order has forgotten), and adores Mrs. Dake and Boo. Frau Bruno says: "Ach, du lieber Himmel! you tink Bruno talk fierce? Jest haf you heard him vunce ven ve in St. Louis been! But now — pshutt, he is like de sheeps!"

Aunt Betsey, however, is still seeking (vicariously in the person of the unfortunate Mr. Francis) for the book which gave her such lucid ideas on the subject of secret societies. It had a purplish back and a right pretty picture of a skull and crossed daggers outside; and, no doubt, when Mr. Francis shall find it, she will convert Herr Knipple.

THE CONJURED KITCHEN.

<hr>

" THE bread done fell," said Aunt Callie.

My friend Dorothea was standing before the huge cypress log which is our meat block. A long, thin young colored man in a ragged coat held a quarter of beef on end awaiting orders. From time to time Dora would look from the open page of her cook-book, with its neat diagram, to the unwieldy mass on the block. Her beautiful black eyebrows were slightly contracted. Usually, Dora is calm as moonlight.

" I dare say," said Dora.

" Looked like 't had a notion er risin'," continued Aunt Callie; " went up all right, but cud n't make out, some way."

She folded her arms as one that washes her hands of fate. The loose ends of her turban hung down over the nape of her neck; such a headdress, with the inscrutable melancholy of her barbaric yet regular features, made her head suggest the profiles on an Egyptian frieze. Being short and round, her shape was not imposing; but she carried her head with a grand air, and took long steps — again like the figures on a frieze. She had large, prominent black eyes, the balls of which moved slowly; and there were little bunches of wool on her cheeks below the ear. About her work, she wore a red and black striped cotton gown and a faded blue turban; but on Sundays, marching in the van of the dusky procession which went from the plantation to " preachin'," she was arrayed in a decent black gown, a plaid shawl, and a bonnet with feathers. Aunt Callie lived with her daughter in the cabin back of the cotton-field on the river-bank. Originally she came from Mississippi. She had always cooked for the quality, was a widow, a good church member, and a woman of property, having money to her account at the store, and owning two marble-top bureaus and a sewing-machine. No person of color in the county was more respected than she. Therefore Mrs. Francis engaged her as soon as Mrs. Caroll decided to fit up the old house and spend her first winter on her plantation; and we were congratulated with enthusiasm.

For three weeks our housekeeping went on smoothly. The first two of the three we were visiting Mrs. Francis, and Caledonia and her daughter, assisted by the man Jerry, prepared for our coming. After we moved into the house, nothing occurred for a week to mar our enjoyment of the novel scenes and divine weather. But then — how it first began none of us could tell — slowly, insidiously, an atmosphere of disaster seemed to ooze out of our kitchen stove. There was a monotonous round of misfortune, from coffee to bread.

" Will I bake it up, ole miss?" said Callie.

This was her invariable form of address to Mrs. Caroll, for she had been a slave, and as she had always cooked for the quality, she knew what good manners are.

Mrs. Caroll came out of the store-room at her appeal. My friend reminds one of Shakespeare's picture, "a virtuous gentlewoman, mild and beautiful." Nothing about her was ruffled now except her hair, which had caught on the meat hook.

"I suppose there is n't any bread in the house," I observed — *I* was churning milk with the egg-beater. " Did you give my rolls to the calf?"

" T' de pigs," replied Aunt Callie, concisely. " Dey wuz too sour fo' de calf."

" And your puff muffins?"

" Dey all wuz sp'iled up too," said Aunt Callie, calmly. " De chickens got *dem*, got dat ar Graham light bread, too. Dey sho bust soon."

" Well, I am sure I don't know what to say,

Callie," said Mrs. Caroll, mildly. "Mr. Dorr likes corn-cake"—

"But when we had it yesterday he said he thought he preferred 'the closely woven bread.'"

"Poor boy! the bread *was* heavy," said Mrs. Caroll. "Suppose we *don't* bake it up; we can have meat."

"I am not so sure," interrupted Dora. "Do you see any resemblance between that quarter and the picture? 'The hind quarter consists of the loin, rump, round, tenderloin or fillet of beef, leg, and flank.' Where do you suppose they are?"

"Dear me!" said Mrs. Caroll; "it seems a very big piece. I should think they would have cut it up at the store, as they did before."

"Mr. Longmire he kills de beef an' cuts it up," said Aunt Callie, "but I speck he's busy makin' of a coffin to-day."

Dora turned to Jerry. "How do they cut the meat up at the store, Jerry?"

Confusion covers Jerry as with a garment whenever he is addressed by us. He had to turn his head away before he could stammer: "Dey jis chops it off wid de axe. 'Gins ter the berginnin' an' jis chops it off, natchel."

"Do *you* know the least thing in the world about cutting up meat, Jerry?"

"Naw, 'm."

"Cut it up, then!"

"Yes, 'm."

"And you, Freddy," said Dora, politely, addressing me, "how are you coming on?"

"Oh, I'm coming on well enough; it is the butter that does n't come."

"Well," said Dora, "nobody can have more respect for the Dover egg-beater, in a general way, than I, but, as a churn, don't you think it rather lacks scope? Milk, too, does n't quite seem to take the place of cream. Winifred, you make me think of Violet and Lionel in the 'Nonsense Rhymes,' churning salt-water violently 'in the hopes of its turning into butter,' which, you may remember, 'it seldom, if ever, did.'"

"'T ain't de milk, young miss," said Aunt Callie, in a hollow voice; "dey allus chu'ns outen milk yeah. Nur 't ain't de chu'n."

"What is it, then — the climate?"

"Dis heah kitchin," said Aunt Callie, fixing her stony gaze on Jerry, who winced perceptibly, — "dis heah kitchin am — *cunjured!*"

Jerry jumped. We had been in Arkansas long enough to understand what she meant. Dora and I were silent with dismay; only Mrs. Caroll said, "Dear me, Callie, I trust not!"

"Yes, ole miss, me and de kitchin bofe. Ole Man Maggart done it. Dat how come all dese bodderations. Reckon wuss a-comin'."

A little persuasion drew out the details of her misfortune.

Every one in Arkansas knows how wicked negroes can conjure other negroes by charms, or spells, or diabolical potions. Sometimes the conjured have lizards " throwed enter 'em," which, starting in the arms or legs, gnaw their way to the victim's heart, and he dies in torment. Other baleful diseases are at the conjurer's beck, but on our plantation the afflicted commonly had lizards. Thanks to a gifted " conjure doctor," Uncle Rufe Lemew, no one had died, though to my knowledge one woman lay ill for months. Besides sickness, woful evils may fall on the person who offends a conjurer : blighted crops, dying cattle, estranged friends — in fine, no end of mischief. Old Man Maggart was our conjurer, hated and dreaded equally. It appeared that Callie, who shunned him like the rest of the world, had come upon him by accident " down in the cypress brake," where he was gathering roots for his " magic." Now, as every one knows, magic must be wrought in secret; very likely poor Callie, seeking nothing worse than " saxfras," quite ruined a promising charm — at least so I account for the rage into which the old man flew at the sight of her, " Jis stompin' on de groun' an' r'arin' on me ; said de mos' outrigeous tings, sich iz no man pusson darst say to me befo'. 'Lowed I wuz peekin' on 'im. Me! 'I 'll fix ye,' sezee; 'I 'll larn ye quit foolin' wid God's yarbs! Yuh workin' in a fine housen wid dem folkses fum de Norf,' sezee. ' Tink a heap on ye, don' dey? *Dey won' long*,' sezee. ' No good luck come to dat kitchin long iz yuh in hit,' sezee. Nur dey won't, needer."

It was easy to laugh at Aunt Callie's superstition, but I am bound to say that the facts were on her side: we did have an array of mishaps. There was the butter, for instance, ordered a month ago, and still strolling about the country, while we were reduced to lard and tallow. Then the weather turned "plumb cold," and everything that could freeze froze solid. To counterbalance this, something awful happened to the damper of the kitchen stove, so that everything put into the oven used to burn. I dare say we ought to have expected the mice to get at the raisins, but need the shelf holding the coal-oil can have broken down the only night when the crock of mince-meat stood underneath? Dorr is a patient fellow, but he did say that he thought we would better draw the line of flavors at kerosene.

All these and various other trials Aunt Callie bore with darkling composure. They were to be expected. Really, she gave Old Man Maggart more credit for evil than he deserved. That the versatile Longmire — carpenter, blacksmith, butcher, undertaker, with equal readiness and in-efficiency — should be called away from our cow-shed before he could put on the doors was quite to be expected on a plantation. Jerry nailed the cows in every night, removing the boards in the morning, and I do not see anything surprising in our best cow tearing her leg on a nail, when there were so many nails about, new and old. But Aunt Callie considered it a special freak of "de magic."   Dora argued that the cow did not belong to the kitchen : why should she be conjured ?

"But de milk do," said Aunt Callie, solemnly, "an' wharfo de cow."

The same reasoning made Old Man Maggart guilty instead of the minks that apparently killed our fowls. It goes without saying that Aunt Callie's own private ventures were a dreary procession of failures. Did any dish miraculously escape from the stove, it was sure to come to grief before it could reach us — like the delicious caramel custard set out to cool in the woodshed, and there much appreciated by our dog, Fritz. We tried to assist Aunt Callie, but it can't be said that she was grateful; she rather regarded such aid compassionately as "quality ways." "Quality liked projeckin' roun' de kitchin, cookin' outen a book, an' makin' a turrible sight er dirty dishes. Sometime deir bodderations twurns out all right, but dey 's heap apter ter burn 'em, er don' putt in 'nuff flour, er plumb forgit de sody; an' dey alluz jis natchelly sa'nters off an leabe de tings on de stove; an' she 'lowed she cud n't never make out romancin' wid torrer folkses tings, 'tickler when she did n't know nuffin dat dey wuz dar twell she smell de scorchin'. But, laws! dey wuz bawn an' raised ladies, bofe on 'em, right clever too, an' she neber see sich sweet, pretty young lady like young miss, 'cept oncet to de cirkis."

Steadily the situation grew more tragic. Aunt Callie was singularly grave. She had not a trace of that careless, lovable gayety bubbling up into the African face from some internal spring of cheerfulness that it takes so little, poor souls! of the rain of human kindness, to fill to the brim. Aunt Callie never laughed; she smiled rarely. But before her weird troubles her gravity had been of the placid, comfortable sort: now it darkened into a sinister gloom. "The Egyptian's skeleton was lively compared to her," said Dorr. "I say, mamma, do send for Uncle Rufe, and get her unconjured."

Of course we had often talked over the matter, and this was no new idea. "But I have hoped she could be persuaded of the folly of her notions," said Mrs. Caroll. "Don't you think the preacher " —

"Oh, try Uncle Rufe first," cried Dorr; "I 've no use for that preacher."

So we broached the subject to Aunt Callie's daughter. She was what in modest establishments North would be called "our second girl." Her name was Ginevra Virginia, but she was never called anything but Jinny Ver. Whether this was Arkansas for Ginevra, or an abbreviation of the two names, we did not discover. She was a pretty brown creature, gentle of voice and manner, and mirthful as her mother was grave; particularly tidy in her dress also, and always with a bright ribbon tying her queer little woolly braids. Altogether she was a pleasant object, but she was "not much force" in the kitchen. Having learned to read and write, and been at service in Little Rock, Jinny Ver at first rather flouted our plantation superstitions. "Maw jis taken up wid that notion er conjurin'," said she. "I don't believe there *is* like sich."

African skepticism is not robust. Monday, Jinny Ver tittered; Wednesday, she vowed she was not scared, but "a right smart of people ben conjured right in this settlement — say so theyseffs; reckon they had oughter know;" Friday, she came to us in a tremor. "The butter!" she gasped; "oh, Miss Dora, the butter!"

"Well, what of the butter?" said Dora. "The boat has come, and the butter is on it; Mr. Dorr paid the freight."

"Yes, 'm; but the butter ain't thar. Jerry, he done sarch ev'ywhar, an' he cayn't find it. An' maw says — she says it's the magic!"

"But you don't believe in that nonsense, Jinny Ver?"

"I did n't useter," sobbed Jinny Ver, breaking down; "but I'm skeered up, Miss Dora; an' yistiddy I scalted myseff; an' t'-day I cut them fingers; an' maw reckons we all git killed up 'fore Ole Man Maggart gits through."

Jinny Ver could hold out no hope of the conjure doctor's assistance.

"Uncle Rufe Lemew? Yes, 'm; say he's a right good doctor; but he ain't yere; he's gone t' Tennessee t' see his wife."

"But his wife lives here."

"Yes, 'm; but his main wife she lives in Tennessee; an' he's went t' stay with 'er fo' good, 'kase he p'intedly fit with Aunt Lissy; so he gethered his gun an' 'is cloze, and leff right 'way."

"Well, I must say," said Mrs. Caroll, "if this Uncle Lemew is that kind of a man, — with a main wife and another wife, — I am thankful we did n't call him in. Don't you think we might try the preacher now?"

We sent for the preacher. He came in his best frock-coat, with his boots blacked; and we gave him three dollars for his church, and asked him to labor with Aunt Callie. Our knowledge of the interview comes through Dorr, who heard Jerry describing it at the store. In the friendly circle about the store stove Jerry was a different being — a joker, a mimic, though just at present under a cloud.

" I wuz sloppin' the pig," says Jerry, " an' I seen him come at 'er ; so I peeks in frew de winder. By grabs ! Mis' Emmuns she jis natchelly matched 'im. ' Don' yuh b'lieve en de debil an' 'is angils ? ' says she ; ' how come yuh a-preachin', den, ain't no debil ? ' ' Sis' Emmuns,' sezee," — here Jerry struts across the floor, imitating the preacher's slightly pompous gestures, — " ' yuh mistaken. I b'lieve en de debil, mos' suttinly ; but Ole Man Maggart ain't no kin t' de debil. Dem suppersishuns is onworthy a lady er yo' 'telligence, Sis' Emmuns,' sezee, ' an' yo 'd orter git shet er 'em. I wisht yuh 'd come an' heah my sermon on suppersishun nex' Sunday ; I strikes it heavy on conjurin'.' But I don't guess preacher ever preached dat sermon. Huh ! huh ! "

Why that sermon was never preached, Jerry ought to know. Perhaps because she never heard it, Callie continued in her superstition, the sole result of the interview being a suspicion, born then and there in her mind, that the preacher was " biggerty." How much reason, therefore, had Jerry's conscience for twinges? But though a kind-hearted fellow, he hated the preacher. Poor Jerry! his had been a forlorn existence. His mother dead and his father in a convict camp somewhere, he had scrambled through a friendless youth, picking cotton, hauling wood, breaking horses, cheerful in spite of his lonely condition, and so good-humored that he was always liked — and cheated — until finally his thin legs, round shoulders, and deprecating grin drifted into our kitchen. At the first sight of him Jinny Ver giggled; she never stopped giggling. "That Jerry," tittered she, " his knees is on the wrong side er his legs."

In fact, there was a concave look about the profile of Jerry's legs, and they were so uncommonly thin and limp that it was hard to imagine any bones in them; but this was partly due to very baggy trousers, and partly to his habit of twisting and bending and intertwining them in the most extraordinary manner whenever he was confused. Simultaneously he would writhe his shoulders and duck his head. No wonder Jinny Ver giggled. He did not resent the giggles; he was too delighted to have her look at him at all. If *she* giggled, *he* grinned. Whenever he looked at her his teeth flashed. Then he would duck his head, glance at her out of the corners of his eyes, and shamble away. And she would giggle. For a long while he could not muster courage to utter a word. Then we began to notice that no sooner did Jinny Ver enter the kitchen than Jerry would dash at the pump handle, grinning. He would make a daring effort and look at her, saying, " Want water ? " and instantly avert his eyes and twist himself all around the pump, grinning more than ever. The next step was his asking her, " Want wood ? " He used to fall down oftener than any human being I ever saw, and he never could carry a particularly large armful of wood across the piazza without hurling most of it ahead, and sprawling on his back after it; the image of Jerry which we shall carry away is like the arms of the Isle of Man, nothing but legs kicking in the air. Jinny Ver, hearing the clatter, would run to the window and fall into soft convulsions of mirth, while Jerry would rub himself, negro fashion, grinning. *He* did n't mind the pretty creature's laughter.

After he had filled our wood-boxes he always carried a load to Aunt Callie. Strictly speaking, Aunt Callie's woodpile should have been her own private affair. However, one must not examine too closely into such matters ; doubtless Jerry considered us all one family, and there is wood for the cutting in Arkansas.

Jerry stood in the deepest awe of Aunt Callie.

He always addressed her as " Mis' Emmuns,"
and answered " Yes, 'm," and " Naw, 'm," obse-
quiously. Aunt Callie received his timid flat-
teries gravely and coldly — more gravely and
more coldly when he dared to ask for Jinny
Ver's company to a " festival." [1] She bent a
frigid gaze upon him as soon as he entered the
kitchen. " Mist' Jerry Gale," was her greeting,
in a voice chilling as her glance, " I unnerstan'
yuh aimin' ter wait on my da'ter, Jinny Ver ? "

" I jis axed 'er ter the festival," said Jerry,
humbly.

" Oh ! den yuh *ain't* aimin' ter wait on Jinny
Ver ? "

" Oh, yes, 'm. Sut'nly, Mis' Emmuns. Dat
is ter say, ef she — ef I darst." Poor Jerry
lost his voice entirely in an agony of diffidence.
Dora and I, on the other side of the door, could
hear the shuffling of his feet, and we knew that
he was twisting up his legs.

" Mist' Jerry Gale," continued Aunt Callie,
with great stateliness, " I respecks yo' feelin's,
but dese yeah 'tenshuns t' Jinny Ver mus' quit
right straight. She are eddicated, Jinny Ver

---

[1] A festival in the Arkansas rural districts has not its
Northern associations with piety, strawberries, and weak lem-
onade. It is a winter entertainment of a private character.
The negroes combine sociability and business, inviting all their
friends to their houses, and selling them cake and candy. The
amusements are dances and games.

are. She's trabeled a right smart en de kyars. I don' aim fo' ter have 'er take up wid noner dese yeah ornery, triflin', Tennessee niggers, spend deir las' nickel to festivals, an' all fo' runnin' an' havin' deir time an' pleasure. Naw, sir, Jinny Ver ain't fo' no sich. De man pusson w'ich wait on Jinny Ver mus' be a eddicated, settled-down, studdy pusson. Yuh heah me?"

Jerry murmured something about a pair of mules and ten dollars at the store.

"Ef yuh got mewls an' ten dolla', yo' lucky," retorted Aunt Callie, majestically; "but 't ain't no differ. Me an' Jinny Ver ain't wantin' mewls. We-uns trabels en de kyars."

"An' I kin read big print, an' write my name," urged Jerry, piteously.

"Dat 's very pleasant an' 'specterbul, Mist' Gale, an' I wisht yuh well. But dat ar ain't eddication. Eddication are readin' an' writin' an' ciph'rin' an' jogify. Kin yuh tell me whar Aschy ur Rooshy 's *at*, Mist' Gale?"

"Dey sells 'em t' de sto'," stammered the unfortunate Jerry; "dey 's fo' de ladies."

"I 'lowed yuh 'd answer dat a-way, Mist' Gale. 'T ain't no manner use we-uns 'cussin' de questin furder. Ye 'd orter see dat yoseff. Be so kin' not fool no mo' wid my gell. I wisht ye well." With these words, uttered in her deepest voice, Aunt Callie turned her back on him. He was so disconcerted, and he had tied his legs into such a knot during his embarrassed writhings, that, starting to follow her, he stumbled, and plunged headlong into Jinny Ver and the soup tureen. He burned himself; but what was that compared to the ruin of Jinny Ver's new frock?

With an inarticulate howl the wretched lover leaped to his feet and fled. Now began a season of gall and tears for Jerry. Neither of the women would speak to him. If we sent a message or order it was bawled impersonally, out of the door, at the river. "Mis' Caroll want dem molasses fotched from de stor'!" "Whar Miss Freddy's horse at? — she jis r'arin' an' chargin'!" "How come de cows ain't milk yit?" — every sentence in the highest key, though poor Jerry might be at the crier's elbow. He did not resent his ostracism. He was a soft-hearted fellow, with no proper pride in him. He rather tried to propitiate the offended dignities. The wood-boxes almost broke down under the weight of his good-will. Regularly each morning he would black the kitchen stove until it shone, his reward being a gruff, "Wisht dat nigger quit monkeyin' wid my stove; sho debil it, some way."

He bought a dress pattern at the store. On the outside of the bundle he printed mIsjiNyvEr EmUNs in letters of various size, and he tied the whole tastefully with blue ribbon to the rolling-pin, which hangs on the wall opposite the door, just where it would be sure to meet the eye, the instant the door was opened in the morning. Poor Jerry!   Caledonia pointed the finger of scorn at the bundle, remarking grimly, "Do yuh reckon he aims dem fo' *letters?* "   "Te he," said Jinny Ver.   There was a rustling noise in the gallery outside, a scrape, and a thud.   "List'ners don' git no good er deyseffs," said Aunt Callie.

That evening the preacher's mule stood in front of Aunt Callie's cabin for two hours.   We could see Jerry's sorry figure slinking across the cotton rows and disappearing in the shadow of the willows which fringe the river-bank.   The willows face the cabin.   When he came back Dora declared that he had been crying.   Our sympathies were so roused that she offered to teach him to read, and I gave him a dollar.   It was an unwise gift; Jerry straightway bought a second-hand banjo at the store.   He played entirely by the light of nature, and in his case the light was dim.   He never played any tune, for the best of reasons; but sometimes he would sing the " Arkansas Traveler."   No one who has never heard Jerry can have any idea of the weird and heart-broken anguish that is hidden in the strains of the " Arkansas Traveler." The first time I heard him moaning out the song over his woodpile I was sure that he must have cut himself; but Dora said, No, he always sang that way. The preacher, however, had a beautiful voice.

"'Clare he makes me cry, he sings so sweet," said Jinny Ver. She said it in Jerry's presence. The young fellow's eyes flashed; even meek creatures may be goaded into rage. "Dod gum his ornery time!" he cried savagely. "I'll make *him* sing!"

He marched out of the room. Being Sunday, the day was his own. He went to Mr. Francis and borrowed his wildest Texan pony. There was no danger for Jerry, the plantation horse-breaker; and how could Mr. Francis suspect that Jerry would lie in wait for the preacher and join him, and when the preacher admired the Texan, would offer to exchange the fiery horse for the peaceful mule? "He's a sorter ill hoss,"[1] said the artful Jerry; "but yo' sicher good rider, I don't guess he kin devil ye."

By this time they had come to the lane which runs back of Mrs. Caroll's house, and is the road always taken by the colored worshipers on Sunday morning. Possibly the preacher, who was a good rider, was tempted to display his

[1] This word is used queerly. It means ill-tempered, cross. They say of a sick person, "He is so *ill*, he must be getting better."

horsemanship before the sisters. We all saw him mount, Jerry holding the horse. The Texan went on for a little space in a series of mincing hops. Suddenly he flung back his mane and whirled round. "An' *den*" — so Jerry described the catastrophe to a delighted audience at the store — "preacher he kep' hollerin' on 'im an' sawin' his mouf, an' sorter worritin' 'im (me tryin' fur ter ca'm 'im all the time), an' all ter oncet dat ar pony begun to buckjump, an', by grabs, befo' he cud bat 'is eye ter save 'is soul, he throwed preacher clearn across the road plumb into the mire en Mis' Caroll's field. Dat nigger, he sho tore de groun' up ! De wimmin-folkses dey scraped 'm off. Huh ! huh ! "

Aunt Callie, who was among the women, witnessed the scene grimly, making no comment. I am sorry to say Jinny Ver shook with laughter. "That Jerry," said she, "he done it jis outer meanness ! That nigger 's got a heap er meanness in 'im ! " Strange to say, she seemed to like Jerry better for his " meanness " than for all his mild good qualities. She met him at the door with an old-time giggle. Friendly relations were resumed without a word of explanation. Even Aunt Callie abandoned the preacher. " He don' unnerstan' hisself," said she.

Jerry made the next attempt to unconjure the

kitchen. He spoke the devil fair ; in other words, he went to see the Old Man Maggart, and offered him " two good mewl an' a waggin an' ten dolla's an' a banjo," — poor Jerry! all he had in the world, — " ef he would let Mis' Emmuns off."

But the conjurer was obdurate. Jerry came home covered with mud, in a great fright. " He 's a turrible fellow," he kept saying," shivering over his recollections — " turrible fellow. Says he got a ball er devil's yarn en you-all's kitchin, an' he do Mis' Emmuns wuss 'n he done 'er ! "

" Well, yuh done yo' bes', boy," said Aunt Callie, less sternly than usual, " but none er yuh 's sharp 'nuff to cotch up ter de magic. Have ter make out bes' I kin my black seff." She tried some most primitive schemes. Once I overheard her addressing the dough ; " Now yuh git up. I 's gwine outen dis kitchin, stay right smart w'ile. Yuh ain't conjured widout I are yeah. Yuh raise, den ! " Absences of this sort were frequent. The bread was left on the fender and the cake in the oven while Aunt Callie's turban was sorrowfully shaken over the chickens outside. But not thus were the malign powers to be wheedled ; nor was her other device of having Jinny Ver do the actual cooking, Aunt Callie advising her through the window, any more successful. " Mout 's well 'a' putt my han's to 't my black seff," she groaned over some particularly poor cake of Jinny Ver's. "Naw, chile, yuh cayn't holp me; I don't guess nobuddy kin!"

"Mis' Emmuns," said a mild and anxious voice in the doorway — "Mis' Emmuns, I knows sumfin!" It was Jerry, who crooked one ragged leg athwart the door, which he held barely ajar, and thrust his head into the kitchen.

"Does ye?" said Aunt Callie, satirically, "how come dat?"

"I ben down t' the sto'," continues Jerry, "an' they was talkin' of conjurin', and Mist' Ike Miller — he ben conjured p'int-blank — he says ef a person kin smack Ole Man Maggart en the face so 's ter dror de blood, an' kin cotch de blood, 'fore it fall ter de groun', he cayn't hurt 'em nur deir frien's no mo.' Says hit 's sho."

Aunt Callie uttered a kind of grunt of mingled despair and irritation. "An' whut ye reckon happen ef yuh don' dror de blood jis right? *Whut den?*"

Jerry, trembling from the wool on his pate to the last wrinkle of his trouser leg, gasped, "Dun know."

"Yuh dun know?" said Aunt Callie, bending her brows and rolling her eyeballs in a truly blood-curdling manner — "yuh dun know? I *does!*" She shooed a presumptuous fowl away from the window without the least abatement of gloom; then, seeing that Jerry's leg still embraced the door, she added: " Yuh all down t' de sto's turrible brash an' brave, but dey ain't nary un er ye darst mix wid de Ole Man Maggart. Nur dey had n't better, needer."

" Yes, 'm," said Jerry, meekly. But he did not go; he cleared his throat desperately. " Mis' Emmuns, I — I aims t' go see Ole Man Maggart an' unconjure you all."

Caledonia's only answer was the sardonic question, " Does yuh like lizards, boy ? "

" Naw, 'm ; I 's skeered on 'em."

" Den leave Ole Man Maggart 'lone. De cunjurin' he guv me are pleasant an' happy to whut he guv *yuh* ef ye go monkeyin' wid his magic."

" I reckon," said Jerry, miserably; " but I 's gwine unconjure you-uns or git killed up my black seff — one ! "

" Boy," said Caledonia, a little moved by this devotion, "don' yuh go. De road 's mornstus muddy ; yuh mire up, sho."

" De mud 's on'y shoe-mouf deep, Mis' Emmuns; I kin make out. Well, I wisht ye well, Mis' Emmuns."

The ragged leg released the door, and Jerry stumbled down the steps. Shortly after, he presented himself in the library, clad in his Sunday clothes, holding his banjo in his hand.

"Miss Dora," said he, "kin I go over yonder t' Ole Man Maggart's? I's aimin' to unconjure you all."

"Certainly," said Dora, cheerfully — we had both been in the kitchen since Jerry saw Aunt Callie. "Unconjure us by all means. Take the whole afternoon if you want it, and ride the big mule."

"Yes, 'm," said Jerry. He choked a little. "Mabbe I won' git t' come back. Say he's a turrible fellow. Miss Dora, please back a letter fur me — please, 'm." He handed her the banjo, to which was pinned a blank envelope. "I'd like fur ter have yuh put Mis' Jinny Ver Emmuns on it," said he; "she cayn't read *my* letters. The banjo hit's fur 'er. An' dey's my money en de envelop — I drored it from de sto' — fur Miss Jinny Ver Emmuns. An' I got two mewls an' a waggin — fur Miss Jinny Ver Emmuns. Please, 'm, put it down. An'— an', Miss Dora, please write a few words on paper f' me — please, 'm." He stood before the fireplace (and why he did n't fall in I am sure I don't know, he did such terrible things with his legs) as he dictated: "Miss Jinny Ver Emmuns: Dear friend, — I reckon I 'm t' be killed up, so I leaves yuh my banjo. I won't need it in the silen' tomb, an' anyhow they all has harps over yander. Please, Miss Jinny Ver, don' forgit me, 'kase I love yuh true. I wisht I cud 'a' heerd yuh a-laffin' oncet agin. I cayn't say how I feel, I feel so bad. Please, Miss Jinny Ver, forgive me ef I ever done anything t' mad yuh. I 'd like for ter say a heap mo', but I mus' be movin'. Please, Miss Jinny Ver, forgive the liberty I taken writin'. Yo' frien' — Please, 'm," said Jerry, " I kin write my name." So he signed his name, standing on one leg like a crane, and sprawling all over the paper; but he surveyed the result with mournful pride. " Miss Jinny Ver Emmuns got a turrible sight er eddication," he sighed. " I 'lowed I 'd go ter school ef I 'd a-lived."

I don't justify the morality of our next proceeding; I admit we leaned on the Jesuits. One of us — no matter which — took a foreign coin out of her purse, saying, " That is my own private conjure charm, Jerry. As long as that is in your pocket, neither Old Man Maggart nor any one else can harm you. But if you get scared you may lose it, so be *bold !* "

" Yes, 'm," said Jerry.

Anything less bold than he as he shambled off it would be hard to fancy: poor black knight of the rueful countenance going to dare more awful peril than was faced by the white knights in their steel and feathers ! It was real peril to him, however it might appear to us; he was horribly afraid, too. Yet he never flinched; perhaps the grotesque creature was a bit of a hero.

Nothing in particular occurred that afternoon, unless I count the breaking of all the yellow bowls by Jinny Ver, who thought she heard a "screechin' noise," and "'lowed 't wuz Jerry," and naturally jumped. Aunt Callie moved sombrely about the kitchen preparing the prodigal Southern supper. She came in from the storeroom to say that the weather was growing warm so fast that all the meat was " p'intedly sp'ilin'." She went out into the yard for eggs, and reported, " Chickens all layin' unner de house — roosts dar; minks git dem least ones, sho."

" Cows ain't come home, in co'se," was the next bulletin of doom; " need n't speck no milk t'-morrer."

But she admitted that her waffle batter looked "real old timey." Alas, fallacious gleam of hope! We waited to be summoned to the table, but no summons came. Presently a strong smell of burning food was wafted from the kitchen, accompanied by smothered exclamations, and then a clatter of metal. " Waffles fallen into the fire, probably," said Dora. The burning odor grew stronger and more complex. Smoke began to drift through the gallery, through the dining-room, into the parlor. They were running about frantically in the kitchen.

Then the doors flew open, and Jinny Ver rushed through the rooms screaming, "Quick! quick! the stove's afire!"

Not pausing to consider the startling anomaly of a stove afire, we caught up, indiscriminately, rugs, the water jug, and an empty pail, and ran to the kitchen. True enough, a sheet of flame enveloped the stove, smoke was rolling from the charred pores of the mantel, and the air was so murky that we could barely see. Besides, Jinny Ver had dropped the lamp.

Dorr flung a rug at the line of dish-towels behind the stove, which was making the most of the illumination. "Water!" he shouted; "the buckets! — the buckets by the sink!"

"They's empty," whimpered Jinny Ver.

"An' de pump's done broke," said Caledonia, with deadly calm.

"I'll see about that," cried Dorr, grabbing the pump handle. A rattle and a shiver, and a very wrong exclamation from Dorr. Yes, undoubtedly the pump was broken.

Meanwhile the wood-box had begun to blaze.

"There's the water in the rooms," cried Dora.

"Naw, young miss," said Aunt Callie, lifting her hand solemnly; "dat do no good. Dis kitchin sho go. I guvs it up; I's gwine. I ain't yo' cook no mo'."

She flung her apron over her head in a burst of emotion as surprising as it was poignant, and ran blindly to the door.

With a crash the blazing kindlings tumbled on the brick hearth. The line holding the towels, burned to a black wisp, gave way, and the towels sank in a flaming heap beside the wood; there they turned harmlessly to charcoal. A dense smoke succeeded the glare.

Caledonia stood still, and breathed heavily. In a second she clapped her hands above her head, and shouted "Glory!" at the top of her voice. Then, calmly as usual, she pointed to the hearth, saying: "De fire done putt *itself* out. Yuh see, miss, ole miss, yuh all see, we's *unconjured*. Dat boy do like he said. Bress de Lawd!" She made no sort of account of the water Dora and I brought from the chambers and flung on the mantel, though it dripped down and made a perfect pool on the floor. "Yes, ole miss, guv de Lawd de glory. Dat boy break up de magic, else sho dis kitchin go. Jinny Ver, yuh go home right 'way. Putt on yo' good dress an' yo' lace collar, an' put somer dat cologe Miss Freddy done guv ye on yo' hanker', an' come an' set by de fire twell dat boy come home, kase he ar gwine keep yuh comp'ny in macrimony. Dat boy, mabbe, don't got eddication, but he got *sense.* Don' yuh say one word. Yuh don' lay yo' han' on a dish dis ev'nin'. Now I's gwine cook yuh all a supper."

It was a supper to be remembered. Caledonia waited on us herself. Her countenance wore a gracious smile as she brought in the waffles, light, crisply brown, delicious. "Looked like I never git likened ter cookin' in dis kitchin," said she; "but I don't guess we gwine have ony mo' trubbel. Jerry he done come home, an' he's settin' long er Jinny Ver. Says he done de ole man like he'd orter, an' it's all right. He putt out his han' an' p'intedly show me de blood. Dat boy!"

Plainly, Jerry's troubles were over. We caught one glimpse of the dusky lovers, sitting in very much the attitude of lovers the world over, and a few stray sentences floated to us through the window-glass: "Then I guv over pleadin' with 'im, an' I up an' hit 'im. I lope dat mewl, an' I tell ye I spilt de mud — wen' so fas' we burnt de wind. An' I do over agin for yuh t'-morrer — I wud so. Fur — Oh, Miss Jinny Ver!"

Now the readers of this simple tale may think what they please. All I know is that in the night it grew cold, saving all our meat; the boat came back with our butter; our new potatoes and fruit came safely; three minks were caught in our traps; the carpenter mended the pump and finished the shed. Caledonia next morning made bread fit for a king, and from that day to this the conjured kitchen has rested in prosperous peace.

THE FIRST MAYOR.

IT is a large city now, where electric lights blaze all night, and factory chimneys stain the sky by day, and the beautiful undulating river shore is scarred with railway lines, and the architecture has felt the touch of Richardson and the American renaissance. But when Tom and I first saw Atherton, looking from the deck of the ferry-boat across the myriad sparkles of the Mississippi, the time was 1858, and the town numbered barely fifteen thousand inhabitants.

Here and there, only, was the battlemented line of flat-roofed shops and warehouses broken by a structure higher than three stories. The hotel loomed up with its multitude of windows; and higher yet towered two enormous brick buildings, flour-mill and store, from each of which a red flag flaunted, bearing the inscription *Atherton and Temple*. I had my reasons for inspecting these edifices, — the same reasons that sent my eyes searching among the smart villas on the bluffs, until they rested on a great white mansion with the lofty Corinthian columns and decorated pediment of our fathers' architectural pomp, and stately gardens and terraces stepping downward to the glitter below. They also permitted a tolerably honorable young woman to listen eagerly to the conversation going on at my elbow. The interlocutors were two men, René de McCarthy, whom I knew, and an elderly stranger. I paid little attention to René's light figure or handsome French-Irish face, but I looked with all my eyes at the stranger. He was of insignificant presence, short and thin, wiry, however, having broad shoulders and long arms. His head appeared disproportionately large, perhaps because it was so thickly covered with iron-gray locks which he wore brushed in a high wave over his forehead. He had pushed his shining black beaver hat obliquely backward over his ears. His nose was of the eagle type, and his deep-sunken eyes were amazingly bright. They flashed in unison with his strong white teeth when he smiled, giving an effect of brilliancy to his rugged and tanned face. In the same way, when he frowned, his shaggy eyebrows helped the savage strength carved in his jaw and mouth. His dress was of the best material, — a satin waistcoat, and the black broadcloth then esteemed the only habit of dignity; nevertheless, it was so carelessly worn and so dusty that he almost appeared shabby. He wore no gloves, and was paring his finger-nails in the most artless manner. Satisfied with their appearance, he waved his hand at the prospect.

"Don't look much like our rival now, hey?" said he.

The point on the shore that he indicated was a mere hamlet; but once, as he had been telling René, it had been the county seat, a distinction wrested from it by the town of Atherton fifteen years before, mainly through the speaker's own efforts.

"I tell folks that town made me first mayor of Atherton," said he, jocosely; "they elected me then, and they 've elected me every year since. I come high, but they must have me."

I could not understand René's smiling attention and deference; to my mind, the first mayor of Atherton was a vainglorious, vulgar little man.

"They named the town after you, later, did n't they," asked René, "when your store was burned?"

Mr. Atherton flashed his brilliant smile on him. "The store was n't burned, my son, — not exactly. It happened this way. The mill did burn down. It was one of the coldest days in the year, — mercury 'way down to thirty below, and only reason it did n't get lower was we had n't any longer thermometer. I was out on the farm, and I came in on the jump. There stood Billy Temple, covered with icicles, and swearing like only an ex-Methodist brother can swear. I sized up the situation in a minute. Blizzard blowing, and water all froze up, and the houses like tinder. I told Billy the only chance to save the town was to make a hole big enough to stop the fire. We had got to blow up our store. He begun about the stock. 'Look a here,' says I, 'do you think I 'm going to see this town burned to save our stock? D— the stock!' says I. Billy 's *white.* He looked at the wind and he looked at the store. 'All right, J. D.,' says he, 'd— the stock!' We lit the match to our gunpowder — Hullo, what 's your hurry, friend?"

He addressed a stalwart farmer-looking man who ran across the deck, stumbling in his haste and a sort of fury that was upon him. The man shook his fist in Atherton's face.

"Oh, you d— swindler, do you know I 've failed?" cried he. He was choking with passion, but Atherton did not change countenance.

"That 's too bad," he said placidly.

"*You* failed me!" screamed the farmer. "You overbid me with the farmers and underbid me in the market. You make your brags you 'll run the produce business of this town, do you? You said you 'd run me out of business, and you 've done it. But I 'll give you reason to remember Jim Ripley!"

In an access of rage, he flung his great bulk upon the mayor, who leaped nimbly aside. Another onslaught, but more disastrous, since, this time, the big fellow lost his balance and plunged headlong against the frail guards with a force that shivered them. Into the water he crashed. I shrieked for Tom. My husband is a magnificent swimmer. But he was already overboard. Nor he alone; there was a second splash, and just behind Tom's sleek brown head I saw a rift of iron-gray locks and a flash of shirtsleeves forging through the waves (all the while a shout ringing in my ears, " Heave the rope after us ! "), and off in the boat's wake a wild white face tossed like an egg-shell and two black arms threshing the foam. I flew to the coil of rope, to find René's hands readier than mine. It was all over in a moment; and they were dripping on the lower deck, and every one was cheering, and pocket-flasks of whiskey were waving in all directions. René escorted me downstairs. Then I realized that Tom's helper and the man who was vigorously rubbing and warming poor, limp, crestfallen Ripley was no other than Mr. Mayor Atherton himself. His loud tones filled the air : —

"Well, Mr. Ransome, this is a funny kind of introduction, ain't it?"

But he was very cordial, and sent us to our hotel in his carriage. How vividly that carriage appears out of the past, — one of the four then in Atherton, — the horses so shining, the gold-plated harness so showy, the cushions so luxurious, the black coachman so majestic! Livery in those days was not common even in cities; I admired Cato's blue and brass and gold-banded beaver.

Mr. Atherton smiled, well pleased at our surprise. "Don't look much like your notions of the West, young lady, does it!" he chuckled. "I can tell you it ain't much like my first carriage, either. That was a prairie schooner."

I recoiled from the man with his heavy voice and free manner: it was a relief when he went away.

"He is very good-natured," said Tom. He would not join in my mockery. He kept to his mayor.

"He is the great man of the town; in fact, he made it. He has shown some fine qualities," said he; "so much the better, since our future depends on him." Alas, it was true to the bone: on this blustering provincial magnate our future did depend.

It does not concern my story how the ancient

amity of our fathers (Tom and I were betrothed while we both wore petticoats) was distorted into suspicion and resentment. Whose the fault matters least of all, since the old foes and older friends are reconciled now, in that dim land to which they departed content with each other. But for a time the feud was bitter. The elders dissolved our betrothal. We were young, hot-headed; we loved each other, and my mother was dead. One can imagine such a pair's way out of the tangle. We ran away and were married, presently finding ourselves as poor as we were happy. Therefore, when René de McCarthy, Tom's classmate at Harvard, invited Tom to become assistant editor of the Atherton "Citizen" at a fair salary, the offer was promptly accepted. René was a young Louisianian whose father was more plentifully blessed with children than with money; he had gone up the river to seek his fortune. He was editor-in-chief of the "Citizen," which he explained to Tom was the sole property of Mr. Jared D. Atherton, mayor of the town, and its most zealous and vigilant promoter; a man of wealth, also, vast for those times; the owner of mills and farms, and houses and stores. He had lavished his own money on the town and drawn Eastern capital to it, spreading its advantages far and wide, in a fashion very common now, but unusual enough to

be original then. The "Citizen" was merely
another agent in the work. He cared far less
that it should be profitable financially than that
it should successfully advertise the town. Tom
had seen the office and was favorably impressed.
" Everything is on a liberal scale, — no stinting.
Even our editorial sanctum has gilt paper and
Brussels carpet. Colors scream at each other, of
course, and no end of them. René calls it the
Rainbow. Atherton is liberal in other ways;
no interference with the political articles except
that I am never to abuse a good citizen and
maker of Atherton. That sounds well. I am
to be as decent as I please in my language, too:
another distinct advantage. Oh, he is not a bad
fellow, Katy."

Thus Tom talked on, happy and hopeful, and
I shared his mood. But the next day he had
gone to his office, and the exile's homesickness
was twitching my nerves. I was glad to receive the cards of Mrs. J. D. Atherton and
Miss Bainbridge. " Very correct cards," I
thought, " but no doubt they are pompous, purse-
proud, horrid things who have come to patronize
me." So lonesome was I, however, that patronage itself was acceptable; it might give me
something to laugh over with Tom, later.

Two ladies were by themselves in the vast,
gaudily furnished parlors; yet I hesitated to ad-

dress them, unable to believe that either of them could belong to Mr. Atherton. The elder was a slender, dark-eyed, softly smiling, languid gentlewoman, whose head swayed a little to one side, and whose tiny foot peeped out far enough to discover a gleam of white silk stocking above the low-cut and rosetted shoe. She was dressed in one of the bright-hued and ample-skirted silk frocks of the period. What we called a mantilla, of silk and black lace, slipped gracefully from her shoulders. Her black hair was smoothly banded under a creamy Leghorn bonnet trimmed with white ribbon. Every detail of her costume pleased me, being daintily fresh and fine, like her embroidered collar and undersleeves of Indian muslin, which were works of art. For brooch, she wore a miniature set in diamonds; and there were diamonds and emeralds on her beautiful hands, sparkling through the meshes of her black silk mitts.

Such was the costume of a woman of fashion in the days of my youth.

No sooner did my eyes fall on the wearer than I recognized her right to the description, and my admiration of her elegant figure and her toilet was increased by the quickly following discovery that she was a Southerner; for in those antebellum days the planter aristocracy furnished our social ideals.

The younger lady could hardly have owned more than twenty years. Between the two there was a plain resemblance, although the girl was taller, with rounder outlines and a hint of vigorous muscles in her movements, — she was lifting a window. Her dress also was simpler, as became her years, but equally tasteful. She had wine-brown eyes, which shone with a gentle, steady radiance; but her bright color came and went uncertainly, contradicting the repose of her manner and her still eyes.

The elder woman, rising very gracefully, introduced herself as Mrs. Atherton, and presented her daughter, Miss Bainbridge. Miss Bainbridge merely bowed and smiled. It soon appeared that she was a silent person. Mrs. Atherton, however, talked fluently, in her languid Southern fashion. She had a good deal to say about the place. Service was the sore trial of the Atherton housekeepers, and I afterward found it a universal topic of conversation, whatever the time, or place, or social rank; then, I remember, I was bewildered to have Mrs. Atherton give it so much time. She admitted that she herself had little cause for complaint. They had kept their old slaves; that is, some of the house servants. Mam' Chloe really was a right good cook, — she cooked to please gentlemen; she herself preferred lighter dishes; but she hoped we would dine with them on the morrow, and judge for ourselves.

I was won by her cordial manner and her sweet voice. More and more it puzzled me that she could have married Atherton. She enlightened me directly, in the most unembarrassed way. I had asked her if she was an old resident of Atherton.

"Oh, yes, ma'am," she answered, smiling, "old for Atherton. People never stay here long. They are always coming and going. That is why Mr. Atherton is trying to induce the Germans to come here. He says they all will stay and make a kind of anchor for the town. We have been here ten years. We all simply came on a visit to sister Elsa Cunningham, who lived here then. They have moved away since. It was that awful cholera year, and Colonel Bainbridge was taken ill and died. So did Tempe, my maid; and Rose was terribly sick, and sister Elsa's three children. And only me to wait on them, — you can't imagine the horrors of that time."

"We all should have died but for Mr. Atherton," said Miss Bainbridge. It was absolutely her first sentence.

"Yes, he was extremely kind," said Mrs. Atherton.

I fancied myself, in case Tom saved my life,

assuring a stranger that he was "extremely kind"! I stole a glance at Mrs. Atherton's white throat. The face on the miniature was young and handsome; it was not Atherton's harsh features that she treasured.

"Colonel Bainbridge's affairs had been shamefully neglected, and worse, by his overseer," she continued in her plaintive, melodious tones. "After his death we found ourselves almost penniless. Why, Mr. Atherton had to buy our slaves for us; he had, indeed. We stayed here with sister Elsa. Pa had lost so much by our troubles I could n't bear to return to Charleston. So a year and a month after Colonel Bainbridge died, I married Mr. Atherton. He took everything off pa's hands, and somehow — I 'm sure I don't know how — he has made money enough to pay pa back. He always does make money," she added carelessly.

I could see that Miss Bainbridge was wincing under her good manners, though she said not a word. The whole history was clear enough now. The helpless Southern woman had accepted the strong arm tendered her simply because it was strong. She did not love her husband. I made a nervous effort to divert the conversation into safer channels, saying something about Mr. Atherton doing so much good with his money, giving so much to the town.

" I tell Mr. Atherton he is crazy over this town," said Mrs. Atherton, opening an elaborate sandalwood fan and softly waving it. "Pray don't encourage his mania, Mrs. Ransome. He has given a park, and a hospital, and a cemetery, besides subscribing to everything. He gives to every church. He nearly built the Episcopal church. We all are members, you know, — not he himself ; oh, no, ma'am, he *never* goes to church ; stays home and looks over accounts, and plays on the jew's-harp by himself."

I must have stared, in spite of my will to keep my eyes out of the window, for I saw Miss Bainbridge's color rise. Naturally I made the situation worse by an imbecile murmur of not knowing that Mr. Atherton was musical.

"I should n't call him musical," answered Mrs. Atherton, dryly. "He likes nigger songs and hymns. There he is now, Rose, with Mr. Temple. Mr. Temple has all the virtues, Mrs. Ransome. Have you ever observed how uninteresting all the virtues are in a man?"

If Mr. Temple had all the virtues, he had none of the graces. I found him a large, faintly colored, taciturn man, whose only spark of animation was struck out by his partner's sallies ; but my heart warmed to his bashfulness, after Mr. Atherton's bravado. This is ungrateful, since the latter, on this occasion, bragged not at all, and very shortly retired with Temple to the outskirts of the conversation.

We soon grew familiar with the town. It was like hundreds of other Western towns in its stage of growth, — crude, inharmonious ("a tawdry sort of civilization," Tom called it), yet with a sound core of Puritan conscience, and groping towards splendid possibilities. Half the streets were unpaved, in spite of the mayor's efforts, but they were picturesque with "prairie schooners," and resounded with a din of traffic and building. Some of the dwelling-houses were well planned and ample mansions, set back in shady grounds, but the business architecture was mean. One single exception do I recall, — Thorne and Quincy's bank, which had a marble façade, with acanthus leaves carved on the cornices, and imposing marble steps curving outward into the street. Neither Mr. Atherton's mill nor store could vie with this; both being simply huge iron-and-brick structures, bare and ugly to the last degree. The mill was the largest flour-mill west of the Mississippi. The store was a vast bazaar, where everything from millinery to drugs made a grotesque panorama for the buyer. René de McCarthy introduced me to the store. He was in high favor with Mr. Atherton; in fact, it was understood that he was to marry Miss Bainbridge. I had occasion to buy a few small articles, and I was surprised to be handed, in change, two bits of yellow and blue pasteboard: the yellow bit authorizing me to receive twenty-five cents' worth of Israel Finch's " excelsior bread " at the Atherton Bakery, and the blue bit good for " one dish of pure ice cream at the Palace Restaurant." My amazement pleased René, who explained that, silver coin being scarce at the West, the shopkeepers' wits had fallen upon this device. While he spoke, a man in a floury coat walked up to a high desk near us, demanding " the old man." He looked so good-humored that I was a moment or so in recognizing our tragic friend of the ferry-boat, Mr. Ripley. Truly, I was not sure of his identity until Mr. Atherton's head peered over the desk-rail, and he called cheerfully : —

" Hello, Ripley! come for the money? I'll get it. That you, Renny? And Mrs. Ransome? Well, we are favored this morning; sun shines and you come to see us. Don't you two want a peep at my private bank?"

I felt rather dazed, but René, as a matter of course, ushered me up two flights of stairs into a bare room that had been partitioned off from the carpet ware-room. It was not only plainly furnished; the furniture was *bizarre :* there were a couple of shabby rocking-chairs clad in black haircloth, a marble-topped centre-table, and a rickety desk. The walls were plastered and whitened, and against this dead whiteness two daguerreotypes, framed in black, had a sickly yellow aspect. The other decorations were a map of Atherton and a pencil-drawing of a tomb. This latter was a florid design representing a very stiff angel playing a harp with her left hand to a group of children, all disposed about the conventional broken shaft. One of the daguerreotypes was the picture of three plain and solemn children; the other, of one plain and solemn woman; and, as in a flash, it was clear to me that the children of the daguerreotype and the children of the monument were model and copy, while the woman's high forehead and long nose were faithfully repeated in the angel's face. But the angel essayed a smile.

During my frivolous criticisms Atherton was unlocking his desk. He pulled out a great package of crisp, new bank-notes, cutting them apart with a pair of shears, after which he dated and signed half a dozen notes, and pushed them over to Ripley, who departed with them.

"Guess a thief would n't make much breaking into my bank," was Atherton's comment. "Like to see the bills, Mrs. Ransome? Here 's a gold check, too."

The first engraving had all the outward semblance and texture of a bank-note, save that the legend thereon was different, reading as follows: " *Six months from date, Atherton and Temple will pay the Bearer, on demand,* TEN DOLLARS *in current funds.*" The other note specified a longer time, and the payment was to be in gold.

Atherton went on to tell René about the gold checks: how his clerks were instructed to offer the other checks first, and only give gold checks when they were demanded. " Then we can work Florence on them," said he, slyly. " Fact is, our checks are good as any money, — banks take 'em, railroad and ferry take 'em, stores all take 'em ; but sometimes they ain't satisfied ; come in and want money. We hand them over Florence, and like as not they go to Thorne and Quincy with that, and want them to cash it and get our checks. Current funds, you know. We call it swapping oats."

" Where is Florence, anyhow ? " asked René. " I know the Florence money is Thorne and Quincy's issue, but it is redeemable at the bank of Florence, it says on the bills. Where is the town ? "

" Nebraska," answered Atherton, with a grin.

" I thought the Territory of Nebraska was all a wilderness," said I, innocently.

" So they say," said Atherton. " I ain't never been there, so I can't tell you."

" You hardly will go there with your Florence, will you ? " asked René.

" I guess not," acquiesced Mr. Atherton. " Do you know, though, that Billy, last year, sorted out all the Indiana bills we found in our safe, — twenty odd thousand dollars, — take them by and around, worth eighty cents on the dollar ; and I assure you he put them in his carpet-sack, and went all through Indiana to the different banks that issued them and got ninety-five cents on the dollar. Pretty good for wild-cat money, hey ? But Nebraska is too far away."

" Mr. Temple got more out of them then than he would now, I reckon," said René.

Atherton nodded. " Bill 's cautious. But he 's got plenty of pluck, too. Never knew him to be fazed but once : that was just before the Crimean war, when I wanted to buy up the wheat crop."

" He did feel shaky then ? "

Atherton showed his brilliant smile. " Well, you see there was a thundering big wheat crop that year, and prices were 'way down, and nobody believed there was going to be a war but me. When I saw how Billy took it, ' All right,' says I. ' You stay out. I 'll go in on my own hook.' But Billy says, ' No, sir ; it has been Atherton and Temple too long for that ; we 'll see the circus together.' That 's Billy. Well,

Mrs. Ransome, he went in and worked like a beaver. We did n't do so badly, neither. Wheat we paid fifty cents for sold in New York for two fifty. Mighty interesting while it lasted."

He smiled again, and we went downstairs together. But when I told Tom about it all, and how nice it looked to see Mr. Atherton tearing off money like postage-stamps, he did not smile. Indeed, I had already noticed that while Mr. Atherton grew on my imagination, Tom's admiration seemed rather to wane. I described the visit, sitting at ease in the Rainbow, where I was often admitted to the privileges of the symposium. Ah me, what innocent little revels we had there, when René would bring the beer foaming in the water-jug, and I supplied the reversion of our best dinners! I often think, recalling those kind men's plaudits of my cookery, that the hopes of youth are only equaled by its digestion. To-day, however, Tom seemed in a desponding mood. "Confound all this wild-cat money!" he burst forth. "Atherton ought to know better than to encourage such a craze. He wants me to write an editorial in the 'Citizen' about the money here, showing how solid the security is. What do I know about the security? I won't do it!"

"Oh, hush thee, my baby!" sang René, mockingly. "Don't fly off the handle, Tommy; I 'll write the unprincipled financial articles, because I don't know enough about finance to have any principles; and I believe in Jared D. Atherton, of Atherton. He made this town, and I don't reckon," said René, slipping into the vernacular, "he 'lows to ruin it."

Mr. Atherton was a favorite theme with us. He towered above the other local personages. There were half a dozen lawyers and doctors, the owner of a steamboat line, and, notably, Thorne and Quincy, the bankers. General Quincy kept a hospitable house. His table, his carriage, his handsome wife's jewels, were the town's admiration. His partner, the Honorable Rufus Thorne, was a dignified old gentleman, who clung to his shirt-ruffles and walked with a gold-headed cane. Though a bachelor, he gave splendid entertainments in his great house, and his wine cellar was famous. Every week, also, General Quincy, Mr. Temple, and Mr. Atherton met in Mr. Thorne's parlor and played whist with all "the rigor of the game." But neither General Quincy nor Mr. Thorne could vie with Atherton in the popular affection. They were both proud men, hugging all their Eastern prejudices of birth and breeding, holding the society of the frontier at arm's-length, even while they feasted and amused it. René ironically compared them with the Roman emperors lavishing corn and pageants on their subjects. Atherton, richer than any of the other rich men, had not an atom of *hauteur* about him; if he bragged, it was in the most sociable way in the world. He may have been a bit of a charlatan; he certainly was not squeamish; he could be cruel; but he was open-handed as the day, gay, good-humored, magnificent in his schemes, and devoted to the interests of the town. As a citizen, only William Temple had any comparable qualities, and he was content to be Atherton's echo.

"He is Atherton's first citizen because he deserves to be!" declaimed René.

"I don't question his devotion," said Tom, — this was on a later occasion; indeed, the speech was one of many that our friend was wont to pour on us, — "the end is very laudable; but I do question his means. I don't believe he is going to advance the interests of this town by lying about it: those circulars" —

"I admit they are not true, just at this present," laughed René, flinging back his black curls, "but Atherton argues that they are bound to be true very shortly. He is only anticipating."

Tom gave an impatient sigh. "You are all anticipating. That is the mischief of it. Your banks issue money that they can no more redeem than they can fly. Your farmers are paying twenty and thirty and forty per cent. on borrowed money. Your merchants are in the same box. Why, man, I was in the county clerk's office, the other day, to look up some titles. The whole county is mortgaged! It is awful! What do you expect will be the end of it all ?"

"Riches and prosperity," answered René, gravely ; "that is what I expect. And Atherton also. You don't consider our resources. When Atherton came here, there was only a little huddle of houses. To him more than to anybody else the change is due. He saw the possibilities. He bought land steadily ; and he sold it seasonably, too. He saw that if this country was to be opened up, the farmers must have a market for their produce, and he bought the first wagon - load of grain hauled to town, — bought it without knowing what he should do with it. That's the way he got into business. It was the same with pork-packing. Nobody else ventured, so he went in. I know now he makes an end of the small dealers very summarily " —

"Take Mr. Ripley for example," said I.

René, as his custom was, walked the floor while he talked ; he stopped short to face me. "Yes, Mrs. Ransome, why not ?" he cried. "He ran Ripley out of the business. No doubt about it. Then — I don't say a word about the saving his life, because that 's irrelevant — then he takes him into his own employ, pays him more salary than he could make money out of his old business, and lends him money to lift the mortgage on his house. Ripley never would have succeeded in business for himself, — he knows it as well as anybody; but he makes a first-rate man under some one else. And I can tell you Atherton has n't a warmer or more loyal partisan in this town than he."

" I 'm not denying he is a leader," said Tom.

" Well, I should say so! " cried René. " Just let me tell you something. At one time, early in his mayoralty, there was a lawless organization in this county; robbery and murder and all sorts of wickedness kept honest men in terror. Well, he, more than any one man, put it down. He planned a foray against them, starting out apparently alone, with a heap of gold in an old rawhide trunk. Every year he did go to St. Louis for gold (he ran a sort of bank until he got Thorne and Quincy to start one), and there was no suspicion. He bagged half the gang; killed one man with his own hand in the skirmish, and brought the others back to town, where he had the court sitting, and the jury ready, and a man hired to hang them; and hanged they were, every mother's son of them, the next day. There was no more difficulty with outlaws in this county."

"He kill a man himself!" I could not restrain the exclamation. "Does n't it make him miserable?"

"Not him," replied René; "he is n't sensitive; he has lived too adventurous a life. He started as an Indian trader, you know. Every year he used to load his boat with supplies and go up the river and barter with the Indians. Then he made money enough to start a general store, and was married. His first wife was a school-teacher; plain as they make them, but a very intelligent woman. You know Atherton has always been an enthusiast about public schools; gave the land for the first school himself. That is partially due to her. They say that she taught him to read. I don't believe that story; but I reckon she did teach him almost everything else. He has the greatest opinion of her. Did you notice that office furniture, the day we were there, Mrs. Ransome? Queer furniture for an office, was n't it? Well, it used to be the furniture of their parlor before he built Overlook. Those daguerreotypes are the pictures of his first wife and his three children, — all dead. That pencil-sketch shows the monument he built to them in the cemetery which he gave the town. He thinks the poor woman was a beauty, and he insisted on the sculptor making the angel at the tomb a statue of her. She was left-handed, so you will observe that the angel plays with the left hand. It is funny, but I think it is pathetic too. The poor soul loved him devotedly, and slaved herself to death in those hard frontier days for him. I always felt sorry that she must die before Overlook was finished."

" Did Mr. Atherton feel badly ? "

" He was quite broken up, at first. But he rallied, and went on with the house for the children. He is a man of phenomenal vitality. Blows that would kill another man hardly maim him. Take the case of those children. They all three died in the cholera time. He took care of them himself ; and Temple used to come over every day, stand under the window, and get directions about the mill and store. He had the city clerk do the same. One day, he came to the window as usual, told Temple how he had better secure a certain contract, and was going away, when Temple asked how the children were. ' Jay 's dead, and Bella 's dying ! ' said Atherton, and burst out crying. But, great heavens ! think of the iron nerve of the man ! He did cave in when the last child, the baby, died. He seemed sunk in a kind of stupor ; they could n't rouse him. Temple tried the house and business, — not a sign. Finally, in sheer despair he blubbered something about the cholera being awful bad in town. 'And they're just crazy with fright, and you can't help them,' sobbed he, 'and they have n't any hospital.' Atherton popped his head out like a flash. 'Why in blank don't the fools take *this* house?' he growled. Sure enough, the town had roused him. He went out and took charge of everything. Even Tom admits his sanitary measures were wise."

"You know quite well I am only too glad to praise him when I can," said Tom.

René wore an air of raillery. "I must tell you, Tom, that he admires madame; she reminds him of his first wife."

"Who was particularly plain," I observed.

"And madame is particularly the reverse," replied René, making me a very fine bow; "but you will remember that he considers his Nellie the fairest of her sex. Madame is tall and slender, and has dark eyes and long lashes, and, he says, the same kind, sweet smile."

I laughed at René, but I confess that I was softened. Indeed, I had been most ungrateful were this not the case. The Athertons were kind in a hundred ways. How often we had reason to praise Mam' Chloe's admirable dinners! How familiar the luxurious rooms of Overlook grew to us! In how many ways we poverty-stricken exiles were made free of their best! There comes a choking feeling in my throat, sometimes, recalling it all. I had grown well acquainted with both women, especially Rose Bainbridge; and when she told me, in the summer, that her mother and she were going away for some months, my dismay was so great that the silly tears rushed to my eyes. Miss Bainbridge surveyed me with her still face and wistful eyes. Presently she said: "I like you to be sorry; I don't want to go. I know how you feel about being here. When I was first here, I used to cry myself to sleep, every night, I was so lonesome. I hated the people here, and I detested Mr. Atherton." She hesitated, but her unwonted tide of confidence bore her onward as if in spite of herself: "What do you think? I tried to stab him with a penknife, the day he married mamma." She laughed, but with reddening cheeks.

"Oh, you poor little passionate thing!" cried I, and before I knew it I had kissed her.

"Thank you," said she, quietly, and laid her hand a second on mine.

"What did he do?" I could not restrain my curiosity.

"He was very good to me indeed. He held me out with both arms and looked at me. My heart beat so hard I reckon he could hear it, but I would not struggle, only I could n't help trembling. 'Poor little fluttering birdie,' said he, in a very gentle, kind voice, 'you won't mind my marrying your mamma, by and by. We 're going to be great friends, you and I.' " She laughed. "We are, now," said she.

She said no more, being interrupted; but many times did I ponder her words.

They were gone a long time; it was summer when I bade Rose good-by, and the February snows were melting before they returned. René was gloomy; and I know Mr. Atherton missed them, though he never complained. Whatever his feelings for his wife (I admit candidly that I never decided whether ambition, or pity, or affection had most to do with that marriage), he indisputably loved his step-daughter. Poor fellow! he used to brag about her exactly as he bragged about Atherton. He needed her, too, for in December a great blow fell on him: his partner, Temple, died after a brief illness. Before men's eyes Atherton bore the blow like a man of iron. During the funeral services not a quiver disturbed his rigid features. Afterwards, he never of his own accord mentioned his partner's name, and he knew how to check any talk about him from others. But it was observed that he no longer went to the Thorne whist parties; and he was more than generous to Temple's widow. René grew warm over the matter. "Mrs.

Temple always was a goose, but she was an amiable, decent sort of goose " — so ran René's version — "until her brother, East, got hold of her. He does n't believe in Western security, and he is going to get every cent, almost, out of the business; and Atherton won't say a word because she is Temple's wife."

" I am afraid it will cripple him to pay," said Tom.

René replied gayly that Atherton always fell on his feet. Had n't he lost two hundred thousand dollars at a blow, from the decline of prices consequent on the Czar's death, and never cared? " Temple looked awfully blue," said René. " I was dining with Atherton when he came and told him. 'That's bad, Billy,' says Atherton, ' but as there 's nothing we can do about it, you may as well sit down and take a glass of '49 port.' It was n't put on, either; because that night I stayed at the house, and I was reading that confounded ' Uncle Tom's Cabin ' book, and I was up late, when I heard the funniest little drumming, rasping sound, — I could n't make out what it was. So suspecting it might be a burglar, I stole downstairs and peeped into the library. What do you suppose I saw? Mr. Atherton, if you please, playing 'Old Folks at Home' on the jew's-harp. I give you my word, Tom, I thought I could n't get upstairs before I should have to laugh. There he sat as solemn and happy, strumming away, — the funniest sight! But when I did get upstairs, somehow I did n't want to laugh. He had lost two hundred thousand dollars, and he took it as lightly as that. The sight was something else besides funny."

But Tom answered that Mr. Atherton's losses were not entirely past, that he was still crippled by them. Prices had continued low; there had been three years of bad crops. "I don't see the end of it," said Tom. But he kept these forebodings from me, because, in those days, life was bitterly hard to me: my first little son was born in the winter, and lived only a month. Strange to say, one of my greatest comforts was Mr. Atherton's utterly silent sympathy. In February, the Athertons returned. I remember what a brilliant day it was when I saw Mrs. Atherton's languid, smiling face and her beautiful furs whirling by in her new sleigh. Hardly an hour later, her maddened horses flung the sleigh against the railway track; and they lifted her, never again to be glad or sorry or vain in this world. She had been kind to me, and I mourned for her. I must think, whatever the chill of their relations, that her husband mourned her, also. He looked years older, though he kept a stout front; and he complained of physical ailments, — an unprecedented thing with him, — consulted a doctor, and gave up his daily walk to town. But it was now no secret that he was harassed by business anxieties. That year the crops failed again. Up to July there was promise of a bountiful harvest. Then came weeks of rain. The soaked grain was beaten over the fields. The blight, the mildew, the rust, ill-omened names that became so wofully familiar, — what misery they wrought! Some of the farmers did not even try to gather their crop. Wiser they than their neighbors who could not sell their ruined sheaves. The potatoes and the onions fared better, but prices were very low. To increase the disorder of the time, no one any longer had confidence in our money. Banks were suspending everywhere. A bank-note worth a dollar in the morning might be worthless by night. One note that Tom gave me he said was worth eighty cents; they called it fifty at the first store where it was offered, but it was valued only at twenty cents before I came home in the afternoon.

The following day I saw a strange spectacle on the levee. A farmer deliberately backed his wagon loaded with potatoes into the river; then swearing frantically, he kicked out the tail-board and dumped the whole load of potatoes into the current. This seemed so unaccountable a proceeding to me that I described it to Tom.

"Poor beggar," said he. "I suppose he could n't sell his potatoes at any price. I myself saw three loads left on the street. Katy, it looks bad, bad."

Times did not mend with colder weather. More than once was the "Citizen's" rhetoric demanded by "currency riots," and once Atherton dispersed a dangerous mob with the fire department, turning the hose on a few truculent spirits. His influence was still potent, and he was nominated as usual for mayor. Late in the autumn he went East to raise money. During his absence misfortunes thickened about him. Some of his heaviest debtors failed; a cyclone blew down one of his mills in an adjoining town; and the very day of his return home, Temple's nephew, a young man well liked and trusted by him, ran away with several thousand dollars in gold, hoarded to pay the gold checks. Tom said then that further fight was useless. Even René looked haggard and dejected. "Thorne and Quincy are in the hole, too," he muttered. "They can't help. They 're looking to Atherton to help them."

Little sleep did any of us have that night. Morning broke wan and chill, a true dawn of calamity. Tom went to the office. I went out into the streets, and was impressed by the unwonted throngs on the sidewalks, — like a holiday, only the crowd wore no holiday air. Women hustled the men. The faces of all were sullen and anxious, while some of the women's faces looked bloated with weeping. I observed, moreover, that the motion on every side was towards one central point: the mass of human beings pressed, struggled, and fought onward to the white marble steps of Thorne and Quincy's bank. Near noon, a neighbor ran to my house crying that there was a run on the bank, and that she should lose everything. I counseled her to withdraw her savings at once, since they were deposited in her name. She said that she would only run home to take her bread out of the oven, and then go. But when she reached the street she found herself caught in the crowd as in a wedge, and before she could push forward she heard the roar of rage and misery which told her that the bank doors were shut. Thorne and Quincy had suspended.

The woman esteemed herself ruined. Really her fortune was made, for the bank eventually paid their depositors in full, giving Western lands; and the farm she thus secured is now in the heart of a city. Thanks to that " broken bank " she became rich. But who was to prophesy such mitigation of disaster? The business of the whole town turned on the pivot of Thorne and Quincy's bank and Atherton's mill. At half-past one o'clock the bank suspended. By three o'clock it was bruited about that Atherton refused to cash his gold checks. Tom did not come to eat my carefully prepared chicken-pie. Incessantly people passed, always in one direction, always with haste. I saw Mr. Shiras High, the sheriff, drive by in a buggy with two men, galloping his horse through the half-frozen mud. I could endure the tension of waiting no longer. Faster and faster I saw women flying down the streets, bareheaded in the bitter December air, wringing their hands and shrieking questions that the wind took away. The contagion of fright and excitement seized me; I too ran out on the street.

My first thought was to get to Tom. I found the street in front of the " Citizen " office black with people, a sight very strange and frightful to me. But my heart stood still when Tom came out and addressed the crowd. They would have hissed him, but his first words quieted them. He said that the office and all Mr. Atherton's other property were in the hands of the sheriff; any damage done thereto would only injure the creditors. Meanwhile, the Atherton " Citizen " would be issued as usual. " An Extra containing all the facts of the late failures," said Tom, "is now for sale in our counting-room. Price ten cents." With that he withdrew, and René, in his shirt-sleeves, appeared and displayed a placard with flaming head-lines: —

THE CITY SHAKEN !

THORNE AND QUINCY SUSPEND ! ATHERTON GOES UNDER!

CLAIM THAT THE ASSETS WILL COVER EVERYTHING !

There was more below the shoulders that I could not see. Apparently either the Extra or the editor's coolness appeased the crowd, although they had gathered to mob the editors as confederates of Atherton; for now there arose a rough laugh, and like magic the black mass of hats scattered, while those who remained walked peacefully into the office to buy their Extras.

I now found little difficulty in reaching the building. Tom was for reproaching me at first, but he ended by devouring his pie. But René was past eating. "The game's up, madame," said he, with a miserable smile.

"How does he bear it?" said L

For a little I did not consider the catastrophe to our own hopes. I only saw one figure outlined against the stormy western sky. He was the provincial lord that Cæsar would have been rather than the second in Rome. Behold, his lordship was wrested from him, and his house left unto him desolate !

"He bears it like a gentleman!" cried René. "He mortgaged his farms, Overlook, everything, and he brought seventy thousand dollars home with him, and planked every dollar of it down to save the bank. And it was no use. I tell you it's mighty hard. Poor Thorne cried like a baby when it was all over. 'I wish to God we had n't touched a cent of your money!' says he to Atherton. 'Oh, quit that!' says Atherton. 'I was on your paper enough to ruin me. We'd both pulled through if it had n't been for that young Temple.' That is what *I* call high-toned."

"It was," said Tom. "But, René, what's the feeling outside?"

"Damnable. The town's ruined. The poor devils of farmers have nothing to pay their interest with, and have got to lose their farms, and they all are raving at Atherton. The Democratic committee want him to come off the ticket. He said he did n't propose to resign under fire. I'm sorry too. *C'est magnifique, mais ce n'est pas la guerre.*"

"If the election only were n't to-morrow," said Tom.

"But it is," replied René. "He'll be beaten awfully. You don't know the monstrous lies afloat. They say he's kept the money he raised

East, and that he's in with Temple. They are wild, Tom. Oh, it's hideous," René groaned, dropping his flimsy mask of levity, "the stories I've heard, the sights I've seen to-day! Poor women, — widows who thought their narrow incomes safe, — laboring people who brought their savings to Atherton, thinking he was safe, anyhow — My God, what a load for one man to carry! And we can do nothing."

"Nothing but write the morning editorial," said Tom. And the New Englander went doggedly to work, while the Southerner paced the floor, aflame with rage and grief.

The next day I shall remember all my life. Writ after writ poured in on Atherton. He sat upstairs in his office, and rocked in the worn armchair, and tried to explain the great pile of ledgers before him, while outside a mob of desperate men and women howled their curses at the man whom they had loved and trusted to their own undoing. One Irish washerwoman who had a crippled son to keep, and who had loaned all her savings to Atherton, clambered through a locked window and ran upstairs, all bleeding from the broken glass, to grovel at his feet, shrieking for her money. They had to take her away by force.

"It will be all right, Mrs. Kelly, — it will be all right," he kept repeating, while the struggling, frantic creature was dragged down the stairs, cursing him. "Now, gentlemen," said he, calmly, "where were we?" But Tom, who was there to explain the "Citizen's" books, could see that he furtively wiped his face with his hand, yet the men were wearing overcoats in the room because of the chill. He betrayed no other sign of distress. Only when the winter day had waned, and lamps were brought, and he rose to find another ledger, he fumbled a bit over the leaves, saying, "I don't know as I can go straight to the place, gentlemen. Temple used to take these accounts. I — I miss Temple a good deal."

On the streets, the tumult waxed more furious every hour. Half a dozen firms had failed. Men whose credit a week before had been unquestionable were pleading as if for their lives with the stanch little bank that weathered the storm. In fine, the town believed itself ruined by Atherton and his friends. One weapon to strike the arch-traitor lay ready in every voter's hand. Long before dark the Republican candidate for mayor was elected by an overwhelming majority. Poor Ripley, whose loyalty was not discreet, was beaten into a pitiable object at the polls. Atherton heard of the fray. His comment was bitter. "Rats are wiser than men: they skip out of a sinking ship."

Rose and I called for him with the carriage after dusk. Tom jumped up on the box, and René appeared at the same time and jumped in after Mr. Atherton. " *Quick!* " cried Tom, in a sharp undertone. Instantly I knew why he spoke; then it was too late. The street at right angles to the little dark street where we waited was all at once luridly gay with the flare of torches, and penetrated with the tramp of feet, shouts, yells, the clangor of brass, the throbbing roll of drums. The light blazed on a great white banner, dancing aloft so near that the hateful black sentences jumped at our eyes : —

HONEST JOHN HARTER THE NEXT MAYOR OF ATHERTON !

HONEST MONEY AND AN HONEST MAYOR !

NAME OF THE TOWN TO BE CHANGED !

We were turned, the next instant, and splashing through the mud, our backs to the procession.

Atherton spoke first, to René : " Is Harter elected ? "

" Yes, sir," said René.

" What are the figures ? "

René lied unhesitatingly : " I don't know, sir."

There fell a heavy silence before Mr. Atherton spoke again : " Do they think of changing the name of the town ? "

"Oh, that's only some fool talk of the rabble," said René.

Mr. Atherton did not make any comment. The rest of us kept up a feeble chatter at first, among ourselves; but we were sensible that it availed nothing. Soon, therefore, mute as he, we looked out on the dwindling line of lights, the sombre hillsides with their fret of black boughs against a leaden sky, and at last the dark oaks of Overlook and the stately white columns and pediment, unsubstantial and faintly drawn in that waning light. Mr. Atherton pushed the window slides down and gazed long and steadily. God knows what his thoughts were. The lamps along the drive were unlighted. Only the glimmer of a candle met us at the great door, which Mam' Chloe unbarred with doleful grunts of exertion. She told us that the other servants had hidden in the cellar on an alarm that a mob were coming to tar and feather Mr. Atherton.

"But," said Mam' Chloe, piously, "I does know I cotch my deff, foo' sho', in dat cole; so I done putt my trus' in de Lawd, an' hide up sta's in de shoe closet!"

She had prepared hot coffee for us, and a meal of some sort which we were too excited to eat. Mr. Atherton refused everything, peevishly, and strode off to his library. Tom followed him, because we could hear sinister noises and shouts borne on the breeze. He found him seated at his writing-table. A sheet of paper, scrawled all over with figures, had been pushed away, and his head was sunk on his arms. Unconscious of any auditor, he muttered to himself, "So many poor people — to lose all — no use — no use ! " Tom must rouse him, no matter how he recoiled from the task. He spoke to him. Mr. Atherton unsteadily lifted his face, which was flushed a dark crimson. He stared at Tom with glazed eyes. Tom tried to say something about a sure reaction to the injustice of the present feeling.

"Why, d— it all," cried Atherton, hoarsely, "do you think I mind their turning on me? Good Lord, they 're right, — I 've ruined the town ! "

He put out his hand to draw his papers nearer to him; instead, his fingers scattered a pack of cards. He looked at them with a strange smile. "Billy's cards," he muttered. "Ain't it a good thing old Billy 's out of all this? I think of that when I miss him. We were together twenty years, Renny, and never a word. See if you can match that with your wife." He did not seem to know that it was Tom, not René, before him. All at once the vacant look slipped out of his eyes; he sprang to his feet, alert and composed, lifting his hand.

"They 've come," he said calmly.

We all heard the noise that had roused him, the thud of feet on the soft earth, the stifled cries and commands.   Tom and René would have persuaded him to escape to the yard, where the horses were ready; but he pushed them both aside.   " I 've talked to the boys before," said, he.

"Never mind," whispered René in my ear; " we are both armed, and the sheriff and a lot of his friends are coming."

The crash of breaking glass and a hubbub of screams from below stopped more words.   René and Tom, pistols in hand, ran out on the porch.

"Stop!" thundered Atherton.   "You boys sha'n't do any fooling with pistols!"

He pursued them as lightly as a lad.   Rose and I flew after.   Outside, the mob seemed to press to the very floor of the portico.   The lawn was only a surging black torrent of heads. As we appeared, a sheet of flame shot up from the brush-heap that they had lighted; and a shower of stones, dirt, eggs, and dead cats was shot into the air as if it were the foam of this horrible sea.   "Atherton!"   "Atherton!"   "Tar him!"   "Feather him!"   "Kill him!" bellowed the crowd.

He had been the admired leader of these men, veritably a petty god; their rancor now had the venom distilled out of faith betrayed.   A yell of rage and hatred tore their throats, as they saw him, standing there before them, his arms folded across his breast. They flung his own name back at him coupled with hideous epithets and threats. They pelted him with their noisome missiles. An egg struck him full in the face, and they shrieked in savage laughter. Tom's pistol flashed out. But neither pistols nor Rose's white arms could have quelled that uproar of hate; what did quell it was the patient composure of the hated man. Calmly, slowly, he wiped his stained cheek with his handkerchief. There was blood on it now from a gash made by a well-aimed piece of glass. Then he lifted his hand — and they listened.

"You know very well," said he, in his loud, unmodulated tones, "that I could have run away from this. I refused to have the sheriff come out with me. I don't want protection from the men of Atherton. I've worked for the interests of this town ever since I was twenty years old, — done my best for it."

"You've ruined it!" a woman's voice screamed, and some boy threw a stone. It must have hit him, but he stood firm.

"Another stone and I'll fire!" shouted René.

"*Never!*" called Atherton. "It's all a mistake — a mistake" — He stopped, passed his hand in a bewildered way over his face; his

voice shook. "I know that I appear to have —
to have ruined " —

But his strength was gone. Rose and René
caught him as he swayed forward. They laid
him on his back; he lay inert and flaccid; his
eyes rolled, then they closed. Rose wailed that
he was dead. René, a planter's son, had a tinc-
ture of medical knowledge. "No," said he, "he
is n't dead, but he has had a stroke of apoplexy."

To me it was marvelous to witness the change
in the temper of the crowd; they stood silent and
awestruck. It was as if the passion of man
were spent before a vision of the judgment of
God. Most of the people quietly turned their
backs and went home. Those who remained
were vehement in their efforts to help. Ripley
and the sheriff found nothing to do. Thus, very
peacefully, we carried the first mayor of Atherton over his threshold; wondering, some of us,
if it were not a merciful fate should he never
need to cross it, living, again. Weeks, indeed,
did pass before such a thing seemed possible;
then the desperately tenacious vitality of the
man's physical powers gave his body force to
crawl out of the wreckage of broken heart and
blunted brain. The doctor pronounced the patient out of danger.

Shortly after this, while Mr. Atherton was
yet unable to transact any business, Tom re-

ceived a telegram summoning us to his mother's death-bed. We left Atherton, not to see it again for ten years. For awhile we heard frequently from our Western friends: that René and Rose were happily married; that Mr. Atherton could not use his mind long at a time, but was growing stronger; that many farmers had lost their farms; that business was dull and houses were empty; that the name of the town had been changed. Then the war came, and Tom volunteered. Some letters must have gone astray about this time; for our letters addressed to René were returned with merely a curt official "Not Found," on the envelope. We surmised that René had carried out his often-expressed intention of throwing in his fortunes with his own section. Such indeed was the case, as we know, for we have renewed the old friendship; and I am glad to say the good fellow has prospered since the war, and his wife is a happy matron. But for years we lost sight of them entirely. Five years after the war, we passed through Atherton, — Atherton no longer. Having an hour to wait, we drove to the spot because of which the city was set apart in our hearts. With a strange, familiar ache, in spite of the laughing baby faces waiting for me by the Atlantic, I looked at the winding river shore and the rich foliage of the hills above.

Overlook, with its stately terraces and groves, was so precisely the picture of the years gone by that a wild notion came to me that Atherton might have retrieved his fortunes, and now was its owner and the provincial lord again. But there was a forlorn change on the other side of vision. Instead of the wide acres, shaded by fair trees or neatly shaven, with brilliant spots of color, — all the brighter for the white flashes among the green, — mills and factories crowded close to a little plot of graves. The rank grass waved a yellow-gray mist of hay-flowers over the sunken mounds; all the paths were effaced by a squalid greenery of dock and plantain and jimson weeds; while the cracked and weather-stained gravestones leaned at every angle. The hackman, carelessly flicking his boots with his whip, at the carriage door, explained that the city had sold all the vacant lots; no one had been buried in the cemetery since 1859.

We asked the man if he knew anything about Mr. Atherton. He thought that he had heard the name, but was not sure.

"'Are we so soon forgotten when we are gone?'" quoted Tom, sadly.

We ascertained that the care-taker whom we trusted had not been negligent, and laid our flowers on the little mound. It was natural that we should linger a moment before the monu-

ment that once had attracted every visitor's
eyes. Though the suns and frosts had dealt
hardly with it, the sculpture had won a touch of
dignity out of its misfortunes : the coarse work-
manship, the florid design, were softened by the
lichens and climbing vines; and I fancied a
novel sweetness in the angel's smile.

"Poor Mr. Atherton!" I exclaimed. "Tom,
do you suppose he has been fortunate again?"

"Yes," Tom answered quietly; "I think that
he has been fortunate. At least, I am sure he
is content now."

His voice rather than his words made me go
to the stone whence his hand had brushed aside
the mask of thistles. Then I saw that he was
right, for we were standing by the first mayor's
grave.

SIST' CHANEY'S BLACK SILK.

Low red partitions separate the bath-rooms proper from the passageways of the bath-house. One morning early in November, when all the mountains about Hot Springs were still aglow with the red and yellow pigments spattered through the enduring pine green, three women sat outside, leaning back in their chairs after their baths. The bath-house was new and smart in all its appointments. The three women paid no attention to the medley of noises which poured through the partitions. A clatter of tongues and a continuous crack of slapping pierced — being of a shriller and higher quality — the monotonous fall and plash of water. So thin were the dividing walls between the two sides of the house that the conversation had rather a startling thread of masculine talk.

"Here, Polk, confound you!" "Yes, sah, yes, sah; in a minute." "Say, Ben, what did you do with my crutch?" "Oh, yes, ma'am; I'm a heap better" (this in a Southern, feminine voice). "Viney, I'm all ready." "All right, darlin', jest set still, an' drink hot water an' sweat; I'm a comin'." "Well, I don't drink any more hot water, anyhow; I feel like a tea-kettle now." "All right, honey; I'm a-comin'."

"Oh, why are you waiting, my brother?"

It is the first line of a popular hymn; a rich tenor voice starts it, but the words are taken up by half a dozen bath-women, until the refrain, with its wailing minor, echoes through the room:

"Why not, why not, why not come to Him now?"

One of the singers has a beautiful contralto voice, possessed of that uncultivated, haunting sweetness one hears sometimes among the negro singers.

"Ain't that Dosier?" asked a woman waiting. She was a large woman, handsome and kindly looking, and while she mopped her face with a towel, she kept up a steady motion of her jaws. In fact, she was chewing gum. An extraordinary abandonment to "the gum habit" is a feature of Hot Springs. Every shop-counter seems to have a little tray of sticks in tinsel. One is told that the men buy it to help them through their deprivation of tobacco, Hot Springs doctors being very strict on this point. But why do the women use gum? They are Southern women

usually, but not always. They have the dress,
sometimes the manners and speech, of ladies, and
they make not the slightest concealment of the
practice. The large lady, as she spoke, offered
a stick of "taffee tolu" to the person whom she
addressed.

This was a thin, dark woman in a red wrap-
per, with large diamonds in her ears and at her
throat. She waved the gum aside, remarking,
severely, "No, I never chew; I have n't any bad
habits."

The other, not at all abashed, answered: "Do
you call chewing gum a bad habit? I don't.
Gum is nice, clean, decent stuff. Now tobacco;
there 's some sense talking against that — chewing, I mean; I don't mind smoking no more
than nothing; but chewing — Colonel Ponder
used to chew till I could n't keep a stove in the
house decent. He did so. I hated terribly to
take away his comfort, but finally I persuaded
him to take up with gum instead. Never chewed
a mite myself, before then, but I did it to keep
him company, and now I like it 'most as well as
him." Therewith she laughed, — a rollicking,
tolerant laugh, having in its melody a note of
something quite innocent and childlike.

The third woman, a delicate creature, whose
maid had wrapped her carefully, looked up at
the sound.   "Were n't you speaking of Do-

sier ? " she said. Her voice had distinctly Northern intonations ; it was rather languid than faint. She had very large blue eyes, and a little wave to the brown hair brushed back from a low forehead. Her face was pretty, though so thin and colorless. She looked unhappy as well as ill. "Is Dosier your bath-woman ?" she continued.

"Oh, yes, ma'am," said Mrs. Ponder, beaming upon her in a motherly fashion. ("Cayn't be more than twenty, and looks like she 'd lost her last friend on earth," was the kind soul's inward comment.) "Why, Colonel would n't let me come to the Springs, I don't guess, if I could n't have Dosier. Not that it would kill me " — she laughed her jolly laugh again — "if I did n't come : I never had a sick day since I was married and come to Arkansas. All I go here for is to reduce ; I get ten pounds thinner every time I come, and last year I lost sixteen pounds in three weeks. Vapor baths. And Dosier's rubbings."

"She is very strong," said the invalid, with a sigh.

"Six feet tall," said Mrs. Ponder, " and can lift me. You 'd hardly believe it, but she 's done it. And the cleanest creature, and as gentle as gentle. She 's a good woman if there ever was one."

"Yes," agreed the woman with diamonds, "I think Dosier is decent. Though"— lowering her voice — "she is the first negro woman *I've* seen in the South that I'd trust."

"Laws! I've seen a heap," said Mrs. Ponder. "I was born and raised among niggers; and they're very much like white folks — they're good and they're bad. You Northern people all 'lowed the niggers were angels during the war; and ayfter the war, when you came down here and found they were n't, you turn plumb round and think they're all trash. Fact is, they're just middling, like the rest of us. But Dosier is the best kind of a colored woman; and when they're good, you won't find anybody better, Mrs. Higgins."

Mrs. Higgins looked strong dissent, but all she said was: "What's become of that husband of hers? — the one that was in the penitentiary."

"Why, she never had but one husband, did she?" said the invalid.

"Well, that one. Two years ago she was spending all the money she had saved up to get him out. He killed somebody."

"He shot one of the worst gamblers and desperadoes ever in Hot Springs"— the stout lady now took up the conversation with decision — "and he had n't ought to have had anything done to him. Anyway and anyhow, they pardoned him out ayfter Dosier had spent more than three hundred and seventy dollars on him."

"Well, what became of him?"

"Oh, he was all broke up in health, and he died."

"Poor Dosier!" said the little woman. "Has she any children?"

"No, ma'am; but she's got a helpless invalid sister, and a niece that's a widow, and two little boys of hers. I reckon Dosier looks out ayfter the whole of them. Well, Nettie she does work about the bath-houses some, but she cayn't more than keep herself."

"The sister's a helpless kind of thing," said Mrs. Higgins; "paralyzed some way. She must be a burden."

Mrs. Ponder's face wore a new expression, a very gentle one. "I'm not so sure of that," said she; "sometimes it looks like folks were n't any comfort because they ain't any help about the house or earning money, and yet they may be a sight of company and comfort. I've heard Dosier say she would n't know how to get along without Chaney."

The young woman looked for a second at Mrs. Ponder. Mrs. Higgins gave a rapid glance downward at her own hands, crippled with rheumatism; then jumped up and began to pace the room. "Well, when I can't help myself I want to die," she muttered.

Mrs. Ponder changed the subject. "Chaney," she continued, in her soft, leisurely tones, — "Chaney gets the funniest notions. What do you think she 's got into her head now?"

"I don't think she 's got good sense," said Mrs. Higgins, acidly.

"Oh, yes, ma'am; she 's got plenty of sense. But this is curious, for she does n't go out of the house once a year. If you please, ladies, she 's plumb crazy for a black silk gown. Ever since Dosier got hers, she 's been craving one. Dosier wants right bad to get her one for a Christmas gift; but you see, Chaney is sick — gone into a dropsy, the doctor says — and Dosier can only work mornings, and there 's the doctor's bills and all: I 'm afraid they will use up all the money she 's laid by."

"It 's a piece of extravagance anyhow," said Mrs. Higgins. "Chaney ought not to ask such a thing, and Dosier ought to tell her flat she can't have it."

She might have freed her mind more fully had not a bath-room door opened and a tall black woman appeared, Dosier herself.

"Say, don't you all go out till you 're right cool," she remarked, shaking her head good-humoredly as she passed. "Miss Maine, you make your gyirl wrop ye up *tight*, ef ye go out."

She had, in speaking, the same rich, melodi-

ous, winning voice as in singing, and her broad
smile and bright eyes made her strong, dark
features attractive. Even Mrs. Higgins looked
kindly after her as she passed.

She walked through the two " cooling-rooms,"
into the office, and so into the street. At that
hour of the day the Hot Springs main street is
a picturesque scene, a kaleidoscope of shifting
figures, all tints of skin, all social ranks: un-
couth countrymen on cotton wagons; negroes
in carts drawn by oxen or skeleton mules with
rope harness; pigs lifting their protesting noses
out of some carts, fowls squawking in others; a
dead deer flung over a horseman's saddle; mod-
ish-looking men and women walking; shining
horses curveting before handsome carriages;
cripples on crutches; deformed creatures hugging the sunny side of the street before the bath-
houses; pale ghosts of human beings in wheeled
chairs, — so the endless procession of wealth or
poverty or disease or hope oscillates along the
winding street between the mountains. The
houses are as different as the people, squalor
and roughness of a mining camp flung cheek by
jowl against brick façades of the American renaissance, with terra-cotta ornaments and low
arched windows. Booths innumerable lean out
over the mud sidewalk; Hot Springs crystals
glitter in jewelers' windows; gaudy garments

swing from projecting stringers; poultry in coops, rabbits in cages, squirrels, opossums, possibly a young bear, increase the lively aspect of the exhibition space of the street, and very much curtail the footman's passageway. Every house that is not a hotel has a sign of " Rooms to Let." Visibly the town lives upon the stranger within its gates.

Dosier, to whom the sight was too familiar for notice, and who was, moreover, absorbed in painful thoughts of her own, moved rapidly along to a cross street.

Frequently she met acquaintances, black or white. They all greeted her with a degree of respect. The negroes said, " Good-mornin', Sist' Rogers!" or " Howdy, Mis' Rogers?" A few stopped to shake hands and inquire about her sister. Dosier's invariable reply was: " Well, she ain't no better. We all gwine have a conserlation dis mornin'. Free doctors."

Admiration evidently tinged the sympathy of the comments. The commonest was: " Is dat so? Well, you suttinly *is* doin' all you kin."

" I *aims* ter," said Dosier.

After awhile she left her friends behind and came to her own house, a neat brown cottage, standing on the side of the hill, in a large garden. Dosier, who was indefatigably industrious, had fine roses as well as a thrifty company of vegetables. A bush of La France roses brushed the window-pane with their pink, exquisitely crumpled petals. The bed was drawn close to the window. Chana loved to lie watching the long stems sway, and the green leaves tap the glass, and the light flicker in the pink bloom. She used to sit up, but of late she had lain all day, too weak or in too much pain to rise. Dosier looked quickly for the face on the big white pillows. It was turned away, and the hands were clutching at the forehead with an unmistakable gesture.

"My Lawd! Chaney's cryin'," gasped Dosier. There was a climbing pain in her throat that choked her. The tears swam in her eyes. "It ben bad, an' dat fool Nettie done tole 'er," she thought. "Yes, thar's them buggies," glancing down the road.

Two buggies, Dr. Green's and Dr. Le Verneau's, were drawn up close to the fence and the line of clover, still fresh and green. The horses were munching dry grass and juicy clover together.

Directly, the little red door of the house opened and three gentlemen appeared. They had the medical gravity of expression over a serious case. On the walk, the youngest man began to talk animatedly, but the others checked him, observing Dosier. Old Dr. Le Verneau raised his hat.

Dosier, even then, did not forget her old-fashioned manners, which prompted the hasty courtesy before she said, in an unsteady voice: " You all ain't no need to tell me, gentlemen. She cayn't get up no mo'. Dis 'yeah her last spell er sickness."

" You see it is this way, Aunt Dosier," said Dr. Green: it was a relief to him to plunge into medical details, knowing that Dosier, the best nurse in Hot Springs, could understand him. Strangely enough, it calmed her also, forcing her into the impartial professional scrutiny of " the patient " that becomes a nurse's second nature.

" I got to give up gwine t' de baths," she said, quietly, after he had outlined the condition of the sick woman and the best mode of treatment to alleviate her suffering; there was no hope of prolonging her life. Then she courtesied again and thanked the physicians, saying that she was sure that they would do all that could be done, and entered the house. She stopped a second outside the door to stiffen herself and fling out her hands. Then she shut the palms tight.

" Bracing up," muttered the youngest man. " She feels *bad*. Queer, too: the woman 's always been a burden to her."

" That 's all you know about it," said Dr. Le Verneau, irritably. " Don't you suppose she 's fond of her kin? That poor soul there has lived with Dosier twenty years."

Dosier's fingers may have trembled a little on the latch, but there was no tremble in her voice as she greeted Nettie; she forced a kind of smile on her face. Ah! which of us is so happy as not to know that pitiful smile of the sick-room?

Nettie was a slender brown woman, never very wise. She "p'intedly did favor her paw," Dosier used to say, and the late Jacob Faury, Chana's husband, was "trifling."

Nettie sat in the yellow rocking-chair, rocking and sobbing, while she strained her youngest child so hard to her breast that he set up a wail on his own account.

Poor Chana was quietly weeping on the bed.

"My Lawd! Nettie," cried Dosier, with the irritation of suffering, "how come you let dat chile beller dat a way in yeah? 'Ain't you got no sense?" Then, her voice dropping to its gentlest key, "Howdy, Chaney? Is you got de mis'ry back?"

No movement, no sound except the low sobbing from the bed.

"You needs some milk shake, dat's wat you does; an' I got some nice new w'iskey to putt in. An' den we'll count de stockin'."

Presently she came back, and gently took the hand down. She had an old yarn stocking hung over her arm.

"Oh, Doshy," sobbed Chana, "1 'm gwine t' die, ayfter all. Ye need n't count de stockin'. I 'll never w'ar no silk gownd."

Dosier, pillar of the church though she was, looked at the quivering face, and for a moment contemplated lying bravely — only for a moment; because something in Chana's eyes told her that a lie would be useless. Instead, she sank down on her knees by the bedside. "Chaney," she whispered, "you like me pray de Lawd holp you tuh bar it ? "

"Naw, I doan't," said Chana.

A thunderbolt could hardly have cloven Dosier's sore heart like those words. Chana, after years of obdurate "stan'in' out agin de Spirit," had been hopefully converted only a month ago. The stumbling-block in the ways of God with men, in her case, had been her own undeserved misfortunes. Finally she had been brought to regard these as a means of grace, but now her faith failed her.

"Looks like I cud bar it better ef I done had my silk dress, an' ben out jes *oncet* in it," she said, after a pause, filled by poor Dosier with desperate mute supplication. "I doan' wanter die."

"Oh, Chaney, tink er de bright worl' above, an' de glori's w'ite ga'ment ! "

"I 'd heap ruther have a black silk," muttered Chana, and turned her face to the window.

All that day she hardly spoke. She could eat
nothing. In vain Dosier went down town and
returned with California grapes, which Chana
used to like. Chana only shook her head, saying, "I'm too busy studyin' t' eat."

Dosier carefully put them away for a more
propitious moment; but it never came. A black
cloud of depression swathed poor Chana's soul.
Every little act of kindness, every sign of affection from Dosier or her daughter, every one of
the small pleasures which they tried so hard to
give her, was like a hand drawing the gloom
tighter, for it made life more desirable and death
more hideous.

"She cayn't seem to get reconciled nohow,"
Dosier confided with tears to Mrs. Ponder.
"She says now we all got so nicely fixed, an' she
got her bed by the winder, an' kin see de roses,
an' folks gwine by on de street, she doan' min'
layin' in bed. Ye know ye fetched a couple er
w'ite figgers, imiges, fo' tuh putt on de bureau,
an' a beaucherful picter tuh hang on de wall.
Chaney she doan' git many presents, and she
ben so pleased when she got dem she jes *cried* —
she done so. An' now she says she hates fo' ter
leave. An' — an'" — Dosier choked over the
words — "she hates fo' tuh leave me an' Nettie
an' de little tricks. She allus uster like tuh look
down de road so she see me comin' nights, an' she

laffed so when somebody give me a present. She
say she won't have no good times in heaben, an'
she cayn't git no satisfaction outer studyin' 'bout
it. She won't pray no mo', neether. Po' chile,
she cayn't git reconciled tuh de Lawd's ways, an'
she faults *Him.* She takes on orful, an' says
He mout of 'lowed 'er live *one* year longer, an'
'j'y 'erself a bit — an' sich. Makes me feel turrible bad." She wiped away the tears that had
been rolling down her cheeks before she continued : " Doan' you be 'maginin' dat I 'm fearin'
de Lawd lay dem bad feelin's er Chaney up agin
her. He knows better. Naw, ma'am. But I
cayn't b'ar havin' her go so oneasy; I cayn't
b'ar it noway, 'tall."

" Oh, hush, Dosier," said Mrs. Ponder, soothingly. " She 'll get reconciled; they always do.
Say, don't she want me to lend her my music-
box? You can keep it ayfter I 'm gone, long 's
she wants it. She used to like to hear the hymn-
tunes. And there 's ' Rainbow Polka ' and
' Sweet Violets ' beside."

But Dosier answered sadly that Chana no
longer cared for hymns. " She jes lays an'
studies," said she.

Mrs. Ponder, not a religious woman herself,
cast about in vain through her scattering remi-
niscences of religious people for some comforting suggestion. The consequence of the inter-

view was that she burst into tears herself, and
sent Chana a large red-velvet pincushion, having a yellow and white bunch of flowers painted
on it, which she had bought the day before at a
church fair, and was treasuring for the place of
honor in her guest-chamber.

She carried an uneasy sense of compassion
with her to the bath-house and to her accustomed
companions, Mrs. Higgins and Miss Maine.   In
the frank Southern fashion she shared her per-
plexities, at once.   "And what would you say
poor Dosier had ought to do?"

"What *can* she do?" added Miss Maine.   "I
dare say Chaney is crazy."

"I don't see what she's got to make such a
fuss about," Mrs. Higgins grumbled.   "A bed-
ridden invalid, I should think she'd be willing
and glad to go.   Why don't they talk to her
about heaven and such things?"

"Well, they have, a heap," said Mrs. Ponder;
"but it looks like she cayn't get up an interest
in heaven.   You see really there ain't so *very*
much we all know about heaven anyhow."

"Isn't her husband dead?" said Miss Maine.
The girl spoke with a vibrating accent of emotion under her indifferent manner.   To her, one
presence filled all her imaginations of the mys-
teries beyond this life: it was that of the man
whom she was to have married, and who had

died a year ago, on the morning of their wedding day. How could any wife — But the instinctive cynical second thought of her class interrupted that first thrill of sympathy. Such people, of course, were different. How *did* they feel?

" Well," said Mrs. Ponder, impartially, " he 's dead, that 's true enough ; but I don't guess he counts much. He was a trifling no-'count nigger, who wanted to wear his Sunday clothes every day, and sit in the store-doors and ogle the yellow girls. I reckon he was n't any too kind to her, either, ayfter she got too sick to earn money for him to spend."

Miss Maine laughed a sharp, quick little laugh. " Then you have to fall back on Mrs. Higgins's panacea — she 's not losing much."

Mrs. Ponder looked rather wistfully from the set young face to the worn older face, with its quiver of irritable pain. " There *don't* seem much we poor human beings can do for each other in trouble," she said.

" I hope, for her own sake and ours too," Mrs. Higgins continued, paying no attention to this, " that she won't have a lingering illness. That new bath-woman we 've got is n't half as good as Dosier."

Miss Maine's eyebrows went up a little ; she directed a side glance at Mrs. Ponder, who had taken out her gum, and was rocking and chewing with unusual vigor.

"She has no heart either," thought the girl, scornfully; "they are all coarse and disagreeable together."

Really, however, she did the worthy Arkansas woman injustice. Gum had become a sort of intellectual motor to Mrs. Ponder, who never felt her mind really working without a simultaneous action of her jaws.

But she said nothing to her companions. Indeed, the notion of comfort that she was revolving would have seemed heartless and ridiculous to one unacquainted with the African "ways." She went to see Dosier on purpose to tell her. "Did you ever think of telling Chaney 'bout the funeral?" said she. "I know you 'low to give her a nice one."

"I does so," said Dosier. She clapped her hands together, though the tears were in her eyes. "De Lawd bless you fo' dat t'ought, Miss Betty; I do reckon I got another myse'f by it, an' dat I cheer 'er up. Come an' see 'er, won't you, Mis' Betty?"

The conversation had taken place outside the house, on the white sand walk. Now silently Mrs. Ponder followed Dosier into Chana's room.

The sick woman had turned her face away from the humble and careful adorning of the walls to the greenery swinging against her window-pane; but her eyes saw the varying shadows on leaf and rose, and the lovely flush of color, as little as they did Dosier's chromos and plaster images. Absorbed in her ceaseless and impotent wrestle with her doom, she would lie thus for hours, hardly speaking. What visions of her thwarted, dim, pain-dogged life, what forlorn gropings among the eternal problems, what wild, half-savage, suffocating revolt against the Power that would not save her, were hidden behind that dull mask which her face had become! Her eyes looked out solemn and turbid with inarticulate thoughts and misery. Sometimes they would follow every movement of her sister, until Dosier would feel an intolerable pity. All her own personal grief and ache of loss was consumed by an overpowering longing to soothe Chana's torment. " Ef I cud only git 'er tuh go easy an' peaceful, I give 'er up. Oh, dear Lawd, holp 'er!" she moaned. " It's wusser dan de pain, kase de doctor kin give 'er opium fur *dat.*" Now she walked up to the bed and gently took Chana's hand. It lay lead-like in hers. " Heah Mis' Betty Ponder, Chaney; she done come tuh see ye."

Chana did not move or turn her head, but her lips moved: " Tell 'er howdy. I cayn't talk."

Mrs. Ponder said a few hearty words, which

passed over Chana's apathy like a breeze over a rock.

Then Dosier's mellow, tender voice struck the new note of thought. "I ben studyin' 'bout you, sist' Chaney. You 'ain't had much good times, has you?"

All the while she was softly stroking Chana's hand. There was no word or sign of response, but Dosier felt the faintest tremor under her fingers.

"Yes, honey, dat so; but ef you did n't have a good time, you shall have de bigges' an' de nices' burryin' of ary cullud pusson in Hot Springs."

Chana lifted her free hand. "Turn me over," said she. Whenever the poor woman would move, she must be helped. Dosier assisted her to change her position.

"Go on," she said faintly. There was no dawning of interest in her face, but she listened while Dosier talked, and it was the first time since the doctors spoke their sentence that she had so much as listened. Dosier had no perception of anything grotesque or horrible in telling her sister about her funeral. The negroes all magnify funerals. She thought simply that Chana might be "chirked up a bit" to know what a nice funeral she would have. Nor was she mistaken. Poor Chana had her meagre social ambitions; she wanted to be well thought of.   Since her conversion she had regularly sent her quarter on Sunday for the preacher.   Dosier had promised her fifty cents to give on the proud day when she should wear her new black silk to church.   It may be that her bewildered soul saw a light of hope in this last chance of display. Death would not utterly crush her, if she might have a " gran' burryin'."

" Br'er Warner shill preach yo' funeral, sister," said Dosier.   " You *shill* go ter church oncet mo' like you wanted tuh, an' you shill w'ar my bes' under-cloze, an' — an' my black silk dress."

There was no mistake now; the sick woman was listening.   " *What!* " she cried hoarsely; " you' —   Naw, I cayn't take hit, sist' Doshy; you' onlies' good dress, an' you spendin' sech er heap er money on me now.   Tuh *burry* dat beaucherful dress!   Why, 't wud be plumb wicked."

But there was a light in her eyes, a flickering, timid hope.   Do not despise it; behind the barbarian greed for show was the human longing to be mourned by her kind; to touch them, move them somehow, leave some more vivid impression behind her than merely the image of a bed-ridden old black woman out of the way.   Who knows that poor Chana's funeral was not to her that one enchanted moment which we all, in some wise — being mortal — must covet, the moment when we are the central figure of our world?

More and more did the hard pain soften as Dosier went on, taking no denial: "You shill w'ar my new ruche dat Mis' Higgins give me, an' de pin, an' be clothed in silk from head to toe. Oh, Chaney, honey, ye doan' know how willin' I gives it up, ef it on'y ease you' min'. I tanks de Lawd ever' night I *got* de money tuh spend on ye."

"An' me tinkin' ha'sh tings er de Lawd kase He call me 'way!" sobbed the now entirely overcome woman. "When *you* is so good tuh me, I give up, sist' Doshy; I reckon He does love me; I is willin' tuh go. Mabbe — mabbe He let me outer Heaven oncet in a w'ile, an' I kin git back an' see you all. Doshy, den I aim tuh shake dat rosebush agin de winder. Den ye know it 's *me*."

Miss Maine stood at her window in the hotel and watched the long procession of Chana's funeral creeping up the hill to the church. The last buggy had turned the corner, and still she stood, held motionless by the sombre reverie that was her usual state of mind — a dismal day-dream where the sorrows of others always were merged into her own grief.

Thus Mrs. Ponder found her, when she was ushered into the room, breathless with her rapid ascent of the stairs, and red in the face from a combination of weeping and fast walking.

"I've just come from Dosier's," she said, after the formal greeting, unaffectedly wiping her eyes, "and I've cried so I'm not fit to be seen. Besides, it's a long walk."

"I thought I saw you in a carriage," said Miss Maine.

"Oh, I left the carriage for Dosier; and Mrs. Higgins sent a carriage too."

"Mrs. Higgins!" cried Miss Maine, surprise overcoming her reserve. "Why, I thought she — she said — I didn't suppose she would care."

"Oh, she's right kind-hearted," said Mrs. Ponder, easily; "only she hates to show. Why, she's gone up to Dosier's a heap of times. She and I. We were there the day she died. She'd jest gone, and Dosier told us about it. She died just as peaceful! After Dosier had that talk about the funeral with her she didn't think of nothing else; saw the preacher, picked out all the hymns — her mind was just full of it; and the morning when she died she had Dosier lay out all her things on the bed, the black silk and all, and Dosier said she actually laughed, and said, 'Will I look nice in it, sister, clothed in silk from top to toe?' That's what Dosier had said to her, you know. And when Dosier replied, 'Yes, she would look beautiful,' she laughed again, and went to sleep holding Dosier's hand, and she passed away in her sleep. There could n't be anything more peaceful. And really, Miss Maine, it was a beautiful funeral — such quantities of flowers, and so many closed carriages, and she did look so nice and happy in the black silk! Poor Dosier did give her her best, that 's a fact."

"What a pity Chana could n't see her own funeral!" said Miss Maine, rather dryly.

"Well, I don't know; perhaps she did," said Mrs. Ponder.

THE LOAF OF PEACE.

IF the kitchen-door stand open — and the door of an Arkansas kitchen is likely to stand open on a late February day — you can look from the kettles of the big stove to the bend of the Black River, to the steep bank where red willow twigs top the velvet down which will be grass, and across the gray waters to willows and sycamores and canebrakes and a few cabins in the clearings. Should you step to the door, you can see the plantation-store and mill, and a score of gambrel-roofed white houses. In the fields, the whitish-brown cotton-stalks lie on the dun-colored earth. The birds are singing in the cypress forest, and a red-bird flutters his gorgeous wings on a stray stalk that has escaped the cutter.

Aunt Callie, one day in February, saw the fields and the bird, and also a little girl whose flannel cape was the color of the bird's wing, and whose thick hair had a gleam of the same tint.

"Humph," said Aunt Callie, "reckon by her favor, dat ar's Haskett's gell comin' by."

"Haskett's gell," otherwise Mizzie Haskett, came awkwardly and shyly down the walk, and balanced herself on the kitchen steps. She wore her holiday attire, a blue-and-white cotton frock, red flannel cape, and a large bonnet (evidently made for a much older head) decked with red roses. Her hair was tied with a bright new green ribbon; and round a soft and snowy little neck was a large white frill in which glittered an imitation-gold pin. Certainly her pretty skin did not need it, but she was powdered (or, to be accurate, floured) profusely; this last Southern touch of art being added, injudiciously, after the putting on of the red cape. She was, moreover, consumed with embarrassment, which sent a flood of blushes through the flour layer, over her skin, from the roots of her hair to the nape of her neck.

"Ye seekin' ary pusson, Sissy?" said Aunt Callie, frigidly. She had cooked for "the quality" twenty years, and she knew her own dignity.

"I be'n seekin' Miss Dora, please," the little girl answered meekly, in a very sweet voice.

Miss Caroll, overhearing both question and answer, hastened to invite the child to come in, which she did after a long interval of scraping her shoes outside.

Once in the kitchen, seated, and her feet twisted behind the rungs of a kitchen chair, Mizzie gasped twice, then said, " Paw sent me. It dropped through."

" What do you mean ?" said Miss Caroll.

" It was sorter sad lookin'," continued Mizzie, on the verge of tears. " Paw made out to eat it, but I knowed 't was n't right."

" Eat what?   I really don't understand."

" The brown bread, ma'am," sobbed Mizzie, big tears rolling down her cheeks, but persistently gasping her way through her sentences. " I put it in the steamer, like — you all — tole me ; but — it dropped through an' spread out. Did n't raise up high like you all's."

" You unfortunate child !" said Dora, " do you mean that you poured your brown bread into the steamer — without any tin ?"

This, it appeared, was precisely what Mizzie had done.

" 'Cause Mis' Caroll did n't say nuthin' 'cept ' Put it into the steamer.' "

" Paw and me made it together," said she, taking out a square of cotton to wipe her eyes ; " an' when it come out so sad an' curis lookin' he said for me to come here to-day, 'cause you all wud be makin' of you' bread, an' mabbe wud n't mind me lookin' on.   Tole me to shore wipe my feet dry.   Paw 'd hate terrible for me to pester ye."

Aunt Callie visibly softened under this humility. "Dar, sot still an' watch me, den," said she.

"I 'll tell you," said Dora; "I taught Aunt Callie our New England bread."

She could not have asked a more attentive scholar, Mizzie watching every motion of the great wooden spoon with the eyes of a hawk, and her lips moving at intervals as do those of a child who inaudibly repeats a lesson to himself.

Presently, the brown batter being safely in the tin mould, and the mould in the steamer, the small maid asked : —

"Please, ma'am, cud we all buy a tin trick like that at the store?"

Being informed that she could, she sighed with relief, extricated her feet from the chair, and "made her manners."

"I 'm much obliged to you all, ma'am, an' I wish ye well."

Hereupon she would have gone, had not Dora detained her to slip a slice of cake and some apples into her hand.

They saw her stop, a little distance from the house, and carefully wrap the cake in a piece of paper.

"She 'll never tech a bite o' dat ar," said Aunt Callie, — "jes' tote it home to de young uns. She do dem chil'en good as a mudder. Dey ain't got any mudder, ye un'erstan'. She keep de 'ouse alone ebber sence her maw died. Dar's her paw; and Sal' Jane, dat's goin' on ten; and de baby, dat's two; an' her, dat's mabbe fo'-teen. De cookin' an' scrubbin' an' makin' de cloze, she an' her paw, dey do it all. When he makin' a crop, den *she* do it all. But in winter he makes out to sen' 'er ter school mos' days 'cept washin' day. He guv 'er dat pin, but mos' times she lends it ter Sal' Jane. Sal' Jane's all fur havin' 'er time an' 'er pleasure; but Mizpah, she's studdy."

Certainly she looked steady, too steady for her years, as she picked her way through the mud. She had stopped at the store, and the "tin trick" glittered under the crook of her elbow. Passing through the "settlement," she went over the brow of the tiny hill, down into the cypress brake. She hastened her pace, tripping along the dim forest ways. Beautiful ways they are in February, with the white bark shining like silver, and the velvet moss coating the north side of the cypresses and sycamores, and the glitter of red berries on the blue-black twigs of the hackberry-trees, and the ferns waving in the damp places, and the little "bluets" which deck the ground, first of all the brave company of spring flowers; but none of these did brisk little Mizzie see, because she was too busy planning for the two younger children and for "Paw."

"We cud make out right well, ef 't was 'nt fur that thar cotton," she said to herself. "Well, I wud n't keer 'bout losin' the cotton, either, ef 't was n't fur such a sight of bad feelin's. I jes' take the all-overs [1] every time I see paw getherin' his gun to go out. An' it used to be so nice!"

Mizzie sighed heavily. By this time she had come out upon a clearing and cotton-fields. On the edge of the cotton-fields stood a bright blue house. Evidently it was a new house; not only was its color a surprise to the eye accustomed to the universal whitewash of plantation taste, but its snug architecture and straight chimneys proclaimed its recent building. A little girl sat on the porch beside a lank Arkansas hound. The hound rushed across the fields with joyful yelps. Mizzie hushed him as best she could.

"Down, Jeru! Down, charge! You 'll fotch him out, shore."

The little girl had followed the dog. She was about Mizzie's age, and her black curls streamed out behind her as she ran.

"My, how long you was!" she exclaimed. "Did she tell ye?"

Mizzie nodded.

"Yes. You be thar, this evening," replied

____
[1] Shivers.

she, solemnly; and she added, "I reckon I'd best fetch 'long the baby. Sal' Jane has had 'im all the mornin'. You must n't ax too much of them little folks."

"All right. I'll fetch 'long my doll."

The little girl looked about her with a hurried and stealthy air, then pushed her pretty face through the fence rails to kiss Mizzie, saying :—

"You' right good to fix it for me so nice! An' I do love you better 'n any gell in this worl' " —

"O Doshy!" cried Mizzie, "I see him comin'. Oh, fly!"

Instantly she herself darted across the road and plunged into the brake. Doshy ran swiftly toward the house. A voice commanded her to stop; she had been seen. She turned and went back to her father. He was a short, dark man, who snapped an ox-goad against his boot-legs in an unpleasant manner.

"Ain't that gell Dock Haskett's?" he inquired. "War n't that her here yisterday, too?"

"Yes, sir," said Doshy.

"Did n't I tole ye I did n't want ye to have no more talk with Haskett's folks?"

Then Doshy plucked up heart to answer. "Paw, I cayn't help it. She's so good. An' I like her better 'n any little gell in school."

"Good!" repeated the father, with strong derision. "Good! Ain't she a Haskett? Ain't she got a red head like his'n? Aw, them red heads kin talk an' git 'roun' decent folks, but they 'll do ye a meanness whenever ye trust 'em. Look at me! Kin I walk right yit? Confound him, I 'll tote that ar bullet er his'n 'roun', long 's I live! An' my gell a-wantin' ter run with his gell! I ain't got patience to enjure hit. Go 'long!"

The child made no answer, but, stifling a sob, flew into the house.

Sullenly the father limped about his work. He was not at all a harsh father, and that unusual look of fright and hurt that his girl had worn smote his heart.

"Now I made the little trick feel bad. Blame it all!" he muttered, while he saddled his horse; and he felt all the more bitter toward Haskett, the cause of his ill-temper.

Everybody on the plantation knew that there was open war, a strong and bitter feud, between Luther Morrow and Dock Haskett. Yet, not six months before, they had been warm friends. The quarrel began over a trifle — a dispute as to which of the hunters was the better shot. There was a match which decided nothing, and a hog-hunt in which each shot the same number of wild hogs, and both claimed the last boar. The two men's tempers waxed warmer, and, by consequence, their friendship cooled, and foolish friends made the matter worse. And, finally, Jerusalem Jones, Luther's pet hound, must needs choose this season of wrath to steal a ham from the Haskett gallery. Dock Haskett, unhappily, snatched up his gun and shot at the beast. He missed Jerusalem Jones, but he hit Jerusalem's master, who was on his way to the Hasketts', bent on conciliation, owing to his wife's entreaties. (He even had it in mind to tell Dock that he was in no hurry for the payment of a certain note that would fall due in February. In their friendly days, Luther had lent Dock money.) Enraged at such a reception, Luther brought his own gun to his shoulder, and there was a very pretty fusilade before Mizzie and the neighbors could reach the place from the cotton-fields. Dock had a shot in the shoulder, and Luther was on the ground with that shot in the leg, which was not yet healed.

To-day, for the first time, Luther was able to ride to the store. He went on no pacific mission. Dock was saving his last bales of cotton for the higher spring-prices. They were at the gin, near the store. Luther's business was to have them attached for his debt. The very first person whom he met, after he had concluded this business, was a tall man, lean and awkward, with a kindly freckled face and red hair — in short, Dock Haskett.

He had heard about the cotton. He rode straight up to Luther. "This yere ain't no place for talkin'," said he. "If ye reckon I done ye any wrong, I am ready to have it out with ye any time an' place ye like; but I promised my gell to fotch her some flour, and I got ter git it back to her fust."

Before the two men separated, they had agreed to meet "an' talk 'bout things" that afternoon, at a lonely spot in the cypress brake, midway between their houses.

Then they rode home, carrying no very good appetite to their dinners.

Dock found the new brown bread over the fire when he entered the room at home which was the Hasketts' kitchen, dining-room, and bed-chamber all in one.

The baby toddled to meet him, babbling an inarticulate welcome which Mizzie interpreted at length — the baby was sixteen months old, and more fluent than intelligible of speech.

An apple and a piece of cake had been saved for the father.

"Ye all had some?" said he. Sal' Jane assured him they had, "all 'cept Mizzie, an' *she* fotched 'em."

"Mizzie an' me 'll go shares," said Dock. "Ye are allers good to the little tricks. Reckon I kin trust 'em with ye."

He sighed in a curious way, Mizzie thought, as he spoke, and as he kissed her. While she was laying the table for dinner, he helped her, as usual, but more than once he caught himself standing still, dish in hand, staring around the room. To a mere stranger, it might have seemed bare and comfortless. The bricks on the hearth and in the great black throat of the fireplace were uneven and broken. It was a meagre array of tin and delft that was ranged on the shelf above. The walls were unplastered, and their sole ornaments were two colored cards, — one, presented with a box of soap, representing a very chubby infant washing himself; the other, the gift of a stray insurance agent, a red and black sketch of a burning house. The floor was in waves, and the only piece of carpet was before the bed. Dock himself had chopped the rude bedstead out of white-oak timbers, and Mizzie had stuffed the pillows and the mattress with cotton. The great cracks in the walls where the clapboards were warped or broken had been plastered with mud. There were barely two panes of glass in the single window of the room. But Dock looked fondly at the red cushions covering the broken seats of the cane-bottomed chairs, at the figured brown oilcloth on the table, and the bright tin spoons which shone in the blue glass jug bought by Mizzie's cotton-money, and the lamp filled with real coal oil, and it seemed to him a truly luxurious and beautiful apartment, only he used no such fine words.

" Don't it look good ! " thought Dock, sorrowfully. " Ye feelin' puny[1] to-day, paw? " said Mizzie, with an anxious look.

" Naw, honey, I war jes' studyin'." In a minute he added, in a serious tone, " Mizzie, do ye set 's much store by Doshy Morrow now'days ez ye use ter ? "

Mizzie came up closer to him and leaned her head against his arm, while she answered, " Yes, paw. *She* ain't hurted you, ye know." She twisted the cloth of his sleeve, and went on, " Paw, wud ye — wud ye mind my learnin' Doshy to make this 'ere bread? "

" In co'se not, honey. I ain't no ill-will ter the little trick, nur to her maw neether. She war powerful kind to us all, onct." He muttered under his breath, " May be she 'd be kind ag'in, if " —

Instead of completing the sentence, he kissed the anxious little face.

Mizzie thought that he was even kinder than usual that day. After their simple dinner, she saw him chopping wood. He chopped a great pile, enough to last a long while, in the mild weather of February and March. Then he

[1] Ill.

brought the sack of meal into the gallery from the shed. "Handier fur ye," he muttered; and he cut up the half a pig which hung in the shed, so that it was ready for cooking.

By this time, the hour was near three by the wheezy old clock on the shelf. Dock returned to the house.

Sal' Jane was poking the fire, at that moment, with an important air which was explained by her first speech.

"Mizzie 's gone with the baby, an' I 'm to keep the water b'ilin', so the bread won't spile."

"That 's right, honey," said her father. He kissed her and went out again.

She thought nothing of his having his gun over his shoulder.

About the same time, Luther Morrow, also carrying a gun, was shutting his gate. He looked grimly and sadly at the cotton-fields and the house, but he forced a smile when his wife nodded to him from the doorway; and after he had walked a little distance he turned to wave his hand.

"Mendoshy 's alluz b'en a good wife ter me," he thought; "mabbe she 'd like fer ter 'member that 'ar, ef anythin' happens."

The place of meeting was marked by a blasted

cypress growing on the edge of a ravine or "slash." A tangle of thorn-trees, papaws, and trumpet-vines made a rude hedge above the bank on the roadside. Luther's first glance showed him Dock's tall figure in blue jeans, outlined against the chalk-white of the cypress. At the same moment, Dock perceived his enemy, and both men advanced, frowning. Half-way they stopped as abruptly as if shot, with a curious embarrassed, shamefaced look. Yet that which had stopped them was but a child's laugh. Immediately it was answered by another childish laugh.

"They 're down thar in the slash, I reckon," said Dock. "Say, war n't that yo' gell's voice?"

"Yes; war n't t' other un *your'n?*" said Luther. He was seized with an absurd and incongruous curiosity.

"Cayn't we get nearer to see?" said he.

Dock jerked his thumb over his shoulder, saying, "Thar 's a opener place a piece back."

"All right," said Luther.

Neither man caring to walk ahead of the other, the two marched peaceably side by side.

Just so, — the abrupt remembering it and the sting of it made Dock wince, — just so they had walked over that very road a year before; then they carried a coffin between them, and the coffin was that of Dock's wife. She was buried out in the woods, as she had wished. The spot was not twenty rods away. Luther had been Dock's good friend and neighbor then, and it was Mrs. Morrow who brought the bunch of holly and red berries that was lying on the coffin. " And how comes it we b'en walkin' yere to-day, seekin' each other's blood ? " thought Dock.

Luther's reflections were of another nature.

" Thar ! if that ar bad little trick are runnin' with Haskett's gell agin, ayfter my tellin' her — I jes' *will* guv 'er the bud [1] — leastways, I 'll skeer 'er up, a-promisin' it to her ! "

Dock soon halted where the underbrush was less dense.

Each of the men eyed the other sharply before getting on his hands and knees to crawl through. Luther, half-way, met with a mishap, catching on a thorn-tree. A smothered exclamation from him attracted Dock's notice.

" My foot got cotched in the elbow-brush," he groaned, " and that ar blamed thorn-tree 's got hold er my breeches; I cayn't reach it with my han's, nur I cayn't kick it 'way with my foot. Say, kin ye cut the ornery branch off ? "

" Waal, ye *be* helt fas', ain't ye ? " Dock answered, hastening to his aid, without a sign of levity. He solemnly cut away the limb of the thorn-tree.

[1] Switch.

" Thank 'e," said Luther, in a surly voice.

They both crawled to the edge.   In some way they both felt a disposition to postpone their quarrel.   They looked over the hedge of " elbow-brush " and thorn-tree and leafless trumpet-vine. Down below, in the hollow, a fire had been built against a log.   Three sticks, crossed above, supported a kettle on which rested a covered tin vessel.   A savory steam arose from this, crisping in the air, delicious to the nostrils and beautiful to the eye.   Close to the fire, Mizzie and Doshy sat together.   The baby sat on a blanket beside Mizzie, hilariously playing with Doshy's new doll.   On the outskirts of the group, the dog, Jerusalem Jones, was chasing a pig.

" Whut they monkeyin' with onyhow ? " said Luther.

" Hush !   Hark to 'em ! " said Dock.

Doshy was explaining something to Mizzie : " An' he loves brown bread a turrible sight.   He eat some to Mis' Caroll's, an' he b'en talkin' 'bout it ever since.   An' I 'll have this yere fur supper, an' he 'll eat it, an' he 'll say, ' Who made it ?' an' I 'll say ' Me ; ' an' I 'll say *you* learned me, an' then he 'll 'low you' a real nice little girl."

" I 'm 'fraid he won't," said Mizzie ; " my paw don't mind a bit my likin' you ; but you' paw 'd like for to set the dog on me."

"Naw, he wud n't neether," cried Doshy. "He jes' lets on ter be cross; he 's *real* good, inside. Don' ye mind how he gethered them pecans fur we - all afore they had the trouble? He 's real kind; he never whips none o' us. Jes' *sez* he will — but he *don't.*"

"Blame it all, the pesky littly trick! She b'en 'cute nuff ter fin' that out," cried Luther, while Dock stifled a chuckle.

"My paw 's good, too," said Mizzie. "He chopped a right smart er wood fur me to-day. I never have to chop wood."

"Neither does maw," said Doshy, proudly. "My paw always does hit, an' he done a heap to-day, too."

The two fathers exchanged glances; without a word each read what the other's forebodings had been, by what he remembered of his own. And each felt, in a vague and dubious way, complimented by the other's dread of being killed.

A loud scream from one of the little girls turned their eyes back to the fire. Jerusalem Jones had worked mischief. He thought it was an unprotected orphan of a pig that he was harassing; so, barking and jumping, he had chased the wretched little beast into the brake. But, in a second, he came back faster than he went, and pursued by three wild hogs. These wild hogs are hideous creatures, long, muscular, with great black heads, and tusks like scimiters curling upward out of their jaws. They would have ended Jerusalem Jones's ill-doing in short order, had they caught him. Jerusalem, howling with fright, bounded up to the girls, the wild hogs at his heels, uttering the strange, fierce sound which these beasts make when they rally to face the hunter. It is the note of danger. The girls turned pale. They leaped to their feet. Mizzie snatched up the baby. With a single bound and a mighty swing of her strong little arms, she dropped the astonished infant in the midst of a thicket of thorn-trees. Then, snatching a brand from the fire, she stood at bay.

"Fight 'em with the fire, Doshy!" she said; "don' let 'em git our bread!"

Doshy had bravely caught a stick, but seeing the baby safe, she had flown to the rescue of Jerusalem Jones. The dog was rolling on the ground in desperate conflict with the smallest hog. In his agony, Jerusalem wrenched himself free and made a flying leap through the fire, thereby overturning the gypsy kettle and sending the brown bread tin headlong at the hogs. Doshy uttered a piteous scream: —

"Oh, my bread! my nice bread!"

Mizzie was on the other side nearer the brown-bread. Before the huge black noses could touch the tin, she kicked over the log.

" Gether the bread an' run ! " she screamed.

The two hogs turned on Mizzie. Doshy was running to her playmate's aid ; but she was too far away. Horrified, she saw one infuriated boar strike the burning stick out of the brave little hand. " Jeru! Jeru! " she cried in her despair, while she threw her stick at the hog.

Let it be told to his credit, Jerusalem responded ; though he had run on his own account, though he was bleeding in half a dozen places, the dog leaped back into the fray, drove his teeth through the big boar's ear, and hung there. The boar had caught Mizzie's skirt ; he flung up his wicked head now. But, meanwhile, the other boar, with his teeth clashing, his eyes like red coals —

" Oh, Lord, Luther ! " gasped Dock, " cayn't ye git a sight at it ?   My pore little gell 's square in front o' *me !* "

He shut his eyes for one intolerable second ; the next, the ping of a bullet made him crash his way through the brush, and slip recklessly down the bank. As an apple falls when hit by a stone, the boar tumbled to the ground. Then Dock's bullet laid the other hog beside him.

The sagacious Jerusalem had loosened his hold when he saw the gun-barrel. Now he capered over the body with yells of triumph. But he ceased his dance and looked in amazement at his master, who was actually hugging Haskett's girl.

"Please, Mister Morrow," she said, "look a' the baby. I put 'im in, but I cayn't git 'im out."

The baby, however, was already in his father's arms. Doshy was mourning over her brown bread.

"Put it back in the steamer," commanded Mizzie, adding : "Oh, please, Mister Morrow, 't ain't Doshy's fault, bein' with me ; I coaxed her fur ter learn ter make the bread ! "

"Honey," her father answered tenderly, " it's the bes' bread ever was baked ! — an' Haskett 'n' me 'll eat it together. Won't we, Dock ? "

"We will so," said Dock, rubbing the tears from his eyes, "an' I guv in, now, 'bout the shootin'. *I* cud n't hev made that shot jest un'er the child's elbow ! Why, ye got a han' o' iron " —

"An' *I* guv in 'bout that ar ornery, triflin', no-'count dog," answered Luther ; " ye was right for ter shoot 'im, Dock. Ye kin kill him off, this minnit, ef yer wan' ter."

"Naw, sir. Not ayfter his tacklin' that hoeg ez he did," cried Dock ; "but ye know, Luther, — I meant that shot, six months ago, fer him, not fer *you ;* an' I are turrible sorry I done hit " —

"Shet up!" said Luther, impulsively. "I've done ez mean by you ez you've done by me. Blamed if I know how it come we-uns was fightin', onyhow. Say, let's take the brown bread ter my house an' eat it — an' tell Mendoshy."

Thus it happened that the man who passed the Morrow house that evening had a most extraordinary tale to relate at the store.

"I tell ye, they was all roun' the table, Dock Haskett an' his baby, an' his two gells an' all the Morrowses. An' Luther he kissed Haskett's gell spang on the forehead, an' he war a-cuttin' her a hunk o' brown bread. An' Dock, he says, 'She didn't do no better nor *yore* gell;' an' then Luther he guvs his gell a buss, too, an' they all were a-laffin', an' Mis' Morrow she laffed till she cried."

Aunt Callie's comment was, "Waal, good cookin' 's never wasted, an' them gells ain't likely to fergit how to make brown bread. I ain't sorry I l'arned 'er, though, ez a gineral thing, I ain't no 'pinion er folkses romancin' 'roun' my kitchen."

THE DAY OF THE CYCLONE.

I⟩ was a warm day. Perhaps but for that it
might not have happened, since Captain Barris
is a most temperate man. Unluckily, the day
was warm, very warm, and Archy was tired with
a long ride in the " accommodation train; " and
a vision of a glass of beer — cool, foaming, pleas-
antly stinging — rose before him. He had just
been stationed at Rock Island Arsenal, and all
his knowledge of the town of Grinnell was the
fact that he had inherited some property within
its limits. Quite innocently, therefore, he stared
about him for some sign of refreshment.

The street was like a hundred rural streets in
the West — straight, broad, and shaded by
young trees.

All the wooden cottages might have been de-
signed by the same prosaic architect.

Some of them looked a little rusty; many of
them shone with new paint. They all had trim
gardens in front, oases of verdure in the midst
of the dust. Between the dwellings, every now

and then, there would come a great gap of un-
tilled fields, where no mower disturbed the
riotous plantain, and burdock and jimson weeds
held a kind of squalid revelry over a heap of tin
cans. The contrast between this unkempt do-
main and the tidiness of the dwellings was
queer; but it was as Western as the sea of
prairie around the town, or the fierce sun above.

No quiver in the hot air blurred the shadows
of the maple leaves on the sidewalks. A few
farmers' wagons crawled tediously through the
glare. Just ahead of Archy was the solitary
other footman in sight. He was a big man, thin,
but built on the large and sinewy plan. Though
it was so warm, his gray head was covered with
a soft black felt hat, and he wore the heaviest
of boots. To equalize matters, he carried his
black coat on his arm and had unbuttoned his
old-fashioned waistcoat. He walked slowly,
with the round shoulders and uneven gait of a
man accustomed to watch the ground.

So little did Archy know of the interior of
Iowa that he marched up to this old man and
asked where he could get a glass of beer.

His answer was the view of a gaunt and
weather-beaten visage and a portentous frown.

"Kin I tell you where ye kin get a glass of
beer?" repeated the man, who frowned as the
keen gray eyes under the beetling brows took in

Archy's elegant figure, from the white Derby hat of the period to his immaculate gaiters. "No, young man, I cayn't; and I'd advise you to quit huntin' up beer, or ye won't wear sich good clo'se long. Anyhow, ye won't find no beer in Grinnell?"

"What's the trouble with Grinnell?"

"The trouble is, it's a prohibition town; and prohibition in Grinnell does prohibit. There ain't a saloon in the place. Ye cayn't git a drop of intoxicatin' liquor, not a drop" —

Here his underjaw fell, his eyeballs fixed themselves in a dismal stare; and the didactic forefinger, that had been sawing the air, was paralyzed midway, so that it pointed straight at the red-faced man reeling round the corner. The look and the swagger of him were unmistakable.

"Perhaps *he* could tell me," said Archy.

He made the old man a very fine bow and walked away, smiling.

But when he returned to Grinnell, a year later, he was more serious. "I dare say Rachel's father is another of the same sort," he reflected; "if not — by Jove, that would be too much, though!"

He laughed a little lugubriously. Rachel was beautiful enough, and, what was better, sweet and good enough to justify any man's passion;

and he was as much in love as a man can well be ; but he thought of her people with a qualm.

" I grant that Rachel is an angel " — so his mother had talked — " and the angels are above social distinctions ; but her father and mother ? "

" Her mother is presumedly an angel, too," Archy had replied, " she has been dead these ten years."

" Well, there are her father and two brothers. And she told me that there was a cousin visiting them whom her father was going to marry. *She* comes from Vermont ; but I don't believe the boys have ever been out of Grinnell in their lives. You can't judge these people by the Ramsays, Archy ; the Ramsays have been everywhere. It was only a freak of Mr. Ramsay's, sending Ethel to Grinnell. Archy, I feel sure her people are *impossible !* "

" I sha'n't marry her people," Archy had said, lightly.

But now, with some misgivings, he scanned the elderly men coming home to their midday dinners, any one of whom might be *her* father. Sedate, prosperous looking men they were, very like men of their years in a New England village, except for a slight Western negligence of dress.

" Ramsay is right," mused Archy ; " Grinnell is a Puritan colony in the prairie."

He was in the college campus, now. The ugly, square stone building he judged to be the college hall, and from the number of heads at the windows, he surmised that a tall brick building was a kind of dormitory. The pretty cottages about must be the professors' houses, and the young men and maidens among the trees must be the students. He thought that the youths had rather a rustic air, but some of the girls were admirably pretty, and the ripple of their gayety spread to the faces of the passers-by.

"But not one of them," was his comment, "can compare with Rachel — Hallo! here's the house."

A doorplate left him in no doubt. The house was of wood, of two stories, and had two bay-windows and a piazza. It was painted gray, and the blinds were red. There was a garden before it full of rosebushes, and the roses were in bloom. Archy grew a little dizzy; he had not seen Rachel for a week; he would see her in a moment, and being a modest, true-hearted young fellow, very much in love, his soul abased itself before this delicate and radiant creature that he was daring to make his own.

"My white rose," murmured the lover, "I am not worthy, but I will try."

"Cayn't ye make nobuddy hear ye? That gong's intended to ring," remarked a harsh, deep voice at his elbow. An old man had come around a bay-window to find Archy smiling tenderly at the doorplate. It was the same old man whom he had met before.

"I am looking for Mr. Jared Meadowes," said Archy, whose heart sank down to his boots.

"Well, you 've found him."

Inwardly Archy groaned. Outwardly he bowed, and said, "I am Captain Barris."

"Walk in," said Meadowes, throwing the door open, but with no gleam of cordiality on his face.

He strode on before, Archy thinking how familiar his back looked, for he was in his shirt-sleeves. He had also dispensed with shoes, and his white socks glimmered in the obscurity of the hall. Archy followed him into a pretty room, and took the chair pushed forward. The old man seated himself opposite, planted his hands on his knees in the fashion of a rustic photograph, and proceeded to subject the young officer to a grim and leisurely scrutiny. Decidedly, it was not a promising welcome.

However, one cannot sit indefinitely staring at one's prospective father-in-law, so Archy cleared his throat and began. He presumed Mr. Meadowes knew the object of his visit. He had met Miss Meadowes at her friend Miss Ramsay's.

"Six weeks ago," interrupted the old man, "and now ye want to marry her."

A trifle disconcerted, Archy next tried to explain his position and prospects. "He was in the army, stationed at Rock' Island Arsenal. The quarters there" —

"That's all right," said the old man, "I've been on the Island. Big thing. Big arsenal. But I want to hear 'bout *you.*"

"Oh, I? I am twenty-eight years of age. My father was in the army, General Barris. He was killed in the war. It is rather an army family. My mother is a Massachusetts woman. She was a Miss Saltonstall."

"Dependent on you?"

"She has about half a million dollars from her father. I have one sister, who is married, and lives in New York. She is not dependent on me either. My mother lives with me. She — everybody thinks my mother a charming woman."

"But Rachel ain't goin' to marry your mother. Cayn't seem to git ye to talk 'bout yourself. Ramsay gives you a fine send off in his letter; but things don't strike him and I just the same. I guess you're a desirable husband as the world looks at things; but I ain't one of the world's people. Never was. You ain't the kind of husband I'd pick out for my daughter.

Nor yours ain't the kind of life I 'd choose for her. But if you 're a good man, and likely to make her happy, I won't stand in the way. It 's nature, I s'pose. I took her mother off to Kansas, 'way from her folks, an' now you want to take her, an' she 's glad to go; but 't ain't nature I should be glad to have her. Well, now, s'posin' you stop to dinner an' give me a chance to sorter size ye up; an' if I like the look o' ye I 'll go down to Rock Island, and if you 're satisfactory all 'round, it will be time to talk of marrying."

" I shall wait until after dinner, then," said Archy, smiling.

No answering smile relaxed the other's iron features as he replied: " All right. Make yourself to home. I 'll go tell the folks."

He left Archy in a frame of mind about equally compounded of irritation, amusement, and consternation. The young man could not help laughing as he pictured his mother's horror when she should see Meadowes. " Well, anyhow, I don't blame him for not wanting to give up Rachel," he thought, gazing about the room for some trace of this one sweet presence. He rightly judged the soft hues of the walls and draperies, and the pretty feminine fancies of wicker-work and ribbon, to be of her choosing; but he gave old Meadowes full credit for the plaster group representing the signing of the Emancipation Proclamation, and for a huge, pale engraving of Lincoln in the bosom of his family. Above the mantel-piece hung a water-color portrait, sumptuously framed, with a jar of roses before it, like an offering before a shrine. Plainly, it was the important object in the room. The portrait was a man's head. The features, the brows, and the contour of the face, which was clean shaven, reminded Archy of those multitudinous busts in the Vatican. Like them, also, was the singularly calm and determined expression. But the blue eyes were mild, sad, and dreamy. Archy had risen for a nearer view, when the inmates of the house appeared. They were Rachel, her future stepmother, and her two brothers. The future stepmother was introduced as Miss Baker. She resembled Rachel in figure and carriage, rather than in features or coloring; and Archy had a fancy that her gentle, faded face looked a good deal as the late Mrs. Meadowes's might have done at the age of — say forty. But, naturally, his glance only lingered a polite instant before it sought Rachel. Her lover had often compared Rachel to the wild flowers growing in the clefts of New England rocks. Her extraordinary beauty was of that fragile type that has a pathos in its very charm. Really, Rachel was both healthy and happy, and her father loved to boast of her prowess in mathematics at the Grinnell College; yet, whoever looked on her exquisite, pale face, with its wistful eyes and sensitive mouth, felt an involuntary sympathy, well enough interpreted by Archy's mother's remark: " That is the kind of girl who can break her heart!" She was a creature to whom one is gentle by instinct. Nevertheless, such creatures have their own strength. She was graceful because she could not help it, and had a natural sense of beauty. Archy felt a fond pride as the lovely shape approached. Nothing more than a white frock and some red roses; but how they suited her!

By this time he was back in his chair, beaming with great friendliness upon the two youths, Ossawatomie (" Is he named for an Indian chief?" wondered Archy) and Jared. They were twin brothers, two years younger than Rachel; both tall, slim, and shy; having their sister's fascinating combination of bronze hair and dark-brown eyes, but with features that were a softened copy of their father's. Jared did not open his lips; Ossawatomie made some timid advances. To help on the lagging talk, Archy spoke of the water-color. " It was painted on East," said Ossawatomie, " from a daguerreotype. It is John Brown."

" The Queen's John Brown, or John Brown's body?" Archy asked, with his fatal levity.

" That, sir," said a deep voice, " is John Brown of Ossawatomie, the noblest man that ever died for liberty ! "

Archy had not seen him approach, and who can hear the footfall of socks ? There he stood in the doorway, forefinger uplifted, as grim and dark a figure as ever sent a witch to the gallows. " Well, sir," he continued, " what is *your* opinion of him ? "

" He was a hero, certainly," said Archy, " whatever his mistakes."

" *What* mistakes ? "

" Well, Harper's Ferry. And that Missouri affair where they dragged men out of their cabins, and shot them in the hearing of their wives and children " —

The old man interrupted him as usual: " Brown was n't on that raid. But that ain't sayin' he condemned it; he did n't. And you need n't waste much pity on them men. They had blood on their own hands, every one of them ; they had murdered Free State men ; and they were judged, condemned, and killed for it, as they had ought to be. That 's all there is to that affair. Those border ruffians used to ride over into Kansas, and slay, and steal, and burn. They 'd come over and vote, and make our laws for us. Then they 'd shoot us 'cause we objected. Did n't ye never hear of the sack of Lawrence? A neighbor of mine was shot down, right before his wife, by three men. Three to one, those were their odds. I know all about it, for I was one of Brown's men. I was only a stripling, but I had the luck to be in four fights, and I got a bullet in my leg that, like 's not, saved my life, for else I 'd a gone off with Brown to Harper's Ferry, so I guess I owe one good turn to a border ruffian. But, I tell you, I did n't thank him for it when I read in the papers how those he counted on failed him, and he was trapped and lay wounded in prison, and then how he — died. I 'd lay on my bed and cry, 'cause I could n't be there and fight it out with him. Say, sir, you that call Harper's Ferry a *mistake*, say, did you ever read the letters he wrote when he was in prison in Charleston?"

"No, I don't think I have; I don't remember them," said Archy, meekly.

"Then you 'd better, 'fore ye discuss Brown and his mistakes again," said Brown's old follower.

It was a welcome diversion to have Rachel, who had left the room for a second, return to announce dinner. Archy managed to get near enough to her for a whisper; but she only gave him a frightened glance and said, "*Please* don't talk about Brown to pa until you know more. Ossie 's named after him. Pa thinks the world of him!"

The meal began ominously. Archy had been praising the pretty town.

"We owe our prosperity to our liquor laws," said Mr. Meadowes. "Humph, did ye find any beer that day?"

So he had remembered! Archy, blushing in spite of himself, said no, he had n't tried.

"You drink to home, I s'pose. Have wine on the table?"

Archy confessed to an occasional glass of claret with his dinner.

"Them boys," said the old man, slanting his thumbs at the twins, — "them boys ain't never touched a drop of spirituous liquor in their lives."

"Indeed," said Archy, trying to throw a sympathetic accent into the word.

"Yes, sir. And the majority of the boys here have the same habits. That's the great advantage of a prohibitory law; it makes a town safe to raise boys in. I would n't raise a family in Davenport if you gave me my home."

"But Davenport is a delightful place, don't you know, Mr. Meadowes; and, in spite of their saloons, there is n't a town in Iowa with a smaller percentage of criminal business."

"All the same," Meadowes retorted, sardonically, "we'll try to improve it a bit. We are going to pass a law that will wipe out the saloons all over Iowa. P'raps you don't believe sich a law kin be enforced?"

" Well, it never has been. Why don't you try high license ? "

"Because I don't believe in compromising with evil. That's why ! I fought slavery in my youth, an' I 'm fighting rum in my old age. And I 've been a no-compromise man straight through. I learned that from old John Brown. There was n't much compromising about *him*. It was a grand thing to see him in battle. And they say it was grander to see him die. And yet there was n't a man was gentler or kinder-hearted. He never took no thought of himself. Look at that letter he wrote his wife from the prison, beggin' her not to come to him, 'cause it would use up all her little stock of money, and she might be insulted or hard treated. But I 'm wandering. Brown 's only a fanatic to you. He was not of this world, and the world martyred him, an' you compromise men stood by consenting unto his blood. You 're a high-license man yourself, I take it. Believe in doing evil that good may come, hey ? "

"Oh, no," said Archy, smiling. Somehow during the last few moments his thoughts had grown kinder to the loyal old partisan. "Oh, no, I merely choose between a little evil and a great deal. I 'll take less than the earth. But, really, Mr. Meadowes, I have n't studied the subject enough to discuss it. Can't you ask me something easy ? "

Ossie ventured to laugh. Jared frowned. "What are your politics?" said the old man, sternly.

"I am not sure that I have any. Sometimes I am a Republican, and sometimes a Democrat. I believe I was a Democrat last."

Now, in the interior of Iowa Republicanism is, still, a species of religion.

A gasp of dismay ran through the circle.

"Those are your opinions, are they?" said the old man, sternly. "A trimmer. Well. Will you have any more meat?"

Archy declined, and Mr. Meadowes only spoke to him once again during the meal. The once was when he observed Archy shredding his salad with his fork. "Ain't ye got no knife?" called he. "Lowisa" — to the red-haired maid — "give Captain Barris a knife."

"He's got a knife," the girl said sharply; "there's your knife!" — pushing the blade at Archy, who silently cut up his lettuce. But Rachel reddened up to her eyes.

The dinner was excellent. I don't know how many hours Rachel and Miss Baker had spent in the kitchen with "Lowisa." The linen was dainty, there were flowers on the table, and the cut-glass tumblers, and the carafe. Rachel had tripped out of the room with a happy smile, thinking: "Archy will see that we can have pretty things too."

But now, seen through a stranger's eyes, everything was wofully changed.

The oilcloth, to which her father clung because he had always had an oilcloth on his dining-room floor ever since he was married; that preposterous sideboard, and those portraits of Mr. and Mrs. Meadowes that a gifted sign-painter had done just before they left Kansas — did Archy notice them, was he laughing at them? Even the table appointments were not an unmixed triumph. Jared asked, where was the " water - pitcher " ? " Lowisa " forgot the white apron that had been furnished her. She piled the dishes noisily into dizzy towers, and it was almost an interposition of Providence that she did n't slay Mr. Meadowes outright, as she swung the meat platter above his head, with the carving-knife prancing on the edge, while he sat below, like an unconscious Damocles. It was no use trying to catch " Lowisa's " eye; her mind was on the sweets in the kitchen, and you must speak to the point, and in a good round tone too, or she would glare at you and say " *How ?* " Rachel thought of Mrs. Barris's dinners, the beautiful room, the glittering table, the noiseless service. Every rough gesture of her father's was like a blow. She could have groaned when he brandished his knife at Archy, in the courage of his opinions, or mopped his face with his napkin. His blunt discourtesy was worse than anything else. "How could he? How could he?" she kept saying to herself, in a spasm of mortification. Yet, all the while, she was angry with her lover. That indefinable thrill of kindred, of the blood that is thicker than water, was sending hot flushes of mingled shame and indignant affection to her cheeks. What could Archy know of her father, of his heroic devotion to principle, his honesty, that was a proverb in the town, and of how under that harsh exterior was the tenderest, faithfullest heart — why, though he talked so fiercely about saloon-keepers, he had half-supported Gus Timm's family after they sold him out and poured the barrels into the street! What did Archy know, sitting there so easily, sneering at his spiritual betters?

Meanwhile poor Archy, ignorant of this tumult of feeling, was congratulating himself on having kept his temper so well.

The dinner, at last, came to an end. Instantly Meadowes spoke to Rachel, "I want to see you a minnit, daughter."

They went out together. Ossie and Miss Baker exchanged a sorrowful glance; and Miss Baker said, "Won't you please step into the parlor, Captain Barris?" in much the same tone in which one might say, "Won't you walk into the silent tomb?"

The air had grown close and warm. Jared flung off his coat without ceremony. Ossie sat on the piano-stool making aimless half-circles of motion and looking dejected. Miss Baker essayed a few commonplaces on the late magazines; but her eyes kept wandering to the door, and Archy's best efforts at sprightliness fell flat; in fact, his listeners gazed at him more and more compassionately. It was a distinct relief, after half an hour of this, to see old Meadowes reappear. Simultaneously, as though they were puppets on a single string which he had pulled, the others jumped up and filed out of the room.

Archy felt a dismal presentiment. It was no false prophet; in the fewest and curtest sentences Meadowes told him that his proposal must be rejected. "I 've looked ye over and ye wun't do," said he; "you 're a drinkin' man "—

"I beg your pardon, Mr. Meadowes, I was never under the influence of liquor in my life. I don't care for the stuff."

Unconsciously Archy squared his shoulders; he had risen on Mr. Meadowes's entrance, and was still standing. The old man looked at him — a gallant figure, erect, athletic, with his fair skin flushing, his handsome head thrown back a little, and his frank blue eyes sparkling. Old Meadowes drew an abrupt sigh. "I did n't say you got drunk," he replied; "I said you was a drinkin' man, a moderate drinker, if you like that expression better " —

" *Very* moderate."

" I don't take no stock in moderate drinkers ; if they 're too cold-blooded to go to perdition themselves, they lead other people there, and I ain't sure but that 's worse. You are a Democrat and an aristocrat. Ramsay says you ain't a professor of religion — jest a sort of 'piscopal. We ain't got an opinion in common."

" I beg your pardon, we have *one,* your daughter " —

" That ain't the same thing, even. You think you 're in love with her now, but when you find her principles interferin' with your amusements, and your fine friends are laughing at you behind your back, you 'll git angry with her. I would have more hopes of ye if you 'd stood up fair and square for the bad things you believe in ; there 'd be some chance of convertin' you to righteousness ; but you 're like the Lacedamonians the 'postle talks of. Ye shew what was in ye at the dinner-table. Ye did n't want no disputin' ; oh, no, you was willin' to make any concessions, till ye 'd got Rachel 'way ; then I guess you 'd sing another song. But I tell you, Captain Barris," — he drew himself up to his full height, his countenance grew rigid, and he made a single downward stroke with his forefinger, —

"I tell you, I 'd ruther see my innocent child dead, right here, than married to a cold-hearted, unprincipled, sneerin' aristocrat that will break her heart, or else ruin her principles."

"You can hardly expect me to take this as final," said Archy, coldly.

"Oh! ye kin see Rachel, if ye wanter," the old man answered. All at once he looked desperately tired and spoke wearily, quite without anger. "It will be an additional pain to her; but you 've both got it to go through, and ye kin talk it over together. I 'll call her. Good-by, Captain Barris. I expect ye won't care for it, but I 'm sorry for you." He extended his hand. Archy felt the same odd movement of friendliness for the stanch old soul that he had felt before, struggling up to the surface of his sensations through all the anger and sting of the moment.

"No, Mr. Meadowes," said he, "I can't shake hands, for I mean to do my best to persuade your daughter to marry me."

"Try," said the old man, stonily, walking off.

Then Rachel came. She looked white and miserable, and had a package in her hands. Archy would not look at her face; he caught her in his arms, whispering, "You won't be so cruel, my love; it 's nonsense my giving you up — I can't!"

"You *must*," said Rachel, trembling, but trying to release herself; "please let me go, Captain Barris."

The young man stepped back rather an exaggerated distance. He looked at her steadily.
"You don't mean that you will throw me over
like *this*," said he.

Rachel made a great effort and controlled her
voice. It was just the soft, caressing, plaintive
voice that one would expect of her; but now it
was on that level of intonation that comes when
the will has to hold every word steady, lest it
turn into a sob. "My father," said she, — "it's
all true what my father says; we are altogether
different. The people you go with laugh at the
things I have been taught were the most important. They call earnest Christian people
'prigs;' and your mother was so surprised when
I told her I belonged to the W. C. T. U., and
said, 'Oh, my dear, don't; that sort of thing
stamps one!' She made me feel as though I
had confessed to having been in jail. Captain
Barris, your mother is ashamed of me. And
you would be if you married me. You *are*
ashamed of my folks" — She choked with the
remembrance of the torture of the dinner-table.

Archy looked at her in a confusion of anger,
pity, and despair. "But, Rachel," he cried, ve-
hemently, " you knew all about this before, when

you promised to marry me. What does all this r— stuff matter when we love each other? Come, my darling, when you know us better you will find we have our principles, too, though we may seem to make light of them."

"They are different; *everything* is different. I was afraid always, but I— You had n't seen my father, then; I told you if he consented. But he would be wretched"—

"You would rather make *me* wretched than him?"

Rachel was standing; she sat down before she answered faintly, "Yes."

"Then," said he, "when you told me that last evening on the island that you"—

"Please don't," she whispered; and she said aloud, "Jared!"

Archy did not know that she felt herself fainting, and her cry to her brother, passing by the door, was only because of this. He thought that she wanted to cut the interview short. He was stung to the quick.

He caught up his hat and bowed. "In that case," said he, "I will not prolong an interview that seems to distress you. I wish you every good fortune, Miss Meadowes."

Not daring to raise her eyes, she dizzily lifted the package in her lap. But he had turned his back. The poor girl had put a few tear-stained words between the lids of her Bible, and placed it with his notes and the trifling gifts that she had allowed him to give her; the little bundle slipped from her limp fingers, and, just as Archy's footsteps pounded along the walk, Rachel's head sank on her brother's arm in the first swoon of her life.

Archy went striding down the street. Well, to this day he has a little tightening of the throat recalling the next few hours. He was in a fever of wrath and anguish: furious with Rachel, who could give him up so tamely, raving at himself for flinging up his chance in a fit of temper. Then he essayed a cynical gayety, and felt his eyes smarting with tears because he had remembered some trumpery incident of the past weeks and the cadences of Rachel's laugh. Ah! have n't we most of us just such moments to remember, with their sickening oscillations of love and anger and despair! How long Archy walked he could not tell, but when he resumed a saner mood enough to look about him, he was among the low hills, covered with wheat and oats, outside the town; and night was falling. Clever alienists have their patients walked to exhaustion sometimes, and perhaps lovers, who are in a measure insane people, may be helped the same way. At any rate, by this time Archy's sweet temper had acquitted Rachel. He even had a glimmer of the truth, and he began to hope again.

He turned himself about, resolved to walk past the Meadowes' house. He would not call, but if by accident —

As he passed through the college campus he heard a girl's laugh.

"See how funny the sky looks!" she said to the young man beside her. "Look — you are not looking at all!"

"I have something better to look at," said he.

Archy brushed past them impatiently. Yet it was a strange sky. Although the sun had set, the western sky, up to the zenith, burned with a lurid radiance. Funnel-shaped clouds, inky-black, dipped into this unearthly brilliancy. While Archy looked, he became aware of the utter stillness of the air. Not a bird's chirp, not the hum of an insect. He had a peculiarly ghastly sensation, as of one that feels for a pulse and there is no throb. "What a cursed night!" he muttered. It was the night of the 17th of June, 1882.

He went on. He passed the Meadowes' house.

Then he turned, saying to himself that he would go to his hotel and write to Rachel; he even remembered that he had missed his supper, — when he saw Rachel come out of the house. It was too dark to see her face, but he knew her figure and a certain blue shawl that she used to wear. Afire now with hope and impatience, he pursued her. Suddenly that dear form grew dim. The strange light was fading, the black funnels dipped lower, lower into the glow, and the dark tree-leaves began to rustle. Directly, the air vibrated with a horrible grinding noise, compared, afterward, to many sounds, like them all, yet most appallingly different from all. And then — it came! Earth and air were rent into chaos. The tall trees swayed, snapped, fell. Houses were swept from their moorings, and whirled shivering and crashing away. They were chopped into splinters. They were scattered like a handful of dust. There was no more space; the air itself was a tumult of darting shapes, a horror of woful sounds. Archy was within arm's length of Rachel. He caught her waist; he flung her, or they were thrown together, against the roots of a great elm. " Cling ! " he shouted ; " lie flat, and hold on for your life ! "

Her head and shoulders being in a hollow of the roots were partially protected, and he could further shield them with his own body. He felt the wind of death swaying their limbs; he was struck heavy blows, he was flogged, battered, stung ; his tense muscles were ready to snap with the strain, but he clung with the immense energy of despair. The cyclone shot a hundred objects over his head — rafters, branches, the marble top of a table, a beast with hoofs and horns, the pillows of a bed — there was no counting them. A house to his right was smashed like an egg-shell; a row of houses to his left fell in amid frightful screams. Balls of fire were skimming the ground. A girl's face, the face he had seen a moment since, flashed by all white and crooked, and vanished. Not a rod away a man ran toward them, screaming. The wind took him, and he was gone. Somewhere among the trees a piteous little voice cried, "Mamma, come! mamma, come!" Back of him were some people in sore plight, who groaned unceasingly, and a woman shrieked, "Oh! my baby." The storm went roaring over them, houses, barns, trees, hurled on either side of its track. It struck the college, leveled the brick building like a house of cards, peeled roof and upper story off the stone building, and flung a shower of blinds, glass, shingles, and bricks out from the professors' houses.

But surely now the worst was over; they could lie still on the ground, and the voices about them were plainer.

"It's over, thank God!" cried a man's voice.

"Well, it's finished me, anyhow," another answered; "my legs are both broke, and my back, too, I guess. Anybody got any legs to get up and look after that woman's baby?"

The cyclone had gone; but the wind in its wake was blowing furiously, and the rain fell as rain never had fallen in Grinnell before; in fact, a water-spout had burst. One could scarcely stand for the wind or breathe for the rain. And the darkness was horrible.

Archy managed to get on his feet and to raise Rachel. She held on to his arm, sobbing, "Oh, my land! Oh, who is it? What has become of them? Oh, Captain Barris, what has happened?"

It was not Rachel's voice.

At that moment, the heavens blazed from horizon to horizon, while a clap of thunder drowned the multitudinous din of human agony. Who that saw it can forget that woful battle-field, struck into sight, then swallowed up in blackness — wreck and carnage such as cannot be pictured, and white faces glaring out of their death-traps. Yet Archy could only see one object, Miss Baker's terrified face. "For God's sake, where's Rachel?" he groaned.

"In the house, and he — he — Oh, look! Oh, look!"

Through the sheet of rain, as the lightning flashed again, they both looked. The house was gone.

Miss Baker showed herself the stronger of the two now; it was she who suggested that they might have reached the cellar.

"Let us go," said Archy; "but I can't leave that baby up in the tree. Wait a moment!"

The little captive luckily was so wedged in the branches (held fast by his frock, which was torn in two and rolled round a limb, as if the cyclone had deliberately tied him) that he was merely bruised a little, and easily released by the simple expedient (suggested by Miss Baker) of cutting off the buttons and pulling him out of the dress. Archy stumbled across to the cellar, and at the first sound of the child's voice, a woman caught him, and wept over him. She said that they were all out of the cellar. Only one was badly hurt, and he was calling to them to leave him and go to others who could be helped.

"I wish we could stay," said Miss Baker; "but we must go on, Mrs. Dane. Our house is gone. And Rachel and Mr. Meadowes " —

"Oh, God help you!" said the woman; "go, do go!"

Though they used all possible speed, they had to go slowly, the ground being full of great holes where trees had been uprooted, or fence-posts torn out, and encumbered, moreover, with the trunks of trees, and rafters, and piles of brick, and splintered furniture of every kind and shape. Once Archy stumbled over a dead horse, very comfortably disposed on a feather-bed. His next stumble banged his knees against a kitchen stove.

A second later, a lantern was flashed in their eyes, and a wild-faced man shouted, "Is Thomas Reynolds's house down?"

They could not tell him, and he ran by, with his wild face behind his lantern. Somehow, this increased their anxiety. Indeed, there was something very ghastly and awful about the way they would be suddenly close to a fellow-creature in dire misery, and, in the space of a thought, he would be gone, and the rain and the blackness about them again. During all this while, also, there was no diminution of the uproar of shrieks, yells, groans; rather its volume was swelled by new voices, because helpers were seeking for the wounded and the dead, and shouted their presence. Lanterns now twinkled in every direction. The men of Grinnell were very generally in the business streets when the cyclone came, and this part of the town had escaped. They heard the storm, and saw it break. As soon as they could stand in the gale, they were out with lanterns. A second and a third man passed Archy. The fourth man wrested Miss Baker from his arm, crying, "God be praised!   Here, hold these," he said, thrusting an axe and lantern at Archy.   The action, it appeared, was to free his arms, that he might embrace Miss Baker, which he did most tenderly.   Of course, it was old Jared Meadowes.

"Rachel?" gasped Archy.

"Rachel's all right, safe and sound, thank God," Meadowes replied; "we got into the cellar.   But you, Lida"—

"I should have been killed but for Captain Barris," said she, solemnly; "I never could have held on but for him."

The old man wrung Archy's wrist; he could not wring his hand, since the right held the lantern, and the left the axe.

"She's to be my wife," said he, hoarsely. "I thought I'd lost her."

He made no other attempt at thanks, seeming to think that sentence explained everything. "But my boys, Lida," he continued; "they're both up to the college.   I must go to them. Kin *you* take her home?"

"Nobody need take me home," said Miss Baker, who had acted with unexpected spirit and coolness all along.   "I know every step of the way, and I ain't a mite hurt.   You both go along; you are needed here, and I don't need you.   You only hinder me; I cayn't hold up my dress or nothing, getting over the logs, with you 'round!"

She would not even take the lantern, protesting that they would need it in their work, which was so much the case that they did not insist; and so they parted. The two men turned back to the college. They had not gone very far before Meadowes began to swing his lantern, yelling, " Hello, Ossie ! This way ! "

A young fellow, bounding recklessly over the logs, stopped with a cry of joy; plainly Ossie. He explained hurriedly that there were five students under the ruins of the brick building, and at least three buried under the roof of Central College. He himself had leaped out of a window as he felt the building lurch. He was bruised and cut, but he had come down all right by the bell. Jared's leg was hurt. Ossie had gotten him out somehow, and he was picking bricks off the other boys; he said that he could do that since his arms were sound : Ossie must get help and find out about the family. " Run on, my boy," said the father. He looked in an appealing way at Archy. " I guess his eye ain't out, don't you ? It 's only the eyelid got tore, ain't it ? I would n't stop him to ask."

" It was only the eyelid. I could see plainly."

The old man drew a deep sigh of relief. " Come on," said he, " you 've got mighty good eyes."

Then ensued a night, the most terrible, the

most pitiful, and the most noble in Grinnell's history. Well had it been named a colony of Puritans; for that night, amid desolation and horror, these plain people rose to the stature of heroes. Fortitude, serenity in danger, courage, good sense, magnanimous civic devotion, all the rugged virtues of the Puritan were there, and with them an open-handed generosity and a jocose philosophy born of the prairie air.

Archy and old Meadowes worked side by side the night through. They worked amid scenes so awful and so piteous that all the disguises in which we Anglo-Saxons like to muffle up our hearts were torn away.

Archy was prepared to find the old John Brown man a cool, long-headed fellow, brave and patient, in fine, a good comrade; but he did not expect to see him as gentle as a woman with the wounded, and he opened his eyes over the sum that the old man put down on the first subscription paper. "It 's a thank-offering to the Lord," said he, solemnly, "for his mercies to me this night."

The two men had worked in the greatest harmony. Indeed, if anything could have amused Archy during those dreadful hours, he would have been amused to observe how Meadowes presently came to rely on his quick eyes and strong muscles. Several times the old man jerked a gruff word of approval at the younger one. Finally, he tapped him on the shoulder, saying, " Had 'bout 'nuff of this, ain't ye? I 've just got word from Rachel that our barn 's all safe, and she an' Lida have got an oil-stove up, and some hot biscuits and coffee and cold ham ready. It 's broad daylight, an' I guess we better quit for a while. Jared 's there; I 'd kinder like to see how his leg 's comin' on. An' Lida 's waitin' to thank you." His tone changed to one of grave and deep feeling. " I ain't rightly thanked ye for that yet, myself," said he.

Now, several times during the last hours it had occurred to Archy that he was sailing into the old man's favor under false colors. There is a well-defined difference between risking your life for another man's sweetheart and for your own.

It was a temptation; he could see Rachel, and the barn, and the steam of the coffee, and the turn of her white throat as she would look up, and her brown eyes shining. Then he said, sulkily, " That 's nothing; I — I ought to tell you I mistook Miss Baker for Rachel."

Meadowes's lips twitched with a grin of humorous appreciation. Though a Puritan, he was a Westerner.

" I 'll bet a cooky you 've been on pins and

needles," said he, "thinking whether you had ought to tell me, or could git off without." His face softened. "Lida does feature Rachel, an' they 've got the same way of walkin'. 'T was that first turned my mind on her." He hesitated. "I guess you 'd have done 'bout the same if you had known."

"Of course," said Archy, indignantly.

"Then I don't see but what the obligation 's just where it was. I 'm glad ye spoke, though; glad ye would n't take gratitude ye thought did n't b'long to ye. My main objection to *you,* Barris, was your bein' so unprincipled; but I guess you 've got a conscience, though it 's considerable darkened. You 've shown yourself a man to-night. I mistrusted you had n't much of a heart either; but when I saw you cryin' over that poor little blinded baby tryin' to make its dead mother hear, an' wipin' your eyes on the sly with your fists, not knowin' you was leaving a black mark every time — oh, ye need n't go rubbin' your face! Bless you, man, you 're mud and soot all over, and your coat 's bu'st down the back. Your own mother would n't know you! But I guess Rachel will. Come along, come along. You and she will just have to settle your concerns yourselves."

It does not need telling that this settlement was satisfactory. Only it was embarrassing that the old man would not let him go to the hotel, or give him time for the rudest toilet.

But Rachel threw her white arms about that dreadful coat with a sob of happiness.

" And you won't send me away again? " he whispered. " We are to settle it ourselves, your father says. He and I are great chums. Though I must admit," he added, " it took a cyclone to make us so."

"WHAT should we do without you, Jerry?" said Phillipson, the prosecuting attorney; "the only murder case on the docket for years, and you have n't been running a week."

Jerry only smiles a wrinkled kind of smile, pushing his hands deeper into his pockets. Then he and the two men with him watch Phillipson and his companion as they enter the court-house. The companion is a Northerner, a director in the railway which may run through the town.

Neither poverty nor a grudging spirit is responsible that the L—— County court-house is Barker's old all-sorts store. Some years ago lightning destroyed the old court-house, which had a portico and a wide hall and a white cupola, and was the pride of the country-side. Now a brick court-house is rising in its place, an ambitious estray from some Northern architect's brain, with Tudor windows and Gothic gables; and in the interval, Justice balances her scales in Barker's store.

From the doorway one has a good view of the
town. It is an ancient town for Arkansas: in
keelboat times it was bustling and prosperous;
but the railroads passed by on the other side,
and it fell into a gentle decay. Those old-fashioned Southern houses, with their modest pomp
of column, architrave, and gallery, and those
dingy "all-sort stores," the gambrel roofs of
which project at each end to shield loiterers
from the Arkansas sun, are a kind of high-water
mark of the vanished prosperity. But a change
has come; there is talk of a railway; hence the
few smart modern cottages elbowing their gay
sides through the pines. Something alien and
picturesque mingles everywhere with the Southwestern roughness. Perhaps it is because the
narrow streets wind so crookedly up round the
hill, or because a rope ferry spans the river
below, or because the near hills are checkered
with vineyards and wheat-fields, and the far hills
have a dark haze of pine, and across the swift
green water an old turnpike draws a straight
line down a shining avenue of birches, until,
swerving suddenly, it is lost in the forest. Over
the river are the cotton plantations, the rich
black loam where a ploughshare will never be
dulled by a stone; the vast, dim woods of oak
and gum; the canebrake and the cypress swamp.
Here the boulders grind through the soil, as

plentiful as oaths in a river captain's talk, and each farmer tills his own tiny farm. The railroad villages of the bottom have newspaper offices and meat markets, but the old hill country county-seat reads its Arkansas "Gazette" once a week, and when a farmer "kills" he hawks his meat from house to house. None the less, however, does the octopus of civilization fling out tentacles into the wilderness: witness the flaming circus-bills, plastered over Jerry Milligan's saloon; witness indeed the saloon itself, which stands, appropriately, next door to the court-house.

"Looks smart, don't he?" remarked one of the men. "Say, he allus wears them lawyer clothes." He spoke, after an admiring glance at the snugly fitting seams of Phillipson's coat and the glossy white rims showing below his black sleeves. "Pore Dock!" he added, spitting gloomily at the short-skirted lady on the white horse. "He fell on downright hard luck in his lawyer. Hops round like a chicken with his head cut off every time Phillipson tackles him. Don't guess Dock got much show."

"Aw, I dunno," said the second man, more cheerfully; "the jury had orter consider how rilin' it's tuh have a feller skin ye out er fifty dollars — all the money ye got."

"He 'lowed tuh buy a mewl with hit. They

all was fixin' tuh go tuh the cirkiss, an' he come
yere fust. Feller got everye cent at three cyard
monty. Yes, sir. I kin see jes' how Dock
looked. He sot right thar, an' the feller was
a-sa'nterin' down the street easy 's you please.
Dock was n't r'arin' on him 't all. All the word
he sayd was, ' Lord, whut 'll I say tuh Sis?' "

" That 's his wife, hay? "

" In co'se. Minute I heerd tell 'bout it I
knowed how he be'n done, ca'se I lost three
dollars an' fifty cents onct that away. Feller
changed the cyards an' plum left out the one
I bet on ; but Dock 's a turrible simple kind er
feller, an' he never mistrusted tell I tole him."

" An' more 's the pity ye ondesaved him,"
muttered Jerry.

" How c'u'd I know he 'd gether you' new
gun offen the byar an' light out that away? "
the other demanded indignantly.

" An' we all ayfter 'im, hollerin' with all the
power," said the second witness, with a chuckle.
" Did n't he burn the wind, though! Ketched
up tuh the feller 'fore we got tuh the cote-
house. 'Member how he sayd suthin' an' the
feller slid his hand back tuh his pocket? Dock
war tew briefly fur him, fired 'fore ye c'u'd bat
you' eye. Feller keeled over dead 's a hammer.
Never seen a purtier shoot."

" Yes, sir, it was so," agreed Jerry; " an' by

that same token 't is a shame to be sindin' him to prison fur a thrifle like that."

"Say Mis' Muckwrath goes tuh the trial ever' mornin' in the world," Dock's first mourner observed. "That's her now in the blue sun-bonnet, totin' the baby, an' the tew boys hangin' on ahind."

The woman passed the men, unconscious of the observation. Her short cotton skirts, limp with dew from the grass and the dog-fennel through which she had walked, were flapping against her bare ankles and coarse shoes. The fat baby hung over her shoulder, and beat her thin back with a muddy stick. Evidently the stick was coveted by the younger boy, for he made futile jumps after it while he ran, until greed overreached itself and landed him in a mud - puddle, whence he was dragged by his mother with a shake. The action disclosed her face — a narrow, pale, freckled face, with anxious brown eyes.

"Thar, Luke, quit you' meanness," she cried fretfully. "Take Bud's han' an' walk quiet, or they all will put ye in jail."

"I don't keer," the child answered; "paw's thar!"

"O Lordy!" cried the poor woman; "but he'll come out; he'll shore come out!"

"Do hush, the pitiful critter!" muttered the nearest of the witnesses.

There were other observers of the scene near enough for sight, if not for hearing. First walked the judge, a tall man, carelessly dressed, holding a rose in his mouth. Behind him, the sheriff was conducting the jury from the little hotel to the court-house. They paced along, two by two, Captain Baz Lemew's head towering above the soft hats. It was a fine, massive head, covered with curly black hair, that shone like a coal against his white hat-brim. All the Lemews were property - holders, men of substance and dignity, Captain Baz in particular owning one of the best plantations on the river. There was a tradition of a wild youth passed away from home; but years of kind neighborliness, and good citizenship, and generous service in the church had so blurred the old rumors that they retained only enough of their erratic outlines to excuse a familiar affection; Captain Baz he was, not Captain Sebastian Lemew.

Arm in arm with Captain Baz, the foreman, came Dr. Redden, slim, agile, with keen eyes, and a yellow beard that curled upward at the ends. He had a trick of clutching his beard, and then flinging his palm outward for a gesture. His loose coat fluttered as he walked, and he swung a branch of dogwood like a cane. The two men following in order were a farmer from the hills, and the shrewdest horse-trader of the bottom. The former was sighing : —

" Hick'ry buds all out. Mighty purty cotton-plantin' weather. Bright er the moon, tew."

" Tew airly," grunted the horse-trader. " April cotton 's apt to git the sore shin."

" Waal, onyhow, I wan't out," declared the farmer, kicking his heavy heels among the bluets that besprinkled the wayside.

" No, sir," the doctor was saying in a hortatory tone ; " no, sir, on principle I avoid looking at the prisoner's wife. Really, it 's no palliation of his offense that he has got a wretched woman mixed up with his lot ; yet that 's the way people argue."

" There she is," said Captain Baz ; " the woman in front. I know her ; Muckwrath is one of my renters." [1]

The doctor's eyelids dropped, and a flash like the flash of a knife-blade stole out of the half-shut eyes. Every other juror's position he could gauge to a nicety ; but the workings of Captain Baz's mind were, so to speak, under water, and left no trail.

Now, Dr. Redden desired a conviction ardently. His motives were the cleanest in the world. Of the new South himself, he believed in immigration, enterprise, and their natural promoters, law and order. His zeal was fanned by a pigmy breeze of opposition from one or two

[1] Tenants.

in the jury. So was his vanity. Dr. Redden plumed himself on his deft handling of prejudices; here was a chance for tact. But Captain Baz — where did he stand? What was he studying at this minute, for instance? He had turned round on the court-house steps — for the little procession had reached the door — and was gazing absently at river and fields. The landscape had the lovely freshness of morning and spring. Drops of rain glittered in the water-oak leaves, the roses in the gardens wore a richer pink for last night's shower; even the furrow-slices and the blunted edges of the cotton-hills were dyed a deeper tone of brown.

" I love this country," said Captain Baz; but it appeared more to himself than to the doctor. " I was born and raised here. I should hate terribly " — Then he stopped.

" Come on, gentlemen," called the sheriff, jocosely. " Mr. Phillipson won't want to speak without you."

Entering the court-room on a warm morning — such a morning as that which saw the conclusion of the case of the State of Arkansas *vs.* Muckwrath — the first impression is of cool dampness. The room is long and scantily lighted, unplastered and unpainted. The authorities have removed, as unseemly, the rosy damsels who lent their charming presence to praises of starch and baking-powder, but the public is still informed by three-foot letters on the joists that " Oliver Chilled Ploughs are the Best ! " and still can read a small placard spared by the hand of reform, — perhaps for its wholesome moral, — affirming that if you pay as you go, then you won't owe.   Decorations of a more legal cast are not lacking ; from estray notices, advertisements of sheriff's sales and delinquent tax lists, to embossments of tobacco quids and gum.   The lawyers sit around a rude pine table, the judge presides in a pine armchair, and there are chairs without arms for the officers of the court ; the rest of the world must content itself with benches.   There is a fiction of inclosing the prisoner according to the venerable usage, an uncertain structure of fence palings guarding his chair, and giving him infinite trouble if the habit of a lifetime assert itself and his heels swing up to the top.

This morning the room was crowded, for it was known that Phillipson was to conclude his argument, and he had a reputation as an orator, to which, rather than to the intrinsic attraction of the case, was due a sprinkling of the gentry of the region among the shirt-sleeves and sun-bonnets.   Immediately after the court was opened Phillipson rose.   He had a fascinating voice — sonorous, musical, flexible.   Convinced of the prisoner's guilt, he spoke with magnetic fervor. The jury were palpably impressed, while the prisoner's pale wife grew paler, and the prisoner nervously chewed gum. He was a tall man and well built, although this was concealed by his ungainly posture, crouched over the fence-railing, his feet squeezed between the palings, his elbows on his knees. His long, curling auburn hair fell over his collar. His eyes were bright violet in tint and of a very gentle expression. His face was of a type common in Arkansas among the renters, where the loosely hung mouth will often seem to contradict fine brows, straight noses, and shapely heads. One could see that he was wearing his poor best in clothes, namely, a new ill-fitting brown coat, blue trousers, rubber boots, and a white shirt with a brass collar-button but no necktie.

When the lawyer pictured in glowing metaphors and more glowing statistics the incomparable natural gifts of Arkansas, her genial climate, her wonderful forests, her rich mines and richer soil, her mountains and rivers and healing springs, the prisoner listened with an air of relief and interest. When Phillipson, on tiptoe, swung his fist and shouted that the Black River country was "the best poor man's country in the world," he nodded cordially "That's so!" to the deputy at his side, adding, "Looks like he ar'

lettin' up on me an' talkin' 'bout the craps."
But in a second his expansive manner collapsed;
his jaw fell, and he leaned over the palings, his
lean fingers gripping them hard. Phillipson was
demanding why a State so beautiful, so fertile,
so attractive to every class of emigrants, is neglected.

"Why is it, gentlemen?" cried the lawyer,
waving his white hands at the jury. "I will
tell you. It is because the old taint of blood
and crime clings to our garments still. Years
ago Arkansas in very truth was a 'dark and
bloody ground.' Murder stalked unpunished
through our smiling cotton-fields and noble forests. All that is past. To-day every one of
you knows, gentlemen, that there is not in all
this broad land a more peaceful, law-abiding section than ours, or a section with better enforced
laws. But people in other States are only just
beginning to realize this. Strangers hesitate to
bring their families and settle among us. They
wait even now, even here, to come among us,
willing and able to pour their thousands into
our industries, or to link us with iron bands to
the great heart of commerce and civilization
which throbs outside." There was a general
turning of heads at the Northerner. "They wait.
What for? To learn that life and property will
be respected by you! Gentlemen of the jury,

the honor of the State of Arkansas rests in your hands. The dead man was a stranger. He was not a good man. But the law extends the august ægis of her protection even as the rain is shed over the just and the unjust. You are not to consider his character, but only the question, Has he been wronged? You cannot afford, gentlemen — *we* cannot afford — to let the word go forth to the world that Arkansas does not punish murder." He sat down amid a grateful rustle of applause and many admiring smiles from the ladies in the crowd.

The judge, who had pulled a heap of papers towards him, took the rose out of his mouth and began to read the charge. Captain Baz was listening with frowning attention; the other jurors had been cheered by a bag of peanuts handed up by the amiable deputy in charge. The prisoner was leaning back with folded arms and an expression of eager interest. The judge stated the charge against the prisoner and gave the usual exposition of the law and the usual definitions. He spoke in a slow, gentle voice, and the Northerner's admiration was excited by his luminous and infinitely patient explanations. Indeed, he was so clear that the prisoner himself could follow him, after a grotesque and dazed fashion, tripping now and then over the legal verbiage, but recovering himself at every familiar phrase. He listened to the definition of murder in the first degree with indignant agitation. "All murder which shall be perpetrated by means of poison or by lying in wait" — So far had the judge gone before Muckwrath exclaimed : —

" Why, Judge, I never seen the man afore, an' iz fur layin' in wait an' fixin' tuh pizen, I w'u'd n't do sicher meanness " —

" Shet up !" whispered the deputy. " He 's readin' what you did n't done."

Muckwrath sank back, relieved, to tap his palings with a virtuous finger at every adjective of the " willful, deliberate, malicious, and premeditated killing " described in the statute, and every felony enumerated, " in the perpetration of, or in the attempt to perpetrate " which, " the killing shall be committed." But his countenance darkened at the explanation of murder in the second degree and grew more anxious at the definition of manslaughter, " the unlawful killing of a human being without malice, express or implied, and without deliberation." But he glanced across to where his wife sat with renewed cheerfulness as the judge passed on to justifiable homicide, since here it was that his counsel had made his boldest stand on the right of the defendant to retake his property by force. Muckwrath actually smiled as the judge read : —

" Section 1279 defines justifiable homicide as follows: ' Justifiable homicide is the killing of a human being in necessary self-defense, or in the defense of habitation, person, or property against one who manifestly intends or endeavors by violence or surprise to commit a known felony.'"

The smile, however, faded quickly at the judge's comment: " But, gentlemen of the jury, where it is sought to justify the killing under this statute, the killing must be to prevent threatened injury to property or the taking thereof by violence or surprise, and no more force must be used than is reasonably necessary. The statute, has no application to cases of killing when the deceased has obtained peaceful possession of the property of the slayer by fraud or trickery, without force or surprise " —

" My word ! " cried the prisoner, leaping excitedly to his feet, " 't was surprise. I hain't had nare sich surprise in my life like I got when I seen them kyards. They be'n plumb changed up " —

The deputy pushed him back into his seat, amid a sympathetic laugh from the audience. " And is slain while in possession of the property so obtained," concluded the judge, who then passed on to the duty incumbent on the State of proving the defendant guilty beyond a reasonable doubt, with the explanation of a reasonable doubt. To all this the jury listened with an air of patient bewilderment, excepting only Dr. Redden, an image of the appreciative listener, and an old man in an extraordinarily frayed and rusty black coat, who was sunk into unobtrusive slumber behind a palm-leaf fan. He awakened in time for the peroration, erecting his head and inflating his chest in a dignified manner, as one who had been following the argument closely all along, let appearances be what they might.

"Gentlemen of the jury," said the mild, deliberate voice, "if you find from the evidence, beyond a reasonable doubt, that the defendant and the deceased were engaged in a game of cards in Jeremiah T. Milligan's saloon in said L—— County, and State of Arkansas, and that the deceased had, in a game of cards, by cheating or otherwise, won money of the defendant, and had left said saloon ; and that the defendant was informed as soon as the deceased left that he had been cheated " —

" Yes, sir, so I was," said the prisoner. His attorney, amid various winks and smiles from the lawyers, bent a very red face close to his ear. The prisoner pursed his lips for an inaudible whistle, then nodded.

" And thereupon," the judge continued, "in a fit of passion, he snatched up a revolver from the bar, with the intention of killing or doing great bodily injury to the deceased, and without time for reflection pursued and shot the deceased on sight, you will then, and in that case, find him guilty of murder in the second degree. The fact, if you shall find it to be a fact, that the deceased attempted to draw a revolver, would not excuse the killing, or turn the offense from murder in the second degree to manslaughter. But if you shall find from the evidence that the deceased obtained the defendant's money as before stated, and that the defendant, upon being informed that he had been cheated, was seized with a sudden passion and snatched the revolver and pursued the deceased without any intention of killing the deceased, but with the intention of using threats to make the deceased return the said money, intending also to use the revolver in case he might thereby become involved in a fight with the deceased and need the same to protect himself " (here the prisoner made an expressive pantomime of assent to the deputy) ; " and if you also find that while thus excited, and while acting pursuant to this intention, he overtook the deceased and the deceased attempted to draw a revolver to shoot the defendant, and thereupon the defendant, in the excitement and in fear of his life " (" Jesso," cried Muckwrath, unable to keep still), " shot and killed the deceased, then, and in that event, you will find the defendant guilty of manslaughter" ("O Lordy!" gasped the prisoner), "and fix the penalty accordingly. The defendant's counsel has asked for the following instruction, which is given, with some modifications: If you find from the evidence that the deceased was a man of violent disposition and dangerous character, prone to shoot quickly and without provocation, and that the defendant was informed of this dangerous disposition on the part of the deceased prior to the killing, and that the deceased swindled the defendant out of fifty dollars at three-card monte in Jeremiah T. Milligan's saloon, on the third day of April, 1888, and that thereupon the defendant, being told that he had been cheated, got up to follow the deceased to demand back his money, without any intention of doing any injury to the deceased, or of making any threats of so doing, and that defendant, having in mind the dangerous disposition of the deceased, picked up and took with him a revolver which was lying on the bar, intending to use the same in case of necessary self-defense" (a grin at what to such an audience seemed broad irony, spread from face to face); "and if you further find that when the defendant overtook the deceased the deceased attempted to draw a revolver, and thereby the defendant was placed in danger of his life or limb, and, while acting under the belief that it was necessary to shoot to save himself, did so shoot and killed the deceased — *then* the homicide was justifiable, and you will find the defendant not guilty."

But at this point the prisoner's baby lifted up her voice in a dismal clamor. Vainly the mother tried to hush the child; the prisoner called out, "Gimme the little trick, Sis; she jes wants to get tuh me;" the sheriff commanded "Silence in the court!" and the audience tittered; all of which rather drowned the judge's voice, charging the jury to lay aside all fear, prejudice, or favor, and render a verdict consistent with the law and the evidence and in harmony with their oath.

The jury themselves were generally absorbed in Mrs. Muckwrath's tussle with her baby and the infant's final consolation by a stick of candy, handed over the heads of the audience from some unknown donor. By the time the stir had subsided, the friendly deputy was whispering: —

"You all got to go now."

The Northerner watched them as they were conducted through the side-door to their room, or, to be accurate, their shed. Up to this moment the grotesque surroundings and the prisoner's antics had made him forget that this rough-handed justice was weighing a fellow-creature's life. Now he remembered.

Phillipson was speaking : " Yes, sir, the charge *was* favorable. Splendid charge. Clear, straight to the point."

" You 'll get a verdict if the jury have n't got on to the Coal Hill horror," said the gray-haired lawyer. " Redden is for you, and he 's a stirring fellow."

The Northerner looked from the man behind the palings to the woman, whose eyes were fixed on him while she hugged her baby tighter. Then he asked, " What kind of convict-camps do you have in this State ? "

" All kinds," replied Phillipson, testily.

The jury had taken various easy attitudes about their table, but they all looked serious.

Captain Baz's mild, bright, dark eyes went from one face to another in a glance that was keen without ceasing to be gentle. He settled his large frame back in his chair and softly fanned himself; quite a typical figure of a planter sitting there, with his dainty linen, and cool pongee coat, and the old-fashioned diamond-pin in his blue neck-scarf. It was an attractive face also which rested on his hand — such a face as a lonely woman would turn to confidingly, though she saw it for the first time ; a kind, frank, strong face, handsome in spite of the long scar marking one tanned cheek.

"Gentlemen," said Captain Baz, "perhaps we shall gain time by talking this business over a little before we take a ballot."

Speaking for the others, the doctor assented. For his part, he said, he believed that the prisoner ought to be punished. Why did n't he get the constable to arrest the man? It was this habit of trying to right our own wrongs when the law stood ready to right them for us that had given the country an ill name. Phillipson was right; it discouraged immigration. He had seen Mr. Thornton (the Northerner) in court. They all knew he was fixing to build a canning factory. Was he likely to do that if they convinced him that any of his men could get mad and pop away at him with a gun, sure of getting off? It looked like they might lose their factory, may be their railroad, if they monkeyed with the verdict. Let them remember their oaths and the law; that was all he asked.

The next speaker, who kept an "all-sorts store" at the cross-roads, agreed with the doctor. So did half a dozen others. Their natural sympathy with a defrauded neighbor was offset by the composite motive of self-interest and public spirit to which the doctor had appealed. As the storekeeper expressed it, they all could n't afford to scare off factories and railroads just to pull Dock out of a hole.

The horse-trader was for a verdict of murder in the second degree, on general principles of rigor towards " folks that squealed."

" What in thunder is Dock r'arin' and chargin' 'bout onyhow ? " cried he.   " If he got skinned up, war n't he tryin' tuh skin t' other feller? 'T ain't noways shore, neither, that the cyards war n't throwed fair.   Them fellers kin juggle the cyards roun' so ye cayn't tell Ham from Japhet.   Dad gum me, I los' twenty dollars myself oncet.   But do ye reckon I pulled out my gun and killed the cuss ?   Naw, sir.   I guv 'im five dollars tuh show me how the trick be'n done.   An' he done so.   But, law me, I mout try tell I was wore to a frazzle, I cud n't ketch up with it ! "

" I 'lowed they all allus cheated," said a young rustic whose mouth hung ajar as naturally as a door without a latch.   " Ef Dock ain't be'n cheated that makes a heap er differ.   I don't guess we 'd orter let 'im go.   Hay, Mr. Hogard ? "   He addressed the shabby man in the black coat, who might be called a professional juror, being one of those court-room hangers-on always ready to the sheriff's hand either for jurors or talesmen.   Apparently occupied in spelling out the judge's charge, he merely shook his head.   Really, he was waiting until he could discover the drift of opinion, in

order to join the minority, thereby protracting
the session and enlarging the fees.

His right-hand neighbor, a young farmer from
the bottom, spoke up quickly: " I don't see no
differ if they cheat with their fingers or their
cyards. I observe they git thar jes the same.
Onyhow, Dock, he 'lowed he b'en cheated; an'
t' other feller drawed on 'im " —

" Drawed on him ! " interrupted the horse-
trader, with sardonic emphasis. " By gum, who
would n't draw on a feller runnin' at ye with a
gun ? "

" Waal, I don't keer," said the farmer, doggedly. " I 've knowed Dock risin' er twenty
year, an' I ain't goin' tuh send him tuh be beat
an' pounded in them convict-camps."

" Now ye talk," said the farmer, who wanted
to get home ; " but what fur did he kill the feller ? Why cud n't he of given him the bud [1]
an' taken the money back ? "

" Did get his money back," said another juror,
the blacksmith on Captain Baz's plantation ;
" taken it out of the dead man's pockets, right
thar. Must 'a' had a' anxious notion er gettin'
that money back, shore. Say, did n't no kin er
the feller ever turn up ? "

He was answered by the old juror, who pushed

[1] " To give the bud " or " to give the hickory " is Arkansas
for to thrash.

a loose pile on the table towards him, saying: "Nary. Nothin' foun' on the person er the deceased neether, 'cept this truck — handkerchief, watch-chain 'thout nare watch, revolver, wallet, Hot Springs cyar tickets, two packs er kyards, an' fifty cents."

The jurors, except Captain Baz, fingered the articles with much gravity, and scrutinized them as carefully as if they held some occult evidence of Dock Muckwrath's guilt or innocence.

The old juror brought them back to the question.

"Dock's lawyer," he modestly suggested, "made a right smart outer Dock's right tuh take back his property. Jedge ruther favored him thar, I consider."

"I wisht you all cud fix up suthin' this mornin'," said the young farmer. "I'm right anxious to git to go to Little Rock to-night, an' thar's a long way to ride to the railroad from my place."

"What ye say tuh manslaughter, then, Baldwin," said the old farmer, "an' let him off easy 's we kin?"

"That's two year," said the old juror, always strong on the minor points of law; "we all fix the penalty. Two to seven years."

"Say, the Knights Templar p'rade tuh-night," said the blacksmith.

"Splendid parade, I hear, it's going to be, too," the doctor remarked, with his knife-like side-glance at Baldwin. "Miss Morkin and a lot of our folks are going."

Miss Morkin was the pretty girl whom Baldwin was only too anxious to please. He appealed with a kind of harassed gasp to Captain Baz: "I'll tell you what I cayn't stand. They tell terrible things 'bout the prisons. Say, what's your notion, cap'n?"

The doctor, who had the medical eye for complexion, observed that Captain Baz was certainly very pale. "My opinion, sir," said the captain, slowly, "is that, in the present state of convicts in Arkansas, if you don't find the man not guilty you had better find him guilty enough to be hanged."

"By gum," muttered the blacksmith, "that are a way ter put it!"

The doctor's eyes brightened, a sure sign with him of rising combativeness. "Do you say that because you have been reading the horrors in the newspapers?"

"No, sir," — the reply came very quietly, — "I say it from personal experience."

For once the doctor's wits failed him, but he flinched from his first idea. "You were a — an inspector, a — warden," he said huskily.

"No, sir," said Captain Baz, as quietly as before; "I was a convict."

"Lord A'mighty!" cried young Baldwin, and was instantly red with shame over his indecorum.

The horse-trader, not so sensitive, declared, "Waal, I bet 't war n't from no meanness, onyhow!"

The other jurors exchanged furtive glances, while Dr. Redden took shelter in a handkerchief and elaborately wiped his face.

"P'raps," — this was the shopkeeper's best mercantile voice, — "p'raps, bein' like you interjuced the subjeck, cap'n, you w'u'd tell us some more."

Captain Baz had been watching their confusion, smiling a little bitterly. It seemed to Captain Baz that already they began to wonder over him and look down on him.

"Naturally," said he, "I did n't speak just for the fun of the thing. I had a purpose. I want you to know the kind of punishment you are proposing to give our old neighbor. Well, gentlemen, this was the way of it: I was a wild young man running a cotton-boat, and Owens, my partner, sent me to Little Rock on business. I was young and foot-loose, and I went straight into mischief; got into a gambling-den and a fight before sundown: a man was killed. Of course he was a promising citizen with a terrible sight of kin. I am tolerably sure that I did n't touch the fellow, but I was the only man there too drunk to run away; so they caught me and tried me, and the upshot was I got three years. In point of fact, gentlemen, I have no legal right to sit on this jury, being a convicted felon. However, it was not Sebastian Lemew who put on stripes, but Thomas Jones. I was so ashamed of my being such a blamed fool that I fixed it up with Owens to keep the business from my folks. They sent me, with a dozen other fellows, in a cattle-car to Arkansas River, to make a corduroy-road. There — that is what I am going to tell you. I have been quiet for so long on account of my wife. She hated to have me pointed at as having been to the penitentiary. That 's all right; women think a heap of such things; but I can't keep quiet any longer."

"I kin tell you one thing, cap'n," cried Baldwin, "nobody 'll ever be the wiser for *me!*"

"Nur me," the old juror echoed.

"I say, 't war all a blamed shame!" said the blacksmith.

"You must act your pleasure about that, gentlemen," said Captain Baz; but a little of the color returned to his face. "I was saying they sent me off; I went off with a rough crowd. However, there was one gentleman among them. 'Radcliffe,' he called himself. I never saw him again, nor I don't know his real name; but he did me a good turn with his information. He told me, what I found was true, that the whole convict system is a money-making affair. They are all on the make. The board, commissioners, contractors, lessees, wardens, and guards, — they all just naturally squeeze the convict. He's let and sublet, and every man has to make something out of him each time. What do the lessees care if they work a man to death in the camps? They can get plenty more. It is for their interest to underfeed the men and not clothe them or give them medicines or decent human treatment any way. The real man in charge is the warden, and he has practically unlimited power. All the lessee asks of him is to get work out of the men. They are mostly trifling, shirking fellows, and to make them work he has to punish them; so he gets to crowding the punishment on. Wardens and guards are apt to be a brutal lot — first-class men don't want such a job. But the meanest feature of the whole business is its discrimination. It is a fact, gentlemen, as our prison laws stand now the rich man can do almost anything. Suppose a jury does its duty, and sends a rich criminal to the penitentiary, what then? Why, his friends hire him out, and he lives at his ease. Radcliffe told me of a large number of convicts hired out that way; his uncle was going to hire him to work on his plantation. 'And do you reckon I'll work too hard?' said he. 'No, sir; I'll ride round like a gentleman, and in my own clothes, too, by ——.' He told me about our warden. He seemed to know all about him, and I'm bound to say his information always turned out correct. Captain Moss, our warden, was an Alabama man. He killed two men down there before he came to Arkansas; but he had influential friends, and the matter was hushed up some way. They need dare-devil fellows in a convict-camp, so Moss got the job. Radcliffe said he was rather a quiet fellow when sober, but the devil and any when drunk. Radcliffe advised me to bribe him by giving him my money that came to me to spend. 'He'll take out his commission, don't fear,' says he. 'If you've got money, you're all right. But God help the poor man in a convict-camp!' You may imagine, gentlemen, that such a talk as this did n't cheer me up much. But the reality was worse.

"We got to our place at sundown, and had to walk four miles from the railroad through the swamp. The camp was in a cypress slash. You could cut the miasma with a knife. But what did it matter how unhealthy the place was? You know what the cypress slashes are. Our shed was on a kind of ridge. Higher up from the river there were some houses built — a cook-house, and storehouse, and house for the warden in charge. The shed we had was, I should say, sixteen by twenty feet, and there were thirty-three men packed into it. It was worse built than any of these old cabins which we all think ain't good enough for steady living in, and give up to the cotton-pickers. A few of the meanest, dirtiest mattresses you ever saw were lying on the floor. Not enough of these, even, for half the men. The others had a blanket and slept on the floor. The cracks in that floor — I do assure you they were bigger than my arm! Of course, the shed was simply stood up on four cypress stumps over the mud, and it had settled lop-sided. The roof had no shingles, nothing but scantling; and when it rained it leaked worse than the famous roof of the Arkansas traveler. Puddles of water were standing on the mattresses and the blankets; and with the flicker of the lamps screwed to the wall, and an awful kind of steam rising up from the swamp, and the chains everywhere, — they always chained us at night, you understand, — and the miserable black and white faces all huddled to-gether, oh, it was a hard sight! The men's rags were dropping off them. Not a man among them had a decent pair of shoes. They never

were washed or changed up, and some of them
had been in camp two months. And while I
stood in that hole, half faint, like a flash I seemed
to see my room at home, and the clean, white
curtains, and the big tin tub I had for washing,
and my mother's and the girls' pictures on the
walls, and my father's sword hanging over the
glass, and the honeysuckle outside swinging —
it turned me dizzy. Just then the dogs outside
began to howl. 'Somebody's lit out,' said the
guard. 'Here, get along, 49, I got to go; thar's
you place.' Such a place — a space between
two convicts, and next to it a poor fellow crumpled all in a heap, with his shirt cut into ribbons
and his back the awfulest sight! He lay right
under the lamp. I can see the way his hands
dropped down as if they would drop off his
wrists, and the sharp look of his nose and chin.
Somebody had dipped a hand down through an
extra big crack and plastered him with mud to
ease the smarting. I can assure you all," Captain Baz added, with a very grim and queer
smile, " it helps a heap. The fellow was hardly
more than a boy, and had a right innocent, pitiful kind of face. As soon as the guard was
gone, I asked the man who had put the mud on,
— you could see the mud in his hand, that's
how I knew, — I asked him what was the matter. He was a villainous-looking fellow, looked

like he had some nigger in him.   He was No. 28,
but the boys all called him Chuckey. Chuckey
gave me a scowl, and said, ‘ Got a lickin’.’
Then I saw him shove his own blanket, which
he ’d rolled up, under the poor fellow’s head.
So I helped him, and the poor fellow looked up
and thanked me. Gentlemen, it was sort of
awful to be thanked in that place ; it stirred me
all up.   While I was trying to find out more,
the guard came with my supper.   Radcliffe
had been telling some tall stories about me to
the warden, I reckon.   Well, I was powerful
hungry, for they had skipped our dinner, so I
did n’t look too closely at the salt pork and corn
pone, and was fixing to drink my coffee when I
observed that the poor fellow who had been
licked was staring at me with a terribly ravenous
sort of look.

“ Instinctively, I suspect, I broke the bread
into two pieces, a big piece for me and the
smallest piece for him, — because I was so hungry I was mean, — but, somehow, when I looked
up to pass it, and saw his miserably pinched
face, I gave him the biggest piece instead, and
tore off some of the meat too.

“ Chuckey scowled at me in his way, and said,
‘ He ’s plumb starved ; hain’t had nuthin’ sense
yestiddy mornin’.’   Poor Slowfoot ! ”

“ Was that what they called him ? ” asked
the blacksmith.

“ Yes, sir. He had something the matter with his ankle. The bone was hurt, and it hurt him to walk. Many a time Moss beat him for not ‘ getting about lively enough ’ as he called it.”

“ Probably necrosis,” muttered the doctor.

“ I asked Chuckey if we got enough to eat. He said yes, usually, but mighty poor stuff — bread, meat, and pease. No variety, of course, and the cooking not half-way decent. The man who leased us did n’t care no more for us than for so many pigs. We all were always chilling, but that made no difference ; we had to work just the same. I did n’t fare as badly as some, thanks to Radcliffe’s talking and the money that I got from Owens. The next morning I saw the warden. I ’m not likely to forget how he looked. We were all hustled out at sun-up, and set to work laying the logs in the swamp. The man who walked by me was a strange-looking fellow. I make no doubt he was a bit off in his head ; anyway, we all called him Looney. He was there because he walked into a Little Rock restaurant, got a dinner, and then said he had n’t any money. The proprietor had him arrested, and he was sent to the penitentiary. So he got into our camp. They said that he was so banged about and ill-treated that it had run him distracted. One thing about his looks I remember.   He had a very large head, and kept wagging it about and talking to himself.   The guard who had us that morning was Todd Baxter.   He was a very clever fellow, too, when he could keep away from liquor.   This poor Looney, by and by, lay down on a log and said he would n't work.   Todd was coaxing and threatening when Moss came up, pretty full.   He rode a good horse, and was, I suppose, what you would call a handsome man.   He was fond of dress, and a great ladies' man.   Oh, I can tell you *his* clothes were changed often enough.   He had a palish face, the eyes were always a little red at the rims, the face clean shaved except a mustache, and he had brown curly hair, and always wore some kind of perfumery.   Well, he needed it in that place.   The instant he saw Looney he was off his horse, swearing.   'I ain't going to work,' said Looney; 'I'm sick.'

" 'I know your kind of sick mighty well,' says Moss.   'Git up, or it will be the worse for you.'

" When Looney would n't get up, he and another guard, by the name of Forbes, tied Looney to a gum-tree by strips of pawpaw bark like the niggers make reins out of, you know, and lashed him with ox-whips.   I told Moss, as respectfully as I could, that I believed the man was crazy.   He knocked me down.   Well, gentlemen, some things are too horrible to be described, though they are not too horrible for poor souls to suffer. Moss swore he 'd conquer Looney, if he had to kill him. He did n't conquer him, though you could hear his screeches clear across the slash. But he would n't work. By and by Todd interfered ; they took him home, and Todd put him in his own bed, and he died there. That night " —

The horse-trader struck the table a sounding blow with his fist. " The bloody tyke ! " he cried. " What did they do to him ? "

" Nothing," said Captain Baz.

" Don't you reckon he was ha'nted ? " said the blacksmith.

" Not he," said Captain Baz ; " if he had been that kind of man, the poor fellows he killed in Alabama would have haunted him. Yet it is hard saying what such a man feels ; it is possible one reason for his sprees was a bad conscience. But to all appearance he went on as wicked and careless as ever. He shoved poor Looney into the river and went about with his whip slashing at us just the same. Gentlemen, I can't give you any idea what an incarnate devil he could be. To this day I sometimes wake up yelling and cursing, dreaming that I am back in that hell. To show you the meanness of the man : there was a poor boy there, and his mother sent him a pair of rubber boots and a letter. Todd told me about it; that's how I know. She'd gone picking cotton to earn the money. She knew it was in the bottom-lands, and she sent the boots, begging the warden to let her boy have them. Mind you, too, the poor boy was chilling at the time. Do you reckon Moss gave him the boots? Not a bit of it; he sold them to one of the guards for three dollars. That's the kind of man he was. Yet since his meanness procured me most of my own privileges, I have reason to thank it. Owens sent me money, and he took it; but he made me a trusty,[1] and out of fifty dollars I got a straw hat and a pair of second-hand horse-blankets, and sometimes an extra bite of something which I could share with Slowfoot. He was schemy, too. He let me go to the river and wash. I had pretty good clothes, and he would send me to the settlement on errands. Usually Todd went with me. Then folks would look at me, decently clothed, clean, and all that, and they would say: 'Must be lies 'bout the convicts being so abused. Look at that trusty!' Which was exactly what Moss aimed to have them think. Oh, he was powerful schemy! But I was schemy too. That's how I got out. There

---

[1] The better behaved and more trustworthy convicts are called "trusties," and have certain privileges.

was a new inspector, who lived on the yon side
of the river and had a big plantation. Most of
the inspectors had been so deviled and conjured by the commissioners and by Moss that,
no matter what yarn he told them, they 'd grease
its head and swallow it whole. But this gentleman was sharp. He made some trouble about
Looney, but he could n't get to find out anything. Well, I stole some brown wrapping-paper
and borrowed a pencil from Todd, pretending to
need it to show him a trick at cyards."

"I don't guess ye got time to l'arn it to
we all," said the horse-trader, insinuatingly;
"'t would make the story sorter plainer."

"Oh, the story does n't need it," said Captain
Baz. "The point was, I needed a lead-pencil
to explain, and I just naturally lost the lead-
pencil — dropped it, or a stick, spang into the
mud. Then very cautiously, at odd minutes, I
wrote on that paper to the new inspector to
come and see how we were treated. The next
thing was to get the paper to the inspector.
That came by accident. I was sent to town
with a guard to get some flour. The guard was
in the store and I sat outside holding the horses.
No show of running, for he had his gun. While
I sat there trying to study out a plan to speak
to somebody — anybody — and fairly wild with
thinking, two young ladies came riding up.

By luck — no, by God's mercy — one of them was the inspector's sister. I knew it because I heard the storekeeper call her name when he spoke to her. It was speak to her, some way, or miss my best chance on earth — one! She had a rather ill horse, and he kept prancing about. 'Lady,' said I, though my heart was in my boots, 'your horse has picked up a nail.' And before she could answer I was on the ground projicking round that horse's foot, my back to the guard's back, mind you, all the while. 'There it is. Look here!' said I. Of course it was n't the nail I handed her, but the brown paper rolled into a spike. 'For God's sake, give it to your brother, miss!' I whispered."

"Did she ketch on?" cried the horse-trader, in high excitement, and the other jurors hitched their chairs closer, almost equally moved.

"She did indeed," said Captain Baz, smiling. "She hid the paper in her hand, calm as calm, and thanked me as she would have thanked any gentleman — me, a convict! I don't reckon you can guess, doctor, what balm that courtesy of hers was to me, sore all over with the degradations of my odious life. God bless her! God bless her! I kept saying. And then that great blundering jack of a guard must see me; and he went for me with his whip for talking to ladies. May be it was a fool thing to do, but I could n't bear to be humiliated before those young ladies. Before I knew what I was doing, I wrenched the whip out of his hand and flung him backward into the store. 'I 'm a gentleman,' said I, 'and I have done nothing to forfeit the right to help a lady. If you touch me, I 'll kill you!'"

"Good for you, captain!" said the doctor. The blacksmith cried, "That 's the stuff!" slapping his thigh gleefully. And there was a little chorus of plaudits from the circle of listeners. They had half forgotten the cause of their presence, in the new excitement.

Captain Baz hardly noticed the words. He continued in that white heat of passion which makes the narrator oblivious of everything but the life he is living and suffering over again. "No, he did n't hit me. I could n't have stood that! The girl was looking at me, so gently, so — I reckon I am forgetting myself." He passed his hand over his face, and spoke in a different tone. "She said, 'Don't hurt him, please!'

"'Oh, I won't hurt him, miss,' said the guard. 'I was afraid he was sassy. Look alive, 49, git in!' I got in, wishing myself dead. Well."

Captain Baz stopped again. The circle of faces and elbows was contracted a little by an instinctive movement of sympathy. "Think er bein' hit an' not able to hit back!" said the blacksmith, in an awed tone. "Myme! Myme!"

The doctor was so interested that he flung away his cigar. "Baz," said he, "is the girl Mrs. Lemew?"

Captain Baz nodded. After a second he resumed his story with a hard composure, evidently forced. "I expect there never was a madder or wretcheder man than I the next week. Never before had I realized the infernal isolation of my position as I did then, cuffed and shamed before a woman. Every instinct of manhood in me seemed to blaze up, like a smudge will if you fling on cotton-seed. So I was in a fit frame for anything. As the days went by and nothing happened, — of course I could n't know the inspector was away, — I got nearly out of my head, I was so desperate. The warden promised me a licking if I ever spoke to any one in the settlement again. I believe he had about made up his mind that I knew too much, and that he 'd better pick a quarrel and kill me. Honestly, I think that very idea was in his mind. But he did n't dare kill me without provocation, knowing that I had friends. Those days he was likely to get his chance, for I was determined to make a break for liberty. The worst difficulty was, I wanted to take Slow-foot with me. I had got attached to the boy.

He used to talk to me and Chuckey — you get plenty of chances to talk in camps — about his mother and a little baby sister he had. Poor boy! I believe he was as innocent a fellow as ever lived. He was in for stealing horses, but I think the real thief swore it off on him. If he did, God forgive him; he had better have shot the boy in his tracks. Such a life as we lived! We not only had the tyranny of the warden and the killing work, the filth and cruelty, but there was no restraint put on the brutality of the men towards each other; the bullies used to maltreat the weaker ones, take their rations or blankets or log-poles, make them tote more than their share of the log, pound them, and beat them, and worry them every way on earth.

"Chuckey and I, however, did up a few of the big fellows, and finally even they were sorry for the poor boy with his iron grinding into his sore ankle. But we could n't do up the boss, and it looked like he had a special spite against Slow-foot; he was hammering and beating him the whole enduring time. I have seen that great hulking Chuckey *cry*, telling of Slowfoot's tortures. It could n't last always. One morning — gentlemen, excuse me; I thought I was strong enough to tell this straight, but — I — I ain't. Will you give me a drink of water?"

Silently the old juror took the tin cup to the

bucket, filled it, and handed it to Captain Baz. Not a man there but felt a thrill of sympathetic emotion over the spasm of recollection which drew Captain Baz's features and roughened his voice, when, a moment later, he continued : —

"One morning Slowfoot fainted when he tried to get up. Todd would have let him stay behind, but he said Moss was on one of his crazy sprees, and might take a notion to look in ; and Slowfoot begged to go with us. Todd said he would have to send to the settlement for nails, and he would risk Moss being mad, and send for the country doctor. It was his business to look after us — though mighty little did we all see of him. So we toted Slowfoot out between us, Chuckey and I, and made a sort of bed of leaves. Brutes as we were, most of us, that patient, grateful fellow had so touched the heart left in us that all the men helped. Slowfoot was point-blank bad, burning up with fever, and half out of his head. Todd gave him some quinine and whiskey, and I was wrapping some wet rags round his ankle when the devil sent Moss along. He was just drunk enough to be ugly and utterly reckless. He saw us, and jumped off his horse. Whether he meant to hit me through Slowfoot, I don't know. I have sometimes thought he did. There happened to be an ironwood sapling, we'd sawed off to make gluts of, lying in the road. Moss picked it up, and ordered Slowfoot to get up and go to work.

"'I cayn't,' said the poor boy.

"Then Moss began to curse him. 'I'll break you in two!' And at every word he was banging Slowfoot over the head with that hard stick. I could n't bear it, and jumped at him. He hit me one cut. There it is on my cheek. The blood blinded me, but I wrenched the stick from him — I hit him across the shoulder. Oh, I marked him for life! but he got out his revolver and fired. I felt I was shot through, but I flung myself on him, and got my hands on his throat. But the guards held me, and I saw Moss catch a branch of thorn-tree up, shrieking out oaths and foaming at the mouth, and run up to Slowfoot and strike him. Todd caught his arm.

"'Ye cayn't hurt him,' said Chuckey; then, 'Look at his face!'"

"Dead?" said the doctor, in a low tone.

Captain Baz answered solemnly, "Yes, thank God, they never could hurt him any more."

"Wa'al!" exclaimed the horse-trader, "what did they do to you all — an' to Chuckey?"

"I reckon they did n't want two dead bodies on their hands. They took me back, and the first person they met was Miss Edgerton and an old justice of the peace she had coaxed to accompany her to see the camp — because her brother was n't home yet."

"Then they did n't hush it up that time?" said the doctor.

"No, sir. Chuckey spoke up" —

"Dad gum me, but I like that Chuckey!" cried the old farmer.

"And Todd was so sick of it all he made a clean breast, too. The contract was taken away from the lessee, and the men were hired to some one else. I think they were fairly well treated. The new inspector hired Chuckey and me. Chuckey is with him still. Nobody could ask a better stockman than he is. As for me, as soon as I was legally free, I married Miss Edgerton. You know the rest about me. But men to-day are suffering what I suffered. I won't vote to send a human being to a convict-camp. That 's all."

"Well," said the doctor, slowly, "I don't want to risk it either. And yet" —

"Lord, I cud n't sleep all night ef I done it!" cried the old farmer.

The professional juror studied the agitated faces about him. He could see a limitless perspective of disagreement and fees, if he would take a lonely position against Muckwrath; but under his ragged buttons beat a swindling, eccentric, soft old heart. He drew a prodigious sigh. "Gentlemen, I reckon we're all agreed," said he.

"But, fust, cap'n, 'bout the warden?" said the blacksmith.

Captain Baz rose. "I was coming to that, gentlemen. They got out an indictment against him, but he lit out, and I never heard a word about him until I was in town the day of the killing, and saw the corpse. Gentlemen, the man that Dock Muckwrath shot was my old warden, Captain Moss."

The court-room was hushed as the twelve men filed into their places, and answered to the clerk's call of their names.

"They look terribly solemn," whispered Phillipson's legal friend. "Bet you it's five years, if not second degree."

Phillipson, convinced of the jurors' solemnity, had leisure to feel sorry for the pallid man in the box and the woman whose eyes never turned from his face.

"Gentlemen of the jury, are you agreed on a verdict?"

"We are, your Honor."

A wave of interest, surprise, excitement, swept half the audience to their feet. The verdict was — Not Guilty.

Mrs. Muckwrath insisted on shaking hands

with each member of the jury, lifting a smiling but by this time unpleasantly sticky baby to kiss the dismayed liberators of her father, assuring each that Dock never would so much as kill a chicken again, and he would join the Children's Band of Hope, there being no adult temperance society within reach.　Meanwhile, Dock stood by, shifting his weight from one foot to the other, and grinning sheepishly.

" Say, Mr. Phillipson," shouted the revengeful Jerry Milligan, as the attorney strode past the door, " ye don't 'pear to fale so gayly like ye done; but I 'm thinkin' Dock fales a hape better ! "

The Northerner, who was with Phillipson, laughed outright.　" They do seem pleased," said he.　" See, Phillipson, there go the interesting family home together in one of the jurymen's wagon; Muckwrath is kissing the baby. Well, I confess I am glad he does n't have to go to your confounded penitentiary."

But Phillipson was boiling with vexation, which spattered over the first juror whom he encountered.　He demanded profanely why they all brought in such a fool verdict, plumb against the judge's instruction.

" Wa'al," answered the storekeeper, — for it was he, — " fact er the matter is, we all got to talkin' an' discussin' them convict-camps, an' we 'lowed 't wud n't be right to send a neighbor to ary sich place."

And this is all that Phillipson or any other man outside the jury knows to this day regarding that verdict. Nor to this day does Dock Muckwrath know that he was the unconscious and guilty avenger of innocent blood.

THE PLUMB IDIOT.

THERE was a vast deal of excitement in Sycamore Ridge when it was rumored that Milt Bedford, that jewel of his party, but otherwise not especially respected citizen, was likely to " get the post-office."

The place was n't worth more than nine hundred a year ; but in a Southwestern town where you can buy meat for eight cents a pound, and a boiled shirt is high toilet, nine hundred dollars is a tidy income. Consider, too, the dignity of office, and the patronage. The postmaster of Sycamore Ridge had at his beck one assistant, one janitor, and one and a half scrub-women — the *half* standing for the scrub-woman's small daughter who should " pack up the water." And one must take into account that the present postmaster, Captain Leidig, the incumbent ever since the war, had slaved days and schemed nights until the office was brought into a condition of prime efficiency ; it could almost run itself.

Take the matter by and large, the little crowd of men discussing it on the hotel platform opposite the railway were agreed to swear at " Milt Bedford's cussed luck."

I have waited so often for trains on that platform where they sat, tilting their chairs against the clapboards, that I know by heart the steel streaks and the gaunt, dim sheds, and the infrequent lamps, and the black shadows that crouch like goblin beasts under the eaves, at night, and the wide, wide street that has an uncanny and lonesome air, so spacious is it, and so low are the little brick blocks of shops, and the little wooden houses with their pointed roofs.

Being a December night, — this of which I am telling, — there was a show of Christmas bravery in the windows, and a barrel of holly at the hotel door.

Across the street is a small park with a trim " bow-dark " or osage orange hedge. Two lamps shine hospitably at the entrance. Great gumtrees and sycamores make a pleasant shade for summer days; and *then*, the plash of the fountain entices the ear, but it tinkles coldly of a winter night, and the white sycamore trunks look spectral. And in winter — even the half-hearted, snowless winter of the Southwest — the hillsides grow ragged and rusty, and the houses look bare; and the engine, that every night at

dusk drags its lurid eye and trail of fire across
the bridge between the hills, like a disabled
rocket, hisses and shrieks dismally. At intervals a light streams athwart the skies above the
river, and a steamboat pipe vies with the engine-
throttles.

To-day the air was so mild that no one of the
talkers had buttoned his coat except General
Throckmorton, the congressman from our dis-
trict. He always buttons his coat as a prepara-
tion for a speech; a habit acquired in the court-
room.

"Gentlemen," said Throckmorton,—his voice
was soft as silk and flexible as a whip-lash, the
true Southern orator's voice,—"I reckon Milt
Bedford has got a better bargain than we all."

"He'll sure devil the money-order office *some*
way," a shopkeeper prophesied.

"Why, the scoundrel can hardly read writing," cried Mr. Marsh, the banker.

"An' Cap'n Leidig knows whar ever' town in
the kentry does be," said an old farmer, "state
an' caounty an any. Never does need t' look in
the book. An' he reads them letters right spang
off, no matter how blind they be. More 'n I cud
do."

"He's a nice man," another farmer struck in,
"mighty stirrin' an' liberal."

"Yes, sir," grunted a one‑legged man.

"That 's jest him. Look a' that pyark," — pointing to the sycamores — "that 's his'n, but he keeps it up for the public. Jest as he always keeps them flower-pots in the winders."

" He 's a mighty clever man."

" An' a mighty smart man."

A chorus of praise arose, to which Throckmorton listened, smiling.

He smiled with his mouth, alone ; and to smile under such a drooping, inky-black mustache as his, with never a ripple in the intense black eyes, is to smile like a cynic. Throckmorton looked cynical. He was a slim, erect man, as distinctly a Southerner as a gentleman. His appearance suggested the planter of the caricaturists, without his whip or soft hat, and better treated by his tailor.

" Now I, gentlemen," said Throckmorton, " *I* call Hiram Leidig a plumb idiot."

The crowd simply gasped ; Throckmorton being Leidig's closest friend, and a man not to desert a friend under stress of weather.

" Yes, gentlemen, a plumb idiot," he repeated, in his gentlest tone ; " here he is. He could have made a fortune had he stayed in the manufacturing business. When the war broke out he was getting a salary of twelve hundred dollars, and he had invented half a dozen little tricks, and got patents on them, and saved ten thousand dollars. If he 'd gone back to business he would have had a hundred or two hundred thousand dollars to-day, instead of his little twenty-five thousand. But, no; first he must fight for his country, and then he gets a notion of patriotism and serving his country in his head. Patriotism is worse than a tick, gentlemen. Here 's Leidig has worn himself to a frazzle to do ten men's work for his office. He is a man of talent, a man of inviolable honesty, and yet so courteous, so kindly, that every child in the town smiles at him on the streets. He has done more than any one man of his d— party in the State to make it respectable. And Milt Bedford has done as much as any man to make it *detested!*" ("That's so, blame his skin!" and laughter from the hearers.)

"Well, what does the government or the party give Leidig for his long services? You all know. Half a dozen times he has been within an ace of getting bounced by one party or the other, and now he is going to be pitched out in good earnest by his very own party because he can't be trusted to run the office as a party machine, and Milton Bedford *can!* That 's the size of it. Now, a man who will squander his chances of fortune and the best years of his life on a government or a party which kicks fidelity every time is — a plumb idiot!"

"To my thinking, the government is the plumb idiot to lose such a servant," said the banker.

"And we all ain't far from plumb ijits t' 'low of it bein' done!" cried the farmer. "That ar Milt Bedford ain't got no more honesty 'n a shote. All 's pickin's t' him!"

"Say, gineral, are ye shore certain 'bout it?" asked the one-legged man, Miller, anxiously — he was the postmaster's assistant. "Captain did n't seem a mite skeered up 'bout it."

"Rice telegraphed me not to come on to Washington," said Throckmorton. "It would be useless, he said. Bedford has the pull. It has been a still hunt, you understand."

There were murmurs of dissatisfaction.

Throckmorton unbuttoned his coat. His next words appeared to slip from his lips by accident. "Yes, gentlemen, unless we can persuade Bedford to withdraw, we must have him."

The crowd pushed their chairs closer. "No violence, gentlemen, I beg," said the banker, nervously.

"Oh, violence!" said Throckmorton, curtly, "Violence is played out. The first man on Bedford's side would be Leidig, if we tried that game. No, sir; if we overcrow Bedford, we have got to do it with moral suasion. [Every one looked blank.] For instance, he is the real owner of Hurd's big saloon.   Are we all obliged to buy our liquors at Hurd's?"

A solemn-looking, lean man in a very decent black coat answered: "No, for sure you are not.   You are ruining soul and body drinking his abominable stuff.   I, myself, am the agent for the old-established, square-dealing house of Drake & Makepeace, of St. Louis, which will supply you directly with pure wines, brandies, whiskies, liquors, and malt liquors, at most reasonable prices."

The crowd was tickled by this, and laughed.

Throckmorton had shot his arrow; without any more words he arose, saluted the others, and went away.

It occurred to him that he ought to warn the postmaster, who would not believe in any danger.   At the same time, he shrank from inflicting pain.   He loved Leidig.   The two men had been like brothers since the Federal soldier saved the Confederate soldier's life and cared for him in prison during the war.

His scheme *might* succeed.   There was a chance of intimidating Bedford's bondsmen. He had been quietly working and suggesting for days, and his wits were busy with the details as he walked past the dazzling windows of "Hurd's Palace Saloon."   He was so absorbed that he jostled Milt Bedford, himself, coming out of the door.

Milt gave his stiff apologies a very truculent smirk.

"You 're runnin' into me more ways than one, I reckon, gineral," said he; "but you can't play off any foul on me, by ——, so don't try it on!"

Throckmorton, a lawyer, had no notion of committing himself; he shrugged his shoulders contemptuously, and gave Bedford to understand that he considered him drunk. Then he brushed past, leaving Bedford (who really was half tipsy) to cool his fury at leisure.

The encounter increased his perplexity. For the life of him he could n't decide whether to tell Leidig. Nevertheless, he went to the banker's, where, as their custom was, Leidig and the three others played whist every Thursday evening, in a manner to curdle the blood of a modern combination whist-player. But these primitive players led from "sneaks," clung to their picture cards or trumps like grim death, and committed atrocities right and left with as much placidity as if they had been getting in the finest *coups* on record.

Throckmorton was an indifferent player this evening. Even the long-suffering Leidig, his partner, remonstrated at his recklessness with unprotected queens. Later, on their way home to Leidig's lodgings, he turned on the lawyer with a friendly bluntness: " What's gone wrong, Marion?   You were n't yourself, to-night."

Throckmorton squirmed out of the question, somehow.   Leidig, the least suspicious of men, believed in a knotty lawsuit and a headache, and wanted Throckmorton to stop and get some anti-pyrine.   Throckmorton caught his wistful looks at every lamp-post.

Leidig was not a handsome man, he was too short and too round ; his face had kept its boyish look to a surprising extent, although he was growing bald and wore a big mustache.   He dressed with great care.   According to the black maid-servant, he covered his off-duty coats with a towel, and pressed his trousers between the mattresses of his bed.   Every morning, winter or summer, he used to pick a flower for his button-hole.   He wore a tall silk hat, because, in his youth (when he was a young mechanic, determined to become a gentleman), gentlemen used to wear tall silk hats.   For the same reason, he carried a silk handkerchief. Indeed, Sycamore Ridge considered him a mirror of fashion.

As they walked along, — perhaps it was the full moon pouring a flood of glory over the landscape, — Leidig began to talk about a girl who was to have been his wife long ago.   She had died as his mother had died, while Leidig was fighting on the southwest border. And so hard had he taken the blow that he never would return to Ohio; he gathered together his property, and settled in Sycamore Ridge.

Leidig rarely spoke of that old grief; he never had spoken so frankly before. Somehow, his frankness gave Throckmorton a sinister and creepy disquietude. He interrupted him : —

"Why did you leave the agricultural implement business? You need n't go back to Ohio, of course; but why take our post-office?"

"Marion," said Leidig, solemnly, "the post-office saved me. You don't know. It was awful! I brooded over it until I was fit to kill myself. God knows, I might have killed myself, but they offered me this post-office. They said here was a chance to serve the country. And I seemed to hear my mother's voice, just as it used to sound, evenings, when she would tell me stories about the Revolution. Mother raised me to love my country, ever since I was old enough to fire fire-crackers. I seemed to hear her voice, saying, 'Son, it 's worth while serving such a government as ours.' I had a feeling — well, you know the feeling you have for your country."

Throckmorton's face contracted, while his eyes roamed, in a curious way, from the stars

and the darkling river (they stood on the bridge,
as Leidig spoke), to the lights of the city twinkling like fireflies above the black roofs.   He
made an abrupt gesture, spreading his hands
and clinching them.   Then they relaxed, and
dropped by his side.

"Oh, what's the use?" said he, "I felt that
way when — when I had a country.   Now, I see
how impracticable such sentiment is."

"No you don't," said Leidig, "*I* know you
don't, whether *you* do or not.   Look here,
Marion, the way you felt for the South, I felt
for my country, *our* country.   And I had this
kind of a feeling: the way to obliterate the
war is to fetch people close together.   'You stay
here awhile, old fellow,' says I, 'and do your
best for the old flag.   Be a decent fellow, for
they are going to sample the North by you.
Don't go at them ramping and roaring, and
shaking your opinions in their face like a red
rag, when they're just naturally sore all over.
Here's a chance,' says I, 'to do your country
better service than you did in the war!'   Con-
sequently, I stayed and I tried.   Mother raised
me to be a gentleman.   Leidig is as good a
name as there is in New York State.   I always
remembered that.   A gentleman and a soldier,
they say, you know.   Why shouldn't every servant of the government be as much of a gentle-

man as a soldier? I hope I have n't made my Southern friends ashamed of me. Well, I got to love the work, fairly love it. Once or twice, as you know, there has been talk of removing me, and I can't tell you the feeling I 've had about the whole town standing by me so. It 's the honor of my life. And to show you, Marion, I ain't joking and bluffing, when I pretend not to be afraid, this time, I 'll tell you that if they *were* to turn me out, after all these years, it would break my heart. I never could hold up my head again."

In such a strain Leidig opened his heart, until they reached his lodgings. He had two rooms on the ground floor, with an outside door and a corner of the wee piazza glassed over for a conservatory; and he was considered to live in luxury.

Throckmorton drew a sigh of relief at the sight of the gay window. He parted from Leidig affectionately; but he said nothing of Rice's telegram.

That night is memorable to Sycamore Ridge as the night of what they call " The Great Fire." Actually it only swept one small street, but it menaced the whole town.

Every soul at the fire admired the postmaster, that night; his daring coolness and his chemical-engine saved both post-office and town. He risked his life half a dozen times. The enthusiasm of the witnesses bubbled over. Poor Leidig himself, meanwhile, had been flung from a fractured ladder. He would not go home, but directed his engine, propped up by the janitor and Miller. Throckmorton (who nearly killed a favorite horse to get in at the fag end of the conflagration) fell upon him and forcibly bore him home. Then he hustled the telegraph-operator away from the cinders, and sent off a message to the Post-Office Department, lavishing details of Leidig's bravery, regardless of expense.

The fire called a truce to the warfare against Bedford. Certainly the government would n't have the brass to bounce Leidig after his saving the post-office, Throckmorton assured Roz Miller.

"But I can tell you one thing, Roz," he added, dryly, "you would have to give up Christmas or the place — one, if Milt had come in. Milt aims to do all the Christmasing himself."

"That 's so," acquiesced Roz, looking foolish. He was a loyal soul and full of energy, but he was "just naturally obliged to get drunk Christmas week." "I could n't fault the season, like to go dry through it," he said, long before, to

Leidig. Leidig knew the man. " All right,"
he said, calmly, " it is disgraceful for a government official to get drunk. I shall suspend you
one week between Christmas and New Year's —
your salary to go on as usual. You are *not* the
assistant postmaster, then. If I ever see the
assistant postmaster drunk, he goes."

Thereafter, annually, Miller was suspended,
and, annually, he returned to his post, a week
later, very shaky in his fingers and puffy about
his eyes; but deadly sober. Between suspen-
sions he was the most temperate of men.

Bedford, all this time, kept well under cover.
Perhaps he knew that Leidig's injuries were
turning out to be more serious than any one expected. There were a couple of broken ribs,
and pneumonia had set in, complicating the
case. The doctor talked of " internal injuries."
" Infernal injuries, I say," fumed Throckmorton; " why the —— must *you* be prancing on
a ladder, a man of your flesh? You *are* a
plumb idiot!" He was too anxious, to keep
his patience, and scolded Leidig out of sheer
fright.

Leidig smiled tranquilly. He could not drink
the choice liquors or smoke the expensive cigars
that Throckmorton, the banker, and other friends
were always sending; but he took a boyish kind
of pleasure in watching the wrapping - papers

removed; and he must have all the odd assort-
ment of cards stuck up around his looking-glass,
in full view.

By and by, Throckmorton did not snap at
him, but used a studied gentleness.   But whenever he left the sick-room, and walked through
the little parlor, he would glare at the now
disheveled rows of flower-pots, with the blackest
frown.   Maudy Lize, the landlady's eldest girl,
always a pet of Leidig's, took to red eyes and
snuffles; and the black maid-servant grinned incessantly, and forgot everything that was told
her, which is the African fashion of showing
emotion.   When a negro stops grinning, he begins to howl.

Besides Throckmorton's telegram, the citizens
had sent an elaborate letter to the Post-Office
Department; but ten days passed, and the department made not a sign!   On the tenth day,
Throckmorton saw Bedford on the street.   He
sat enthroned in a red-wheeled buggy, between
two men.   All were smoking, all grinning.
Seeing Throckmorton, Bedford swept his hat
off his black curls with an exaggerated flourish,
and grinned more broadly.

" What does the scoundrel mean by *that?* "
queried Throckmorton.

He understood directly.

Two envelopes were handed him at his office. One was addressed to Leidig (Throckmorton looked over his mail), and had the official superscription of the Post-Office Department. Throckmorton tore out the inclosure, a florid letter of thanks to Leidig. Although a critic in general, Leidig's friend waded through the fine phrases well pleased.

"It will tickle old Leidig," he thought. "Oh, well, they are more decent than I 'lowed they were."

Then he opened the other envelope.

There was a telegram from Rice, concise and to the point. "Bedford has got the post-office. Damn!"

Throckmorton flung the telegram into the fire. He used some vitriolic language about the civil service that would better not be repeated; but he understood Bedford's grin.

Late that afternoon he paid a visit to Leidig. Young Dr. Rollin had just walked away on foot. Dr. Peters was untying his horse at the gate, and old Dr. Farwell sat in the buggy.

"They 've had the consultation," thought Throckmorton; and his heart choked him.

"Well, gentlemen?" said he. Somehow, the sensation that he felt seemed to mix itself up with an old pain, and, again, he was a lad on the battlefield, dizzy with the smoke and roar, and that horrible smell of carnage in his nostrils; watching his brother die.

The old doctor gripped his hand.

"Dear, dear, dear," the old doctor said, "ain't it too bad? Such a splendid man!"

Then they explained to him; but he didn't understand, though he nodded, and said "yes," and went through the manual of intelligence, decorously; the internal injuries rather than the pneumonia that had supervened were killing Leidig, so much he did comprehend, and it was enough. Leidig might live a week, he might die in two days. Throckmorton got away from the doctors and went in to his friend. Leidig lay quite alone, but Maudy Lize cried softly to herself in the parlor, with the door ajar.

When he stood by the bedside, Leidig turned over feebly and smiled. "Sit down, Marion," said he; "no, that's the chair with the broken spring; take another."

Throckmorton is ashamed of it to this day: but groaned, "Oh, d— the spring!" and burst out sobbing like a baby.

Leidig soothed him; yet there were traces of tears on his own cheek. There had been a grim half hour for Leidig after the doctors were gone, alone in his chamber with the vision of death. How does the soul conduct itself, to which, of a sudden, awe and mystery have become the inexorable, next realities? Disease blunts the sensibilities; yet is there not always a chill in this going beyond the shining of the sun?

All Leidig revealed were those tears on his cheek and one speech to Throckmorton. "Don't take on so, my dear; but, indeed, I can't help being glad you 're so sorry. It has been pretty lonesome." But, immediately, he was talking about the post-office, telling Throckmorton his plans. "And, Marion," he added, half apologetically, "would you object to writing the department and just mentioning I did my best for the office — afterward, you know."

Throckmorton, still coughing, and strangling, and blowing his nose, fished the official letter out of his pocket with his handkerchief.

The sick man's limp fingers fumbled in vain at the paper. "I reckon you 'll have to read it for me, Marion," he was obliged to say.

Throckmorton gulped, and desperately went at it. The letters danced before his eyes; he had enough to do to keep his voice steady through the sentences, but he read it to the end. When he looked up he was startled by the rapture on Leidig's face.

"I was n't sorry before, but now I 'm glad," said he. "Marion, it 's worth while to serve such a government!"

Then and there, Throckmorton registered an

oath that his old friend's delusion should not be broken ; and he kept his vow.

It was easier than might be imagined. All Leidig's friends entered into the plot. He still saw a few friends, and still, every morning, Roz Miller reported for directions. He kept on reporting just the same after Milt Bedford's commission arrived ; and Milt himself was swaggering about the office with his hat on the back of his head, cursing the late trains. Leidig could n't say enough to praise Roz. " Why, Marion," was his grand climax, " he is keeping sober over Christmas. He refuses point-blank to be suspended ! "

Christmas morning, for a second, Throckmorton distrusted poor Roz. The assistant came banging and hobbling and pounding down the street, on his wooden leg, hatless and coatless, in the utmost disorder. He tumbled into Throckmorton's office.

" Oh, Lord," he gurgled, spent with his efforts, " the fat 's sure in the fire, *now!* Bedford 's up with the captain ! "

As soon as he could get his breath, he related how Leidig had sent an imperative message to the post-office, requesting him or some one else there (Roz, hard pressed, had set up a mythical assistant), to come directly to the house. Unluckily, Roz was out of the office. Bedford, observing the ambiguous direction, opened the note, and then remarked to the janitor that *he* would wait on Captain Leidig. "And he's gone," said Roz, nearly crying, "and he'll *kill* the boss, telling him! Oh, dad burn his ornery hide!"

He wasted his rage on the two clerks and a much scandalized girl typewriter. Throckmorton was half-way down the street. The lawyer fancied, savagely, that he could understand: Bedford's brutal vanity was in arms; and he would take this revenge. Throckmorton ground his teeth. Ten to one, the cur would blurt out the whole vile truth! All the while his long legs swung over the ground, his mind was gyrating through lurid lies of fires at the post-office, and fights in the street, and sudden deaths of Bedford's nearest kin — *anything* to get him safely outside the house, where he (Throckmorton) could deal with him.

"I'm a right peaceful man," said Throckmorton, feeling for his pistol, "but I've stood all the nonsense from Milt Bedford that I'm going to."

But when he softly opened Leidig's door, no human being could look meeker. The spectacle that met him was amazing. He saw the familiar bed with the long fold of the white sheet over the quilt. He saw Leidig's peaceful face laid back on the pillow. He saw, on the other side, the ragged chrysanthemum petals nodding their white against Milt Bedford's blue flannel legs, as Milt stood, shifting his weight from one foot to the other. His face fronted Throckmorton. It wore the strangest expression : bewilderment and awe, confused by the sense of an ugly kind of comedy in the situation. That was the way Throckmorton chose to interpret it, later. At the moment, his wits were held by the daze of the first words that he heard. They came from Bedford.

"So *you* ben runnin' the office jest layin' here on the bed," said he, slowly; "I expect Roz ben here regular " —

Throckmorton beckoned.

"That 's all right, general," said Bedford, "I catch on. Well, captain, I won't take up your time. I 'm 'bleeged to you for seeing me, and I sincerely hope you 'll feel pearter, soon. I wish you well."

"Thank you, sir. I wish you well, sir," said Leidig. Clumsily Bedford shook hands. Clumsily he tiptoed out, shaking the house at every step. I am told that all the way down the street, he wagged his head and muttered : "Lord, ain't he a plumb idiot! But he 's a mighty nice man."

Throckmorton shot a keen glance at Leidig,

as the door creaked and closed. He ventured to ask: "Did that brute say anything to disturb you?"

Leidig's eyes twinkled. He feebly indicated a package on the table. Opening it, Throckmorton lifted a bottle of rum.

"Very old Medford, Marion," said Leidig; "he brought it for a Christmas present. I expect that was why he came. He began a queer farrago about all being fair in politics, and no personal feeling, and the highest respect for me, and he looked very up a tree, when I condoled with him on his own disappointment; and finally he presented this. It is rather pleasant, don't you think, Marion, to know he does n't keep any grudge about the thing?"

Throckmorton said, "Yes, it was pleasant."

Then Leidig spoke of his message to the post-office, wondering why it had not been answered. It had reference to his will left in his desk. By this will, after legacies to his friends, he left the remainder of his property to the town. The bequest included his little park and about eight thousand dollars. The money was to be used to erect a building suitable for a post-office in the park, and the town was directed to give the use of the building to the government, rent free.

Leidig lived for two days longer. Nothing

occurred to disturb him any more; and his last intelligible words were to Throckmorton, repeating : —

" It is worth while, my dear, to serve such a government as ours."

Perhaps he was right.   Perhaps, again, he may be right, some day.

THE GOVERNOR'S PREROGATIVE.

The Governor was at home. He sat in his library, in a most amiable mood. His eye took a languid pleasure wandering over the familiar surroundings. After the bare and slightly dingy furnishing of the executive office at the capitol, he was glad to look again on the ceiling, with its mahogany bars, the stamped gold and leather behind the glass of the bookcases, and the warm hues of the curtains and the velvet carpet.

"It is pleasant to be home," said the Governor, dropping his newspaper to look out of the window. The paper certainly was not as entertaining as the distant view of the lake, a blue mist breaking into tumbled lines of foam on a sandy beach; or the nearer view of his own lawn, and the groom in livery, leading a wee Shetland pony, with his little daughter for rider, around the drive, while the wind blew the child's yellow curls against her rosy cheeks and carried her small laughter and shouts to her father's ears.

Thus he happened to be looking when an old German woman entered the yard and stopped under the shadow of the *porte-cochère.* She was evidently quite an old woman, with wrinkles and white hair; but her face had a ruddy tint burnt into the brown on her cheeks, and her sturdy shape was erect and vigorous of movement. She wore a black stuff gown made in the simplest fashion, and carried a bundle. With considerable amusement the observer saw her undo this bundle and take out a comb and a white kerchief, preparatory to making a sort of toilet. First, she brushed away the dust which lay thick on her gown; then she smoothed her hair; and, finally, tied the white kerchief about her neck. Having done all this with the utmost gravity, she walked to the basement door.

"Oh, woman, woman," mused the Governor, "how you cling to your little vanities! She is hardly fine enough for a friend of cook's; perhaps she comes to see the laundress. But why did n't she dress at home?" Smiling to himself, he returned to his paper, only to be interrupted shortly by the butler's announcement of a woman to see him.

"She is an old woman, sir," said Hopkins, who had rather a kind heart and knew the Governor's like weakness.

"Show her in, Hopkins," was the reply.

"Ten to one," thought the Governor, "it's my old woman. So the toilet was for me. I wonder what she wants of me. Thank Heaven, the offices are all full, anyhow!"

The Governor guessed correctly; it was the old woman whom he had seen. She entered timidly in the rear of Hopkins. Safely opposite the Governor, she dropped a courtesy.

"Spricht Excellenz Deutsch?" she asked.

"Ein wenig," said the Governor, apparently with the unworthy motive of impressing Hopkins: for the instant that personage had closed the door, departing, he added, "Speak English, if you can; and won't you take a chair, madam?"

"Oh, no, gnädiger Herr — Excellenz; no, I vill petter stan'. Excellenz, I haf von son, er ist einsiges — mine only schild. Dis morgen I vas tell he do *dis* — see, Excellenz." She courtesied again, holding out a carefully folded newspaper to the Governor at arm's-length. Even in youth she could never have been a pretty woman, and years of toil had made her shape angular and clumsy, and tanned and wrinkled the large features framed by the white hair; but her clear blue eyes were as simple and honest as a child's, and they looked up at the Governor so anxiously that, glancing down the page, he felt a sensation of pity.

"Fritz Jansen," he exclaimed; "are you *his* mother?" and to himself he added, "This is worse than the office-seekers!"

The old woman courtesied timidly. She was quick-sighted enough to see that, somehow, he was unfavorably impressed.

Just then there came two taps at the door. The Governor frowned; he recognized his wife's knock. It is not, therefore, to be inferred that his domestic life was unhappy; on the contrary, he was in love with his wife, who returned his affection; but he felt a presentiment that her presence would make infinitely more disagreeable the decision to which he was sure he must come; yet, at the same time, he was conscious of an irritating longing to shift the responsibility of consolation on to some woman's shoulders — besides, his wife spoke German. A third tap sounded on the door-panel; it meant, "Are you engaged?"

"Perhaps I vould go vays," said the old woman. "I kin vait outsides, yet — if Excellenz is pizzy?"

"Oh, no," said the Governor. "Come in, Annie." The lady who entered was young and pretty, and her charming eyes had not yet lost their look of amiable interest. She seemed to have just returned from a walk, for her fair skin had the wind's roses, and her blonde hair

was roughened the least in the world. There
was enough silver braid on her perfectly fitting
blue cloth dress to compel the old woman's admiration and awe.

"My wife," said the Governor, briefly. "Will
you interpret a little for me, Annie? This is
Fritz Jansen's mother."

The old woman dropped her courtesy, the patient sadness of her face brightening a little.

"Ya, gnädige Frau," said she, "I koom to beg
der barton von mine son. He is in brison to pe
hang'."

"You know," said the Governor, "that he has
been found guilty of murdering his betrothed,
Lena" —

"No, Excellenz — Greta," interrupted the old
woman, eagerly. "She vas heist Gretchen; der
baper speak wrong von dat, an' berhaps it vould
be mit oder t'ings wrong also!"

"His betrothed, Greta, then," amended the
Governor, "under very — hem — very aggra-
vated circumstances. He has had a long and perfectly impartial trial, and has been condemned
on overwhelming evidence. I — I really do not
see," said the Governor, trying to bring the
scene to an abrupt conclusion, "how it will be
possible for me to pardon him. Tell her that
in German, Annie."

"Oh, poor thing!" said the Governor's wife.

The old woman had listened with an expression of pathetic attention. Plainly she did not comprehend the Governor's words, but in some way she gathered from his manner that her petition was rejected. She clasped her large rough hands unconsciously as she turned to the lady, whose kind face looked to her then like that of a guardian angel.

" The gracious lady speaks German, is it not true ? " she said in her native tongue. " Ah, gracious lady, it is cruel lies ; my Fritz is not a wicked man. Oh, no ; who should know of him better than his mother ? I will tell it in as few words as I can, if the gracious lady will but listen. My Fritz is the only one of seven the good Lord has let me keep. The father was a carpenter, and he carried me to Munich, and there he fell off a scaffold and hurt his back, and lived ten years but never walked again ; and the cholera came, and four of my children did die, and there was only Fritz and Otto, because the others did die when they were babies. And the next year, in the street a wagon did run over my Otto, and he was sick for three months and died. How could I have lived those days but for my Fritz ? He was but a boy of ten, but he cared for the father and Otto while I was gone to work and scrub for the American ladies. He would cook and make the room neat like a girl, and in the evenings he would study the book to learn. Always he would help me and do little things to please me; and when he was sixteen and the father died, he said: 'Now I will save money, and we will go to America.' And he would work at everything and give me always the money; and nights he would always work also, and at Christmas he comes to me with a fine black gown, saying: 'Thou, too, shalt have a fine gown for the church; this is with the evenings' work, mamma.' Ah, gracious lady, none can tell how good and kind is my Fritz; never idle one moment and never cross, but always singing, and merry, and kind to every one, and not able to go by the starving dog even, but must share his own soup and black bread. And so it was with Greta, too, gracious lady. There was in the house with us a poor woman that made flowers, and she did have a little girl. She was five years younger than was my Fritz, — eleven only was she, — and one day she comes weeping to my room to say her mother is fainted; but it was not fainted; she was dead. The people in the house, they say, 'Now since the little Gretchen has no one to care for her she must go to the waisenhaus;' but my Fritz says, 'Mamma, Otto is dead, and all my little sisters; there is but thee and me: let us take the little Greta for my sister and

thy daughter, and she shall have half my bread
and soup. We shall not go any less soon to
America, and in America will be bread for us
all.' And that was how Greta came to us.
Then my brother writes to me from America,
saying, 'Come,' and we came, and at first we
were all with my brother, and Fritz worked
for him ; but, after a while, Fritz and I, who
also worked hard, saved a little money and we
say we will buy a farm. So Greta, who was like
my daughter, and was fifteen now — Greta say,
'I will go and work at service in the city to
make money, so then we can buy the farm.'
And Fritz, he works here with me to buy the
farm, and so it go on. Greta, she comes to see
me, and always she brings the money. She will
not have enough dresses to be bright and gay
like a young maiden, if I do not sometimes go to
the city myself to buy for her. But I know
that an old woman like me would not know what
would please a young maiden; so I did always
pick out a young lady at the shop that was selling and looked kind, and I told her what money
to spend I had, and how it was for Greta, that
was like my daughter, and would give all her
money to me to buy the farm. And when Greta
would come to see us in the new dress, then
would my Fritz smile and kiss me. At last we
did have almost enough money, and then did

come the bad crops, and my brother he loses all
the crop that he means to sell to pay the money
that he must pay on his own farm, and I feel
bad for him and talk with Fritz and Greta, and
they say he must not lose his farm when we have
money; so we lend to him money, and Greta
tells to us how Fritz, who was like his father a
carpenter, could earn much money in the city.
By this time they were betrothed and to be married when we have the farm. So Fritz — it was
six months ago — went to the city. He writes
to me and Greta writes to me, and twice he
comes to see me, but two months ago I got a letter saying he must go to a city far away and I
will not hear for a long time; and for two, three
weeks when I do not hear I do not think so
much, but then I begin to wonder, and I have
my brother write to Greta, but I get no answer,
and then — then — will the gracious lady have
patience with me that I am so long? — then it
was yesterday that my brother was in the little
town that is near us and a man showed him the
paper, how my Fritz a month ago had killed
my Greta, and had been before the judge, and
was now in prison to die." The old woman's
hands trembled, and her voice, for the first time.
The Governor's wife said something in an undertone to her husband; he nodded and went
quietly out of the room, returning with a glass

of wine. But the old woman, courtesying in her old-fashioned way, shook her head. "No, Excellenz, I cannot trink; if Excellenz und die gracious laty forgif', I vill tell more — in German."

"Certainly, if it is easier for you," said the lady; while the Governor, with a resigned air, sank into a chair. The old woman continued:—

"So my brother cannot show me the paper, when he will come home, but sits in the corner still, with his head down, and my brother's wife cries and will not tell me why, and they do not let the children laugh, and in the morning, when they have talked together, my brother brings me the paper and I see the name. And he tells me how the man says that the Governor is the only one can have my Fritz let out of the prison. So we did go to the town, to the railroad, but the cars have changed the time to go, and we did not know; so we are too late, and Hermann would have me wait for the cars to-night, but I could not wait when my Fritz was in prison, and my Greta was dead, so I did walk " —

"From where?" asked the lady, gently.

"It is from Egmont, gracious lady."

"But it is fifteen miles !"

"Yes, gracious lady."

"Walter, do you hear?" said the lady reproachfully; " she has walked from Egmont !"

"Yes, my dear," answered the Governor, mildly; "it is a long walk. She would better sit down."

Then his wife rapidly repeated the old woman's story to him. "Now, tell him the rest in English," she said to the old woman.

The latter turned to the Governor, and dropped her invariable courtesy before she spoke. "My brother told me dat I vould pring de baper vat say how mine Fritz is not vicked mans. I did go, dis mornin', to der peoples dat know mine Fritz, Herr Excellenz." She took a paper out of the bag that hung from her waist, in plain sight, so that she might always be secure of its presence, and presented it with the courtesy.

Some German had evidently drawn up the humble certificate to Fritz Jansen's honesty, good-nature, industry, and peaceableness. "I kin not for long stay," said the old woman, wistfully eying the Governor's face, "so I go to dem I knows. It is sign py Johann Mueller, dat Fritz did vork py — und Kurtz Claussen, dat have de farm ve puy, und Ernst Bürger, der saloon-keeper dat know Fritz well — in dee olt country also," said she with simple pride. In Germany one may be a liquor-seller and lose nothing in the social scale; indeed, it is a calling of respectability quite above Frau Jansen's former station.

The Governor looked uncomfortable. He gave his wife a glance of appeal. "My dear, I don't see what I can do," he said desperately, rubbing at the wrinkles in his forehead. "There is no doubt about it, the fellow killed the girl out of jealousy, in the most brutal way, and then tried to throw suspicion on an innocent man. The evidence is quite conclusive; the girl lived long enough to identify her assailant. Besides, he is known to the police as a brutal, dissipated fellow; he nearly beat a man to death before. He has been sentenced justly, and I have no right to interfere. Such crimes as his are getting too common."

"Look at his mother," said the lady, gently. She was still standing, her strained gaze bent on the Governor's face, her gaunt, brown hands plucking at the strings of her bag.

"I am as sorry as you are for his mother," said the Governor, staring the other way; "but I have no right to let my pity blind me to my duty. If every jealous brute can kill the woman he is jealous of, and escape scot-free, what security have you women got?"

"I don't believe he killed her at all," said the lady. "Such a good boy as he was could n't do such a cruel thing as that. I 've read it all, Walter. It 's sickening, it 's atrocious; and that 's why I am convinced Fritz Jansen never did it."

" She said he did."

" Then she was mistaken. I don't think much of *her*."

The Governor put his hand over his mustache to hide an involuntary smile. " Well, you see *I* am sorry for her. Apart from the murder, he had not treated her well. He had not even been faithful to her. My dear, there are the police-court records. He has been up before the courts for drunkenness and assault half a dozen times. His mother says he was a carpenter, but he was n't anything so respectable. His principal business seems to have been a billiard-marker, which he combined with much shadier ways of getting money."

" Walter, I can't believe he was so bad, when he was such a good, unselfish boy. Don't you think it was touching the way he helped his mother when he was a child? I don't see how he could have changed so suddenly."

" My dear," said the Governor, gravely, " he may have been a good boy, I don't know; unhappily, there is n't the least doubt that he was a wicked man. You must remember his mother only tells the best of him now; besides, mothers are the last persons to know when their sons go to the bad; probably his uncle could tell a very different sort of story. Madam," — turning to the old woman, — " what did you do with your money ? "

She looked dazed, and her eyes wandered to the lady, who repeated the question in German.

"I gif' all to Fritz, Excellenz," she answered, "und he have it in der pank to keep."

"Humph!" said the Governor.

"It may be all right," pleaded his wife.

"Did you ever hear — well, anything bad of your son since he went to the city?" the Governor went on.

"Bad? of mein Fritz?" said the old woman; "nefer vun vort."

"Can you read English? Have you read the paper?"

"No, Excellenz. I kin no English read, but der man he did tell to mein bruder vat it vas been. Yes."

"You see, Annie," said the Governor, "he might be a thorough-paced scamp, and his mother never know. I have no doubt he has used all the money she fancies is in the bank. He intended this crime; wrote to her he was going away; meant to run away, for that matter. Don't you notice that the murder was committed just after he wrote? I am afraid he is a bad-hearted fellow. I don't see how I can do anything for him. Such fellows as he are too dangerous to be let loose. Decent people have their rights too; they ought to be protected, even if the rogues must suffer. Your good heart" —

"I have n't any better heart than you," interrupted the Governor's wife, with spirit; "only I don't sit down on it, as you do!"

— "Blinds you," pursued the Governor, "to the grim facts of the case. Not only would a pardon be an abuse of the pardoning power, which the people have vested in me, confiding in my honesty and justice; not only would it be a virtual encouragement of a peculiarly brutal class of murders; but, my darling wife, it would be cruelty in disguise to this poor old mother herself. If the boy dies now, true, his mother will mourn him and miss him all her life; think him an innocent victim, and me a cruel murderer. Very well, so be it. She will still have her memories of his youth to console her, and her very conviction of the injustice of his fate will be a comfort to her; while, on the other hand, if I release him, he will dissipate all her illusions, neglect her, ill-treat her, very likely spend every cent of her hard earnings, and at last convince even that trusting soul what a brute he is. It is the truest kindness to her to refuse."

"But I am sure he is n't a brute!"

"Unhappily, I am sure he *is*."

"Then," said the lady, quickly, "you might commute his sentence to imprisonment for life; in the penitentiary he could n't ill-treat his mother, or spend her money, and if he happens to be innocent, you would have a chance to find it out!"

The Governor shook his head. "You want to open the whole question of capital punishment, I think. But, my dear, whatever your view or mine of the advisability of hanging, the laws make hanging the punishment for murder, and I am sworn to see that the laws are executed. And, frankly, I must say that if ever the extreme penalty of the law was deserved, it was in this case. Jansen's lawyer made all his fight on technicalities. He has appealed to me, and I have gone over the ground with him. It was a brutal, unprovoked, deliberate murder — just that. Were I to pardon Jansen, I should n't do it because there was a shadow of excuse for him, but because I pitied his mother. Now, I have n't the right to gratify my own feelings at the expense of the State. I am convinced that Jansen's immediate trial and his speedy execution will do more than anything else could to stop the wholesale murder that has been going on for the last six months in this State. But, suppose I commute Jansen's sentence, and, because of my leniency, a single murder — not to say five, or ten, or a dozen, as is probable — is committed; do you think I can hold myself guiltless of that bloodshed? No, Annie; I can't do it. It hurts me as much as it does you to have to refuse this poor creature; but the law must take its course. Tell her so, please, as kindly as you can."

His wife knew him well enough to perceive that further pleading would be useless. She went up to the old woman and took one of the big brown hands in hers. Her voice faltered as she tried to put into German her husband's conviction that he had no right to interfere; before she was done, the tears were running down her cheeks.

The listener's face lost its ruddy brown color: whether she grasped the meaning of the words is doubtful, but she knew that she had failed.

"Kann Excellenz nichts fur mich?" she stammered, her dim eyes still fixed with the same wistful intensity on the Governor's troubled face, her hands clasped again.

He shook his head.

"Wer, den, Excellenz? who? I vill go to him py de cars."

He shook his head again. "Good Heavens, Annie," he cried, "I can't stand this! Can't you help me out?"

"Alas," his wife said, in German, very gently, "I am so sorry — so sorry for you, but there is no one — no hope."

"No — hope," the mother repeated brokenly;

"und my Fritz"— Taking a step forward, she tried to look more closely into the lady's face, but her strength failed her; she staggered, and must have fallen had she not caught at the corner of the table to steady herself.

Instantly the lady held the rejected glass of wine to her lips, while the Governor pushed a chair towards her. Mechanically she took a swallow of the wine; but she would not sit.

"No, Excellenz; pardon," she said weakly, "but it vas so long vays und I haf veep so mooch for Greta. Now I vill go. I did already dersturp der pisiness too long, und I must see mein Fritz."

"I will give you a note to the jailer," said the Governor, suiting his action to his words; "and"—

He did not finish the sentence; but, when he had written the note, he put a bank-bill into another envelope, on which he wrote a few German words.

The old woman stood a moment, collecting her strength, her face looking old and worn. She made none of the efforts to alter his decision that the Governor had dreaded. When he handed her the note, she took it with a low courtesy, saying, "Excellenz haf been ver goot to me. I bin sorry for troubles him," and placed the paper carefully in her bag. Then she turned to the Governor's wife, kissed her hand, courtesying again and murmuring some low words of gratitude, and passed, erect as ever, though with a feebler step, out of the room.

"Oh, poor soul!" said the Governor's wife. "Walter, send somebody to the train with her, — poor, simple, meek, broken-hearted creature!"

The Governor's face was almost as haggard as that of his petitioner. "If she had only reproached me, I could have borne it better," he muttered. "Now, I sha'n't be able to get the look of her eyes out of my head!" He questioned Hopkins (who was the "some one" sent to the train) minutely about her. Hopkins said that she seemed like a woman dazed, but was quite docile and grateful, and went off on the right train, safely committed to the conductor's care. He spoke warmly of her downstairs; he had a shrewd surmise as to the nature of her errand, and his pity was not lessened by the deep deference of her manner towards himself. The general opinion downstairs, shaped by Hopkins, was that the Governor ought to be ashamed of himself.

Indeed, the Governor found little comfort anywhere, unless it might be in his own conscience. His wife refused to be convinced by the abundant evidence of Fritz Jansen's guilt, which he was at the pains to lay before her. Even his children picked up some garbled version of the story from the maids, and his little girl, nestling her golden head on his heart, stabbed it with the question: "Does it hurt much to be hanged, papa? Wally says it does."

"Wally is a naughty boy to talk to you about hangings," said the Governor.

"It was n't Wally; it was just Sarah, when she and Ellen were making the beds. She said there was a poor man to be hanged, and you would n't prevent it; but you will, papa, won't you?"

"You may be sure, my dear," said the much-tried Governor, "that I sha'n't let any man be hanged who does n't deserve it."

"But, papa," pleaded the child, "don't let him *anyhow!* Wally says it hurts *awful!* he choked himself to see."

The Governor gave a sort of groan, and put the child down; it was a relief to hear the door-bell ring, and have a chance to get away. "I wish that miserable Jansen were hanged and it were all over," he thought; "this is terrible!" He knew that the execution was to follow soon after the conviction; but he would not look at the papers to see the exact date. He could not keep his imagination away from the figure of the old German woman so meekly accepting her fate and going on that dismal journey to her son. Had she staid near him ever since, he wondered. On his part, he had written to the various prison officials, and to the sheriff, bespeaking their kind offices to smooth the prisoner's last days. He had sent money to the jailer for Jansen's mother, "afterward." It seemed to him that he had done all in his power, and now he was only anxious to forget. For a month after the interview he was away from home most of the time, — just a month, to a day. He had come back, and was sitting in his library with his wife, when he happened to notice a paper on the table. His wife's eye followed his.

"It has the notice of Jansen's execution in it," said she; "he was hanged, yesterday."

The Governor dropped the hand that he had extended. "I don't care to see it," said he. There was a wood-fire burning in the open fireplace, and he turned his face towards the blaze. For the next few minutes there was silence. Hopkins's voice broke it. He spoke in his usual quiet tones, but he had a curious look of suppressed agitation on his impassive face.

"It is the old woman who was here the last time you was home, sir," said Hopkins. The Governor turned pale.

"I will see her, Walter," said the Governor's wife, gently; "it will be better."

" No," said the Governor, straightening himself in the chair, with a distinct sensation of wanting to run out of the room. " You are very kind, Annie; but I will see her myself. Show her in, Hopkins."

She came in — behind her a young man with the aspect of a " naturalized American." The Governor had not the hardihood to lift his eyes to her face. He was dimly aware that she was courtesying in the familiar fashion; but his words stuck in his throat when he tried to speak.

" Excellenz," said the old woman, " I haf pring mein Fritz." She dragged the young man forward.

" Your Fritz!" cried the Governor and his wife together. " Ya, Excellenz; ya, gnädige Frau," said the old woman, with a beaming face. " Ya, ven I vas py der prison und see der pad, vicked mans, it vas not mein Fritz; it vas Fritz Jansen, but not mein schild, und it vas Lena und not mein Greta he vas kill, already, ya. Der baper vas tell kein lies. Mein Fritz vas in Canada, und I go by mein Greta und it vas tree days he come, mein Fritz, und I prings pack der money und tanks for him. He can goot English speak to Excellenz. Und, Excellenz, vill Excellenz gif to him different name to dat vicked mans dat is hang? He vish not be heist name of mans dat is hang!"

She paused and courtesied. The young man blushed and bowed. There was a strong likeness between him and his mother. He had the same round, honest face and wide blue eyes. His profuse blonde hair was carefully parted on one side of his head, just above his ear. His clothes retained all the freshness of the shop creases, and his linen was spotless. Greta's hand might be traced in his blue cravat, as well as in his mother's decent new bonnet and shawl. He was evidently abashed by his surroundings, but answered the Governor's questions frankly and to the point. He had written his mother, but the letters were delayed. Had either his mother or his uncle been able to read English, they would have noticed circumstances about the story of the other Fritz Jansen's crime which would have made them suspect the truth. Greta had made everything plain to his mother, and taken her home. He, himself, had returned three days before, and his mother was eager to have him go at once to the Governor and return the money given her, and, also, — this she had greatly at heart, — beg the Governor to change his name. During the colloquy the old woman kept turning her head from one speaker to the other, smiling radiantly, and courtesying whenever either the Governor or his wife looked in her direction.

"I 'm fery grateful," Jansen concluded, "to your Excellency and your " — he hesitated, seeming uncertain what was the proper title for a Governor's wife, and compromised on — "your lady, for all the kindness you 've showed my mother; and I vould like, too, as you should know I ain't that kind of a fellow like Fritz Jansen, but a honest man, like my mother said."

"Ya," said the old woman; "die gracious lady believe, but Excellenz vas not know."

"I am quite sure everything your mother said of you was true," said the Governor, in his most affable manner, "and I shall be glad to see about the legislature changing your name; but you must n't think of returning the money."

"Let it be our wedding gift to Miss Greta," said the Governor's wife, with her charming smile. So, indeed, it was settled; and a certain gorgeous coral and gold brooch figuring at Greta's wedding some weeks later was bought with that exact sum. Frau Jansen was far too conscientious to add or subtract one penny. The simple people went away happy, after Hopkins had served them with wine and cake. The latter mighty personage received their confidences and heartfelt gratitude with stately suavity; indeed, Hopkins felt himself rather instrumental in Fritz Jansen's turning out to be a good fellow instead of a murderer, and an approving conscience swelled his imposing shirt-bosom. Meanwhile, the Governor and his wife were looking at each other. The Governor felt immensely relieved. Neither could he help rejoicing to himself that he had not weakly yielded. Principle had triumphed. Moreover, the triumph had that particular spice that comes from a victory over one's wife. He was quite too magnanimous to say: " Now, my dear, you see I know better than you about my own business. How embarrassing it would be had I followed your advice and pardoned that scoundrel! " But he stole a glance at his wife to see how she was taking things, expecting, perhaps, some hint of contrition on her face.

Instead, she said, " Walter, dear, did n't I tell you so ? "

" Tell me so! " gasped the Governor. " Of course you did n't tell me so! You wanted me to par— "

" But did n't I tell you over and over, and insist, that that pathetic old thing's son *could n't* be a cold-blooded murderer ! "

The Governor stared a minute in dumb amazement before he got breath to laugh.

" Bless your feminine mind, Annie, and did n't *I* insist that Fritz Jansen *was?* Who was right? "

" Both of us, of course," said she.

THE MORTGAGE ON JEFFY.

THERE are few more beautiful sights than an Arkansas forest in late February; I mean a forest in the river-bottoms, where every hollow is a cypress brake. Prickly joints of bamboo-brier make a kind of green hatching, like shadows in an etching, for a little space above the wet ground between the great trees. Utterly bare are the tree-branches, save for a few rusty shreds clinging to the cypress-tops, a few bunches of mistletoe on the sycamores, or a gleam of holly-leaves in the thicket; but scarlet berries flicker on purple limbs, the cane grows a fresher green, and, in February, red shoots will be decking the maple-twigs, there will be ribbons of weeds which glitter like jewels, floating under the pools of water and ferns waving above, while the moss paints the silvery bark of syca-mores, white-oaks, and gum-trees on the north side as high as the branches, and higher, with an incomparable soft and vivid green. The white trunks show the brighter for their gray tops and for that background everywhere of innumerable shades of gray and purple and shell-red which the blurred lines of twigs and branches make against the horizon. Such a forest is in my mind now. What an effect of fantastic and dainty magnificence the moss and the water and the shining trees produce! The dead trunks are dazzling white, the others have the lustrous haze of silver; it is not a real forest, it is a picture in an old missal, illuminated in silver and green. Yet beautiful as it is, there is something weird and dreary in its beauty — in those shadowy pools of water, masked by the tangle of brier and cane; in those tall trees that grow so thickly, and grow, I know, just as thickly for uncounted miles; in the shadows and mists which are instead of foliage; in the red streaks on the blunt edges of the cypress-roots and the stains on the girdled gum-trees, as if every blow of the axe had drawn blood — there is a touch of the sinister, even, and it would not be hard to conjure up a mediæval devil or two behind such monstrous growths as those cypress "knees."

Through this forest winds a rude road, winding because of the river, for these red smears to the right are willow-branches which mark the course of the Black River. On the February day that I recall, a one-armed man was driving a pair of stout horses to an open spring-wagon, the kind of wagon called in Arkansas "a hack." The wagon was new, and the harness had none of the ropes, odd chains, or old straps apt to garnish harness on a plantation. The driver, also, though wearing nothing better than a faded gray-flannel shirt, jean overalls, and rubber boots, was clean and even tidy in his appearrance. His broad shoulders and long back promised a frame of unusual height, should he straighten himself up, instead of slouching forward until his hat-rim and its fringe of black curls made a semicircle between his shoulders. The reins were about his neck, and he guided his horses with his one hand. For all his empty sleeve, Jeff Griffin was the best driver "in the bottom." At the same time his elbow steadied the object on his knees. This was carefully wrapped in a piece of that bagging which is used for cotton-bales. Presently he checked his horses, to very gently remove the wrappings, bending over them a plain, kind, tear-stained face. He was looking at a little coffin. It was simply made, yet in a workmanlike fashion, too, and was painted white, with silver nails and handles.

"Ain't it beaucherful!" he murmured; "it mought rouse 'er!"

"Howdy, Mist' Griffin," called a voice from

the roadside, with those mellow intonations which are as much the property of a black throat as the color of its skin. "Kin ye gimme lift fur 's de twurn ?"

Griffin perceived that he was abreast of an old negro, on foot, carrying a bag of meal on his shoulder. He knew him, Uncle Nate, who worked on the Widow Brand's farm. It was inevitable, according to the customs of the country, that Jeff should let the old man climb into the wagon.

"Ben down ter de Bend," said he, settling himself comfortably on the back seat; "my ole woman ben r'arin' an' chargin' fur mo' meal. Cud n't cotch dat fool mewl; hed tu gether de bag on my wethers an' walk. Whut ye got dar', Mist' Griffin ? Looks like — fo' de Lawd, hit 's a coffin !"

"Hit 's fur — fur little Bulah," said Griffin, choking.

"Not Cap'n Bulah's baby! My Lawd, ain't dat too bad ? W'y, I seen de Eller a-layin' at de landin' dis ev'nin' w'en I come by. An' Cap'n Bulah, don' she be takin' on turrible ?"

"She kep' walkin' the floor with it all las' night, long 's it lived. Never made a lisp er complaint. Done anything the doctor commanded, an' all her word was, ' Doctor, don' let 'er suffer !' but w'en she seen doctor war doin'

his bestmost, she never said nary nuther word.
Looked like she wud n't hinder 'im a-frettin'.
She are mighty fair-minded, Cap'n Bulah, Nate."

"Is so," agreed Nate, sympathetically; " but
whut a sight er turbbel she done hab, fust de
cap'n, an' now de onlies' chile she got dyin' off.
Was hit sick long, sah?"

"On'y two days. 'T hed crowp."

"Dey all b'en stoppin' ter yo' house sence de
boat tied up fur ter hab de b'iler fixed?"

"Yes. The baby b'en sorter weakly-like all
winter. Bulah, she war mighty timid of her —
but did n't do no good."

"Looks like," said Uncle Nate; "sut'nly de
ways er de Lawd is dark, an' we uns cayn't get
round 'em, nohow. Now, dar 's dat ar baby de
mudder leff ter de sto' las' Chewsday; ye heerd
on 't?" Griffin shook his head. "By gum, ain't
dat cuse! W'y, 't war dat ar Headlights, 's dey
calls 'er, kase of dem big feery eyes er her'n.
Tall woman; ye knowed 'er, picked cotton for
dey all at de Bend. 'Peared ter set a heap er
store by de little trick,[1] too; but she taken up
with a mover, an' he p'intedly swore dat w'en he
got married he did n't want no boot. So Headlights, she putt de baby unner de counter an' lit

---

[1] Trick, in Arkansas speech, means a number of things:
a child, an article, a stratagem, a machine; in fact, it is as
hard-worked a word as "thing."

out; an' dey bofe done gone. Mist' Frank, he clerks ter de sto' now, an' he fotched de baby home ter his maw fur ter keep twell somebuddy 'd want hit. An' dar dat baby is, eatin' hearty, dat his own mudder don' keer ter keep; an' dar 's Cap'n Bulah a-mournin' an' refuzin' ter be comfurted, like dat woman in de Scripter — I disremembers her name. Dat 's what tries de fait'; mo' ye studies on hit, mo' you' tried. Darfur, O Lawd, 'lighten we all's unnerstandin's; fur we 's up peart like de grass, an' en de mawnin' we 's p'intedly cut down." Here the stream of Uncle Nate's consolations meandered into the safe channel of his prayers (Uncle Nate had a gift) and flowed placidly on for a while, Griffin not hearing a word.

The latter's thoughts took their own dreary way, in vagrant, unuttered sentences: " She 's rockin'; in the little red rocker, 'sides the bed. She done hilt Bulah en her arms ever sence she dressed of her. She are a-holdin' 'er now. She ain't cried, nur wept, nur spoke; jes' sets thar a-rockin' her baby an' lookin' at its face. Oh, Bulah, won' you let nobuddy holp ye ? Hits pore little han's a-hangin' down — my Lord, how cole 't is ! Oh, pore little Bulah ! pore little Bulah ! but ye don' never need suffer no more, baby. Bulah, won' ye lemme cyar the baby a spell ? " — his thoughts had gone back

to the horrible night just past; he was pleading with the poor mother again. " Ye 'll shore
drop; ye cayn't keep up that-away! Lemme
take 'er; I kin make out 'ith one arm. I done
cyared 'er a heap.   'T ain't no good talkin' —
she don' hear me. Oh, Bulah, she don' have
no more pain; the Lord taken 'er outen it now.
Let S'leeny take 'er; you lay down.   Don' cry
so, S'leeny, mabbe it frets 'er ter hear us; we
kin cry, out-doors."

Now it was the doctor's voice speaking: " You
must rouse her somehow; she 'll die or go crazy
if you don't."

" Rouse her?   Lord God! how kin I, w'en I
cayn't make her hear me? I wish't it b'en me
stiddier the baby, Bulah; I b'en prayin' all
night ter the Lord ter take me stiddier her.
Won' ye jes' lift you' head, Bulah, an' try ter
listin?   It 's Jeff talkin' ter ye! Ye know how
Jeff allus thought a heap er ye — naw, naw, ye
never kin know what I thought er ye! Never
ye min' what I say, honey, I cayn't b'ar to see
ye settin' that-away, an' I say quar things. *Do*
ye hear me, Bulah? Oh, Lord God!" He remembered so vividly just how useless his efforts
were that he groaned aloud.

Uncle Nate stopped short.

" I wuz forgittin' everythin' but my trubbel,
Nate," said Griffin; " wuz ye sayin' suthin'?"

"I wuz jes' speakin' 'bout dat ar baby, sah; sayin' 't war a year 'n' haff ole, jest."

"Yes — the baby — jes' seventeen months," said Griffin, in a dazed way; then, with quite a new expression, he turned his head on the black man. "Ye mean Headlights's baby; what like is hit? Is hit pretty?"

"Iz t' dat," said Uncle Nate, judicially, "I ain't no jedge. Looks right puny an' ga'nted,[1] but I lay it git over dat at we uns'. Yeah 's de twurn, Mist' Griffin! I wish't ye well, sah!"

The "twurn" meant the fork of the road. One of the bifurcations goes on deeper into the swamp, the other deflects toward a clearing wherein, back of cotton-fields and garden, stands a comfortable battened house, the widow Brand's house. A certain trig look about land and buildings may be due to the fact — always kept well to the fore — that the widow came from Georgia. Jeff could see her tall figure on the porch, now; she was caressing a baby. His heart gave a kind of leap in his breast, and he turned white and grabbed at Nate's bag.

"Nate," said he, almost in a whisper, "I wanter see that ar chile! Is 't a boy ur a gyurl?"

"Thar 't is," replied Nate; "li'le boy. Won' ye come by, sah?"

---

[1] Thin; puny is always used for sickly; peart always means lively, well.

The widow came out to meet them, the baby in her arms. She always wore her hair looped smoothly over her ears and fastened behind with a "tuckin' comb." It was black hair, having a shine to it like her eyes. Spare and tanned as her features were, they were not uncomely, and their expression of shrewd alertness softened wonderfully when she recognized her visitors. The boy certainly was thin, — pale, too, — still, a pretty, bright little fellow, who ruffled the widow's sleek hair and slapped her cheeks, in the gayest humor. Griffin could not understand why he felt a curious pang of relief, seeing how unlike the little castaway was to the dead child. He saluted the widow.

"Oh, we 're all stirrin'," she replied. "Aunt Fanny b'en over 'n' tole me 'bout you all's 'fliction. They jes' puttin' the gears on the mewls."

" Won' ye come long er me, Mis' Brand, now!" interrupted Jeff, eagerly ; "an' cayn't ye fotch 'long the baby? Ye heerd 'bout Bulah? I 'm turrible skeered up 'bout 'er, an' I sorter 'lowed mabbe the little trick mought rouse 'er — being leff so lonesome like ; ye know Bulah 's powerful good-hearted."

"We kin try," said the widow, musingly ; "ye got good sense fur a man person, Jeff."

She was very soon in the wagon, on the seat behind Griffin, watching him as they drove silently through the swamp. She thought that his had been a lonesome kind of life. Jeff Griffin had come back from the wars with an arm the less, to support his bedridden mother, his widowed sister and her family, and a forlorn little cousin with no nearer kindred than they — Bulah Norman. "Old Man Griffin" and the "big boys" had been killed long before. Jeff himself was seventeen, but he had been a soldier for two years. The Griffins originally came from Tennessee. They bought a little farm on the outskirts of a large plantation on the Black River. They were all of them honest, hardworking people, and Jeff had a natural turn for business, though he could not write his name. Those days, there was money in cotton; those halcyon days when we burned our cotton-seed for fuel, yet could get more for the cotton alone than we can get for them both now. Jeff toiled early and late. As the widow from Georgia told her son Frank (a good fellow, clever, too, but a bit touched by the climate), Jeff Griffin's one arm did more than any other man's two. He prospered; he bought more land, he built a house for his mother, — just the year before she died, poor soul, — and generously started his nieces and nephews in life. One by one they drifted out into the world until only their mother and Bulah Norman, now grown into quite a pretty lass of eighteen, remained in the house with Jeff. Bulah was eleven years younger than Jeff. He had always been devoted to her. When she was a child he never tired of her prattle; he gave her a calf, a colt, a saddle, a riding-whip, while every other girl in the settlement was content with a pawpaw switch; he could not do enough for her. If he was too busy to go to school himself, he was never too busy to drive "the little tricks" over to the schoolhouse, and every evening, Bulah, "the least little trick of all," used to teach him what she had learned. Bulah was very fond of Jeff, in a filial way; but Jeff loved Bulah with all his heart and soul and strength. He was such a dry, quiet, matter-of-fact fellow that nobody ever dreamed of such a thing; that is, nobody but the widow. How do women manage to discover a reticent man's passion? Jeff had never confided in the widow; but one day she remarked to him, with the calm bluntness of the backwoods, "Look a yere, Jeff, ef you don' make haste an' court Bulah she'll be takin' up with that thar triflin', biggity Sam Eller that she met up with down to Newport w'ilst she's stoppin' with S'leeny's gyurl. She will so."

"Po' Jeff!" the widow was saying to herself, now, "I come too late. He done got her prommus then. Jeff looked like he was jes' gittin'

up by a spell er sickness, them days — p'int
blank gashly; but he never let on, jes' talked
natchell to Bulah, an', law me, what a sight er
truck he guv 'er! An' thar she leff that nice
house that he done fixed up so lady-fine fur her,
an' her room, all papered, gran' 's Mrs. Francis's,
— roses all over the walls, and the ceilin' painted
blew like the sky, — t' go and live with Sam
Eller in a boat! I reckon she found out right
quick that thar war n't nuthin' t' *him* 'cept good
looks an' brags! an' ye cayn't eat neither. Wonder how long 'fore he begun borryin' money er
Jeff. He wuz no force, nohow. Say he war
blin' drunk w'en he tumbled outen the pilot-
house, spang on the deck, an' mashed 'is shin,
and never got up by it. Lived a whole year
ayfter, too. Bulah war mighty long-sufferin'
with him, tendin' on him night 'n' day, an' runnin' the boat, too; an', in course, the baby mus'
come in the thick of it! An' 't made me mad,
seein' him so ill [1] with her. I don' guess a man
person kin holp r'arin' on ye, *some*, w'en he 's
sick, kase he wants out so bad, r'iles 'im all up;
but *he* wuz a-cussin' and sw'arin' the plum'
w'ile, an' steamboat cap'ns natchelly kin cuss
wusser'n anybody else; 'clare, I don' see how she
cud b'ar 't sich a patient way. What wud she
'a' done 'outen Jeff? Keepin' the cap'n under,

1 Cross.

an' lendin' money, and lettin' S'leeny go an' stay on the boat by spells to holp 'er an' cherkin' 'er up — law me, I never seen a man person like Jeff Griffin! An' now that the Lord done took the cap'n, an' she kin have her time an' her pleasure, she won' go home long er Jeff; naw, she mus' run the boat twell she kin pay off the money — jes' biggity, *she* is! How come she don' marry Jeff? That ar'd pay him best. Nex' thing, he mus' coax S'leeny to go long er Bulah, an' leave him 'lone with jes' Aunt Fanny ter 'tend ter 'im. I know *her* cookin'; ye cud build chimbleys outen her light bread. An' now, this have ter come on 'em — po' Bulah!"

She bit off her sigh, lest it should disturb Jeff, for they had come to their journey's end, and the horses were standing. There were the brown cotton-rows and the whitish-brown stalks strewn over them; there, under the elm-trees, was Aunt Fanny's cabin, and there was the house, long, low, with its black roof and white-washed walls. The open gallery in the centre had been decorated with bunches of sweet herbs and strings of red pepper. Two or three saddles and a gun are expected to hang in an Arkånsas " gallery; " they were a little brighter than common here.

The new-comers stepped softly through the gallery into a large room. Bulah was sitting, precisely as Jeff's imagination had pictured her, rocking her dead baby. An elderly woman had her back to them, leaning over the hearth, and the turkey-wing in her hand, with which she was brushing the bricks, moved by jerks as if the hand were nervous.

Bulah did not look up; her head was bent over the waxen face on her arm. The dead calm of her own face was more ghastly and pitiful to see than any anguish. All the while, she was rocking very gently, never ceasing, or in the least varying the motion. Her chair made the merest creak; yet, all at once, the other woman hurled the turkey-wing aside to wring her hands, sobbing: "Bulah, I cayn't enjure t' hear ye! For the Lord's sake putt her down! 'T ain't Christian-like. Oh, dear! oh, dear! she don' hear a word."

She did not seem to hear. To her, in that awful mystery of grief, where her soul was with her dead child and her dead hopes, all this outside jar and fret vibrated so faintly, that before she could comprehend their presence they had ceased. Nor did she seem to notice Jeff when he showed her the coffin, begging her, weeping, to look at it.

The widow, with the child in her arms, stepped across the floor on tiptoe. "Bulah," said she, solemnly, "the Lord taken you' baby, an' this yere baby's mother have desarted him, an' he 's all alone on earth.   Cayn't ye find it in you' heart t' have pity on him?"

She put the child down, close to the strange-looking, silent woman, and, naturally enough, he began to cry.

At the first whimper, Bulah's eyes were lifted; with an indescribably wild and agonizing inquiry, she stared at the small creature, now quite terrified, and wailing, "Mammy! mammy!"

"Ye ain't got no mother, baby," said she; then, with her dreadful composure, "nur I ain't got no baby."   She would have loosened one arm to touch the little fellow, but the action seemed to recall something; for, screaming "How could she! how could she!" she burst into a passion of tears, and while she wept, the widow gently took the dead child out of her clasp.

.   .   .   .

Little Bulah's grave had been green for months, and it was on an autumn day that Jeff Griffin stood on the platform of the plantation store, waiting for the Samuel Eller to round the Bend.   Being Saturday afternoon, there was a pretty bustle about the settlement — a hum from the mill where the cotton-wagons were unloading, a continual ring of the hammer from the smithy, and a far-away song floating up from the cotton-fields filled with pickers. At least thirty horses were tied to the fence-rail on the left, and a score of booted legs dangled over either platform. Occasionally, a sunbonnet might appear in the doorway, but it was likely to go straightway about its business, having possibly more business than belonged to the boots. All about this wee hubbub of human life was the forest; maples and hackberry-trees kept up their autumn revelries in scarlet and gold, and their gay leaves, fluttering amid the sad-colored foliage of the cypress, looked like courtiers dancing with Puritans. To the right, the woods on either side the river-bank seemed to converge; that was " the Bend."

" Yon she comes! " cried Jeff, spying a cork-screw of smoke above the tree-tops. He spoke to the widow from Georgia, who had just emerged from the store, in a very clean and stiff print gown, and was prudently testing some new snuff before carrying it away.

" Cap'n Bulah never misses," she answered; " ain't it amazin' how well she done! Say she done passed her examination, an' got a license reg'lar. The mate says they ain't many like 'er. Expect S'leeny stayed down t' Black Rock 'ith her son. How are you all's little trick? "

" Oh, he 's right peart," said Jeff, his plain

face quite beaming; "gittin' on smart. Talks a heap. Follers me roun' everywhar, laffin', an' grabbin' at my pants — sorter good them little fingers feel, don't they? Putt him on ole Nig, las' week. I wish't you 'd a seen 'im; fust, he looked mighty jubious; then he begins to laff. He 'll git likened to ridin' mighty briefly."

"Yo' mos' petted on him 's Bulah, ain't ye? How come ye don' keep him an' her both with ye, allus? Actchelly, Jeff, my bones is wearin' out waitin' t' dance at yo' weddin'!"

The reply to such jocularity ought to have been a sheepish grin, but Jeff looked very downcast. "Ye won't never dance at *my* weddin'," said he, "an' iz t' Bulah, she have laid by t' stay single."

"Wal, I did n't aim t' drag [1] ye, Jeff, but — law me!" The caustic twitch of the widow's lips disappeared in a gurgle of dismay; she will never be nearer swallowing her snuff-stick. On the landing in front of her was a tall woman, whose wild beauty could not be obscured by her wretched dress — a draggled brown-stuff skirt, ragged blue jacket, and towsled red handkerchief, knotted awry. A mass of glossy black hair was straggling out of its coil over the red triangle behind; her battered hat shaded a bold

[1] Tease.

profile, cut cleanly, like the head on a Roman coin. The sun, which plays havoc with dainty beauties, had only deepened the rich tints of her skin, and brightened the untamed fire in her eyes. She was as graceful and unconscious as a panther.

" Headlights! " muttered Mrs. Brand, under her breath.

Jeff had not even seen her ; all his eyes were for the boat. Yes, that was Bulah on the upper deck, and there was the dear little white head against her skirts. Other people might see merely a slip of a woman, with plenty of freckles on her fair skin, a firm little mouth, and pathetic blue eyes. What Jeff saw — but how can I picture the radiant being as the lover sees her ?

Now the plank is down, and Jeff, with his one arm and his Southern gallantry, is helping the widow across, who does n't need helping one whit, but accepts it as the duty of a " man person." In a minute they are on the deck, and Jeff has little Jeffy on his shoulders and can look at Bulah. But why have Tom Bracelin, the deputy-sheriff, and his two men come on board, and does that shabby woman mean to take passage on the Samuel Eller? She pushed the underlings aside with an imperious elbow, and got close to Jeff and the little fellow.

"That's him!" she shouted, "that's my chile! Take him 'way, boss!"

"Oh!" exclaimed Bulah, and flung herself upon Jeffy's small legs, the only portion of him within reaching distance.

"What ye seekin'?" demanded Jeff, sternly.

"I are seekin' my own chile, thet I leff unner the store-counter," Headlights answered, "an' you uns taken him."

"Ye wicked critter! do ye reckon we all will guv him up t' ye?"

"I reckon ye 'll have ter," said Headlights, composedly; "they 's a right smart er folkses kin sw'ar hit 's my chile. You all ain't 'dopted of 'im, nur nuthin'!"

"Look a yere, you Mis' Headlights, or whutsomever 's yo' name," said Mrs. Brand, "ain't ye got no natchell motherlike feelin's 'bout the po' little trick's own intrusts? Look at him bein' raised so good, gwine ev'ry Sunday t' school or t' preachin', an' gittin' washed hisseff ever' mawnin', an' good cloze, and his knees patched beaucherful, an' look a' them copper toes," — shaking poor Jeffy's foot at her, — "an' you cayn't so much as guv him proper victuals; I seen ye, myseff, feedin' up that innercent chile on gouber peas and hog's melts! My word, I wonder he got any insides leff — he had n't orter have."

Headlights listened quite unmoved to this homily, and equally unmoved she heard the threats of the boat people and the remonstrances of Mr. Francis, who had come aboard. The owner of the plantation was no more to her than the deck-hands. There is a depth of poverty as arrogant as riches, and social distinctions count for nothing in that grave.

"Ye kin r'ar all ye like," said she, tossing her black mane, "I 'm gwine cyar off my boy. Yere, baby, come to mammy, mammy got candy."

But Jeffy gripped Jeff's neck all the harder, whimpering "Jeffy 'faid! 'Way, lady! 'Way, lady!" and, with a very black frown, Headlights beckoned the officer to help her.

He advanced, looking desperately ill at ease. "I 'm right sorry, ma'am," said he, "but she 's got the law on her side, and I have to do my juty."

Jeff and the mate of the boat exchanged glances; they had the simple Southern plan of dumping the officers overboard and steaming off down the river; they were willing, however, that Mrs. Brand should try her device first.

"Wal, Tom Bracelin," said she, as it were clearing the decks for action by throwing away her snuff-stick, "I never did 'low t' see *you* draggin' off a po' harmless little chile int' perdition — fur ye know 't aint no better 'monst them cotton-pickers — you with you' own six little tricks t' home, too! How 'd ye enj'y hevin' them two least ones tolled off by a gang er cotton-pickers? Cap'n Bulah sets 's much store by thet ar baby iz you kin by yourn; and mo' too, kase it 's all she 's got. Nur wud I of b'lieved it er *you*, Lafayette Sands," — wheeling round upon one of the deputies, who tried, ineffectually, to blow his nose to hide his confusion, — "them evenin's you an' Bulah Norman wud come home from school tergether an' be projickin' roun' my kitchin for light bread an' smear. Naw, sir, I did n't guess them days ye wud do Bulah meaner 'n a murderer! Iz fur *you*, sir," — the second deputy jumped, — "I ain't got no acquaintance with ye, but you' a pretty man, an' I jedge ye to be a clever man," — the second deputy rubbed off a smirk with a very big hand, — "an' I don't guess ye aim ter hurt that ar pretty chile, ef 't *is* the law! Onyhow, gentlemen," concluded the widow, in the most unexpected way, "ye won't let 'er cyar that chile 'way th'out payin' Cap'n Bulah board."

"Board!" screamed Headlights, "who ever heerd er payin' board fur a baby?"

"Board war guv that baby," retorted the undaunted Georgian; "good board, too. An' feedin' a chile ain't like sloppin' a pig, neither.

Ye cayn't devil them little stummicks with leav-in's; they has t' have good victuals that cost money. That chile b'en boarded frum last er Feberary to last er October — makes eight months. Call it two dollars a month; that's p'int blank cheap; twicet eight 's sixteen. Then the cloze; Cap'n Bulah done spent most er nine dollars fur truck fur that ar chile, ain't she, Mr. Francis?"

"More," replied Mr. Francis, with a twinkle in his eye — he saw the widow's drift; "she must have eleven dollars charged on the petty ledger, now."

"I 'm blamed my skin," the cotton-picker struck in, "if I ever spent dollar 'n' haff on the chile. Quit yo' funnin', I won't pay board!"

"Reckon some folkses wud count in the boat-fares gwine back'ards and for'ards on the river," continued the widow, "but we uns ain't graspin'. Twicet eight 's sixteen, an' eleven is twenty-seven. That ar 's ciphered right, ain't it?"

Headlights burst into a fierce sort of laughter, crying, "I ain't got twenty-seven cents!"

"Oh, we uns air content t' take a morgige on the chile," replied the widow, calmly, "for six months; an' we 'll keep the chile twell then, an' ef ye don't pay then we 'll keep the chile furever mo'. Mr. Francis is a squire; he 'll draw up the papers. Do you all 'gree to that?"

Bulah released her hold on Jeffy to look around ; her pallid features and entreating eyes said more than her voice : "Oh, gentlemen, be merciful, look how he loves me ; he ain't nuthin' to *her ;* don't part us !   He 's always b'en puny ; he 'll die off in the swamps, like she 'll take him."

The men whispered together.   They were indeed glad of a loophole of escape ; and the upshot of the matter was the production by Mr. Francis (after an interval in the cabin) of a document duly drawn up and reading as follows : "I, Sabrina Mathews, alias Headlights, do promise to pay to Mrs. Bulah Eller, of Lawrence County, Arkansas, the sum of twenty-seven dollars on or before the fifteenth day of April, 18—; and if I do not pay the aforesaid sum of twenty-seven dollars by or before the fifteenth day of April, 18—, I hereby promise to give and bequeath and resign to the said Mrs. Bulah Eller my child, now known as Jefferson Griffin Eller, to keep for her child ; and I do hereby promise to renounce any and all my claims to the aforesaid Jefferson Griffin Eller."

It was only when Headlights was convinced that the sheriff and his men would do no more for her that she consented to make her mark to this paper.   She insisted upon her right to pay before the six months, and Mr. Francis did not venture to refuse. "Oh, let 'er have it her way," said the widow; then, in an undertone to Bulah, "Git shet of 'er now, an' we kin gether the chile an' light out, don' ye see?"

So Headlights had her way, and signed; and every man on the boat who could write his name witnessed, with a dim idea that he was helping Cap'n Bulah.

Having made her mark, Headlights strode up to Jeff, who was still holding the boy. Bulah would have stepped between them.

"I ain't aimin' t' hurt him," said the cotton-picker. "Ye won't stop me kissin' of him oncet, will ye?"

The two women glared at each other, probably with as venomous feelings as those two historic dames who puzzled King Solomon. But Jeff had said truly that Bulah was a fair-minded woman. "Ye got the right to," said she.

Headlights bent over the baby with surprising gentleness. She was so tall that it was easy for her to reach his hair and his little averted cheek as he clung to Jeff's neck. She whispered something, of which Jeff only caught the words "sorry" and "hurt ye," and immediately ran off the boat so swiftly and recklessly that she nearly fell into the water.

"Well, that critter!" said the deputy, "she come to me yesterday. She's got out with the fellow she ran off with. Lum Shinault was telling me *he* heard he gave 'er the hickory, an' she drawed a knife on him. Now, she 's back with the rest of the Missouri folks, terrible anxious to git her baby; she 'd orter b'en anxious a spell back, *I* take it."

After that day the Samuel Eller made her regular trips round the Bend; but no one ever saw the little white curls dancing over the deck. A good many people believed that Jeffy really was on board; if so, he never came out of hiding. Headlights did not go away. She stayed on, picking cotton, until the ragged white streamers were all stripped off the brown stalks. Two or three times Jeff caught a glimpse of her prowling about his own fields. He never attempted to speak to her, and she gave him nothing more than a scowl. He was watching her secretly. He was sure that she must be saving money; for she was sober on Christmas Day, when the rest of the cotton-pickers were a howling mob, and, for that matter, there were very few steady legs left on the plantation. One day, visiting Bulah and S'leeny on the boat (good-by, now, to the happy times when Jeff could watch Bulah, with Jeffy on her knees, on the other side of his own fireplace), he observed that Bulah seemed troubled. Finally, she brought out a little package, and told him that while the boat was unloading at Newport, Jeffy had been allowed to walk in the street with S'leeny ("for the chile's gitting right puny cooped up so, and I had to see to the loadin'"), and a woman had spoken to him and given him the package. "S'leeny don't know her by sight, but she suspicioned 't was *her*, an' she called her to stop and take the things back, but she run too quick. See, Jeff!"

She displayed a flimsy red silk handkerchief and a child's harp.

"Yes, hit war Headlights," said Jeff, gravely; "she bought 'em at the store. Frank Brand tole me. I 'lowed then she got 'em for Jeffy — Law me, Bulah, what ye doin'?"

He caught Bulah's hand just in time to prevent harp and handkerchief going into the Black River.

"Lemme 'lone, Jeff," cried she, with flashing eyes; "Jeffy's b'en talkin' of the critter ever sence."

"Oh, hush, honey," said Jeff, soothingly; "'t is rilin', but don' throw the critter's pore little truck overboard. She got sorter feelin's, I expeck, too."

"I *hate* her," said Bulah; "I 'd like to *kill* her!"

But she dropped the bundle on the deck instead of in the water.

All this made Jeff feverishly anxious, for he was positive that if Headlights did not go away Bulah would sell the boat and hide herself somewhere with the child; besides, he had a dread of some collision between the two women. "An' ef Bulah mixes with Headlights she 'll shore git killed up!" thought Jeff. Therefore it was a mighty relief to him, one day, to see the whole troop of the cotton-pickers, Headlights in their midst, ploughing through the mud on the road to the railway station, six miles away. He rode the whole muddy way after them, to see them safely on the train bound for Missouri. Then he rode home, singing. Possibly he was jubilant too soon, since Headlights got out at the next village.

Jeff went straight to the landing. He heard the refrain of the " roustabouts' " aimless song,

    " Four o'clock done come at las' ! "

and he could see the cotton-bales bounding along the plank; down among them he ran, light as a boy.

"She 's gone !" cried Bulah; "I see it in yo' face ! Oh, Jeff, take us home, Jeffy 's plum' sick. Simmons can take the boat to Black Rock."

Of course she went; and, late as it was then, Jeff rode ten miles for the doctor. The next morning he rode again to the railway station, to telegraph to a larger town for some medicines.

He must wait for the train to bring them, so that it was after noon before he could start homeward. The road is the worst in the country-side, and just then, to use the phrase of the bottom, " 't wud mire a snipe." He was crawling along, two thirds of the way home, when his mule shied, with a great splash, and nearly reared off the roadway. "Dad gum ye!" cried Jeff, irritably, "whut — by grabs, hit's a human critter!"

The cause of the beast's fright lay athwart some logs, her skirts trailing in the mud. No sooner had Jeff lifted her head than he uttered a loud cry: "My Lord, it's Headlights!"

There was no response; the head lay on his arm like a stone; evidently she had sat down to rest, and swooned. Jeff heartily wished that she were dead instead; but he could not leave her thus. He glanced disconsolately about him — at his mule improving the unexpected leisure to munch cane-leaves; at the brilliant, desolate sweep of swamp, silver-trees, green moss, gray pools of water, and the rotten corduroy raised a little out of the ooze. "Wal, the Lord's mussiful," groaned Jeff, "they's a right smart er water 'roun', onyhow."

He got Headlights's head in a more comfortable position, and splashed water on her face until a gasp arrested his hand and she looked dizzily up at him, murmuring, "Then I done got thar.   How's baby?"

"Git whar? You' in the swamp, gyurl. Wake up!"

Headlights did sit up, and moaned.

"I cud n't make out," she muttered. "Lemme 'lone, Jeff Griffin; how come ye done slopped me all over?   I 'll shore be chillin' ter-morrer."

"Ye 'll shore be chillin' ef ye don' git up outen this yere slosh."

"How 's my baby? — least ye mought tell me that much."

"Wal, he are plum' bad, then," answered Jeff, gloomily — angrily, too, since he saw nothing for him to do but to put Headlights on his mule and walk himself; it would be like murder to leave her in the swamp, and the mule could not carry two through such mud.   Yet he felt a twinge of pity as he saw the tears rolling down Headlights's cheeks at his words. "Ye mus' git on my mule," said he, more kindly; "ye cayn't walk, an' ye mus' git outen the swamp."

She struggled to her feet and let him help her into the saddle, saying, "I 'll ride a spell, then I kin walk."   Had she attempted to ride in the usual feminine posture, she would certainly have fallen off the mule, being nearly unconscious; luckily, neither Jeff nor she thought of such a thing.   By and by she began to shiver violently.

"Thar 't is, wust sorter chill, an' we uns' house the nighest by two miles!" At the idea he groaned aloud, for the relentless hospitality of the bottom left him no alternative.

"Mist' Griffin," spoke Headlights, feebly, "I 'll get down, ef you' tired. I kin make out. On'y won't ye tell me more 'bout my baby, fust?"

"Wal, Headlights, he come down yistiddy, an' his fever ain't cooled, an' doctor, he 's skeered er pneumony; but he says he are a heap apter ter git up by it fur havin' of such good 'tendance like his — like Bulah's and S'leeny's. Don't ye go fur to cry, Headlights; ye shake all over, an' I cayn't hole ye!"

Headlights somehow choked her sobs. Jeff went on: "Now, Headlights, I 'm goin' cyar ye home with me, case ye ain't fit t' walk. Now be ye goin' t' devil us, onyhow? try fur t' toll Jeffy way an'" —

"Naw, naw, I ain't no short;[1] I fight fair. I wud n't do ye sicher way."

"Wal," muttered Jeff to himself, "I expeck S'leeny 'll be r'arin' on me, an' Bulah — but Bulah 's fair-minded. Onyhow, cayn't be holped, an' they 'll git over it, some way."

With this reflection, which has eked out many a man's courage on the brink of a tussle with

---

[1] No cheat.

his womankind, Jeff waded along. A good deal
of the time he had to hold Headlights on the
mule or she would have slipped off through
sheer weakness, and all the while she appeared
to be in a kind of stupor. Once he asked her
how she happened to hear of Jeffy's illness; how
she came to be at the station. She said: " I
came ter git Jeffy; I knowed ye 'd have him
back by ye, quick 's ye 'lowed I done lit out.
I heerd the men t' the deppo a-talkin' 'bout
ye. I walked from Hoxie on the track; started
afore sun up." He thought that her mind must
be wandering.

It was a dismal journey, tedious to the last
degree, but at last the mule turned in at his
own gate, and S'leeny, hearing the hounds' chorus of welcome, ran out to meet him. She
lifted up her hands in horror when she recognized his companion. " My, my, my, Jeff Griffin! are ye clean bereft? "

" You hush! " whispered Jeff. " I did n't ax
'er. I run up with 'er in the woods. She war
layin' on a log dead 's[1] a hammer. I cud n't
leave 'er that-away, cud I? "

" Guv me the med'cines, an' you cyar 'er
straight t' Mis' Brand's."

---

[1] They have a peculiar use of the word " dead " for " senseless." " He knocked him dead," they will say, or, " She was
plum' dead for an hour."

"I cayn't. Look at 'er : she are chillin', this minnit."

Headlights had staggered into the gallery; now she would have fallen, had not both brother and sister caught her. "Ye *see!*" said Jeff.

"What'll Bulah say?" groaned S'leeny; "law me, ain't she got 'nuff trubbels an' triberlations 'thouten *you* a-pilin' more onto her?"

But this was only the futile last stroke of a vanquished fighter, the natural impulse of the woman to find the man to blame; S'leeny had her own conscience, and Jeff knew that she would make no more objections. In fact, she helped him to get Headlights to the fire, and got the quinine and whiskey before she went to Bulah. Headlights had revived a little and was sitting in the armchair, when Bulah softly opened the door and came in. Jeff ventured one furtive glance, and began to poke the fire.

"Don't take on, Bulah," begged he, with that artless freedom from tact which is the right of his sex; "onyhow, she's Jeffy's mother"—

"I wanter know 'bout my baby," interrupted Headlights.

Bulah's chin went up a little: "I expect you mean my Jeffy; he's mighty bad"—

"Kin I look on him — jest oncet — jes' fur a minnit?"

"He'd most like be scared up to see a stranger," said Bulah, coldly.

"Law me," cried the helpless man between the two women, "Bulah, how *kin* ye be so cruel?"

It was the first word of reproach that he had ever spoken to her, and it must have gone straight to her heart, for she put both hands there quickly, with a sort of gasp, like a person stabbed; a little flicker of color came into her cheeks and went out, leaving her extremely pale. Jeff was already in an agony of remorse, crying, "Naw, naw, ye ain't! It's me that's cruel."

"Yes, I am; yes, I was," said Bulah. "Come, Headlights, ye cayn't walk; lean on me. Ye mus' jes' look at him an' come out!"

"I kin walk," answered Headlights, shortly. Walk she did, though unsteadily, across the gallery into the other room. It was the pretty room, with the roses on the wall-paper and the sky-blue ceiling. S'leeny could have fainted when she beheld that tall shape, all wet and muddy, and the wild face and burning eyes. Headlights, not venturing to advance, for fear of awakening the little sleeper, stood on the threshold, where she could see the bed, and gazed with an agony of longing at the flaxen curls and flushed cheek on the pillow. After a moment, she bent down very carefully, and began to remove her miserable shoes. S'leeny almost screamed to see Bulah kneel and take off those dreadful, mud-soaked shoes herself.

" Though, to be shore," reflected S'leeny, " they 'd of p'intedly tracked the floor. Mabbe that 's how come she done it." So little do the ones nearest us know of the strange and complex emotions which war in our motives. But Jeff understood. His wet eyes met Bulah's, and afterward she remembered his look ; though then her own feelings were swept away by the spectacle of the overpowering feeling before her. Headlights crept up to the bed. She bent over the sleeper ; and the desperate misery in her face touched even S'leeny. Her breath came in gasps, with the fierce pain which she would not show. At that moment, Bulah, living over again her own desolation, felt a horrible kinship with this mother, suffering as she had suffered ; yet all the while her heart seemed to stand still with fear and impatience, lest Jeffy should wake and be frightened. After all, Headlights only kissed a stray lock of hair. Then she stole out of the room, and, before they could stop her, ran out of the house, just as she was.

Jeff and Bulah found her in the cow-shed, crouched on a pile of hay. Jeff tried to say something comforting, but he stopped as soon as she turned her face.

Headlights spoke: "Yes, I know he'll git well. 'T ain't that. I seen 'im. 'T ain't no good me hopin' fur ter take him 'way. I cud never have thin's fixed up so good fur 'im when he's sick. He's puny. He'd die up, shore." She drew in her breath and said, with a mighty effort, "Ye kin hev him fur good. I won't pester ye no more."

"Oh, my Lord!" said Bulah. The tears blinded her, and they were tears for Headlights; she was disarmed by her adversary's surrender. "Come, ye poor thing," said she, gently; "come in an' get rested, an' then ye can help me tend him."

In her turn, she had made the greatest concession in her power. Headlights rose submissively to follow her, but before she took a step she touched Bulah's arm, saying, "They's one thing more — you uns 'll be gittin' merried."

"Me!" Bulah said huskily, and choked.

"Ye got you' mind mighty sot on 'er, ain't ye?" said Headlights to Jeff.

Surely it was his good angel that prompted his answer: "It b'en sot on 'er all the days I knowed her, Headlights. They ain't nobuddy on earth like 'er, to my mind."

"An' ye jes' done got 'er," said Headlights.

"Wal, I don' keer, all I want's fur ye ter prommus ter be allus good ter my boy, whatsumever"—

"We will," said Bulah, solemnly. "Now, come on in."

Bulah led her into the house. She was burning with fever. Bulah put her to bed, where, almost instantly, she fell asleep. But it was the widow from Georgia and S'leeny who entered presently, bearing each a stick, and, as it were, fished the outcast's clothes from the chair, with countenances on which were vividly painted the sensations natural to two such notable housewives, and bore them out into the yard, and hung them on the line to air.

"An ef it do come on to rain," remarked the widow, complacently, "it 'll holp t' clean 'em all the mo'!"

Bulah had gone back to Jeffy. Jeff whispered to her that he was sure that the boy was better — his breathing was easier, he was sleeping quietly. "An' look," said Jeff, "them little curls er his'n is plum' wet: the fever 's cooled; he won' git pneumony ayfter all!" Bulah looked. She sank down on her knees, and Jeff knew what she was doing; his own heart swelled with gratitude, not the less fervent because confused and dumb.

Headlights was fated to keep her word. Her

chill developed into pneumonia, and as Mrs. Brand (who came over to nurse her) observed truly, " Cotton-pickers never had no ruggedness, an' she cud n't pear ter git up by it." She added : " Headlights war n't a bit ill ; jes' iz easy, patient critter like ye ever seen ; did n't know nuthin' most er the time."

Once, just before the end, she seemed conscious. Jeffy had been brought in to see her — polite little Jeffy, who had been well drilled in his lesson beforehand. " Po' lady, so sick," said Jeffy ; " Jeffy sorry. Make it aw well ; " and, giving her the only remedy his babyish mind knew, he took her face between his little soft hands, and kissed it.

The sleeper stirred in her sleep. " Yes, yes, baby," she murmured drowsily, " mammy knows. 'T is cole in the cotton. Mammy cyar 'im home. Have a fire." Then she opened her eyes wide and saw them all. The spark in her dim eyes seemed to glow again, but no longer in anger or pain ; she looked at Bulah, steadily, with the strange, peaceful, solemn gaze of the dying.

" Yes, I will," said Bulah, as though she had been asked a question ; indeed, it seemed to Bulah that she had.

Headlights fumbled at her throat, with an old shoestring that was around it ; when Bulah drew out a leather bag, she smiled. "Fur — him," she murmured, and her hand groped for the child. Almost before it touched him, she was away from him and all earthly troubles, in the merciful shadows ; and so gently did those waters of oblivion submerge her soul that no ripple was left to mark when it finally sank forever.

"An' I 'clare," avowed Mrs. Brand to S'leeny, "I are plum' surprised by myseff, I b'en cryin' fur that ar critter like she war my own kin. But she war so sorter bidable an' decent, an' done the little trick so decent, ayfter all! I sw'ar some folkses don' git no fair show in this world!"

"Bulah been cryin' too," said S'leeny. "Wal, I don' see no call fur grievin'. All I wisht are that she 'd of leff some money fur the buryin'. Bulah, she will have Mr. Dake make one er his. fust-rate coffins, though I say his second-bes' is plenty good nuff. Jeff done gone fur 't now."

"She guv a little bag t' Bulah ; whar 's it at, Bulah ? "

"It 's Jeffy's," said Bulah, showing it, "but I don't guess there 's any harm in lookin' " —

"My word, *no !* " cried the widow, with her fingers inside. The contents of the bag were a roll of bank-bills and a folded paper. The roll contained twenty-seven dollars. The paper was a copy of the mortgage on Jeffy. The widow from Georgia dropped into a chair, alternately shook her head and waved her hands, and finished by wiping her eyes, without saying a word.

"My, my, my!" cried S'leeny, "ain't it a main mussy the critter died; she cud of taken Jeffy 'way!"

But Bulah, who had grown very pale, said, "S'leeny, ye don't know. That woman trusted me. I'm a-goin' to tell Jeffy all 'bout 'er when I give him this. Headlights, can ye hear me? You paid the mortgage, an' he b'lougs to *you*, too!"

www.ingramcontent.com/pod-product-compliance
Lightning Source LLC
Chambersburg PA
CBHW051134120726
47905CB00005B/1540